21 Steps to Happiness

21 Steps to Happiness

F. G. GERSON

RED
DRESS
I N K
™

21 STEPS TO HAPPINESS

A Red Dress Ink novel

ISBN-13: 978-0-373-89583-0
ISBN-10:   0-373-89583-6

© 2006 by Francisco Gerson.

www.RedDressInk.com

Printed in U.S.A.

Acknowledgments

Thanks to Kate Silver for her incredible help and insights;
Farrin Jacobs for her courage and commitment;
Selina McLemore; Kathryn Lye; Ruben Gerson for
his kindness; Franklin & Dulce Gerson for their love
and comfort; Lukasz & Veronica Karwowski
for their warm support.

Also, thanks to my wonderful agent, Julie M. Culver,
and everybody at Lowenstein-Yost for the caring
support, unlimited enthusiasm and hard work.

For Maria & Ilo,
the two authentic ingredients for happiness

"You're on the next flight, leaving at 5:40, Miss Blanchett."

Listen to her French accent! It's so...

"I can check in your luggage straight away."

"That would be just fine," I say with a suddenly posh voice.

I make a mental note: easy on the posh voice.

I pass her my bag. She frowns. Okay, it's not one of those fancy Frenchy-looking kind she expected from someone like me. It's more like a little Adidas job I used to take to yoga. And yes, it looks horrible, like an old sheep stomach stuffed with clothes and underwear. But darling, you should take a look at the rest of my life.

I have no time for futilities such as traveling wear anymore. I'm so desperately busy right now!

I am a *businesswoman*.

Going to Paris!

"You may wait in the Premiere Lounge and I'll place a

call for your boarding," she says extra gently as she points at
some sort of classy hotel-reception area behind her.
"And…Miss Blanchett?"

"Yes."

"I love your mother's work."

"Sure, thanks," I say, stepping cautiously into the lounge
with the feeling that I'm entering a sacred place.

Hello? I mean, *Bonjour?*

L'Espace Première is a magnificent lobby full of aging
golden boys playing with their cell phones and computers,
reading French newspapers while drinking scotch on the
rocks under appropriately dimmed lights.

I make another mental note: Lynn, you must get used to
these swanky places. Because, right now, I feel as comfortable as a monkey sitting on a rocket.

Oh!

A waitress brushes past me and places a basket of pastries
on the buffet table. I move closer. I'm guessing they were
baked in Paris this morning and flown to JFK.

"Are they from Paris?" I ask.

Silence.

"The croissants?"

"I don't know," she says. "They deliver them by truck. We
heat them up in the microwave. I'm new here, anyway."

"Thank you." I grab one of those ridiculously tiny plates
and fight a natural instinct to beat the cake-eating record,
which is actually held by a Japanese woman, or so I've seen
on the Discovery Channel.

Since Jodie asked me to behave like a young lady of the
world, I put the tiniest of all the croissants on my plate, ignore
the tray of éclairs, and find a seat next to an elegant woman.

She is all I would like to be. Startlingly beautiful. Confident. At home in such surroundings.

She is *much* older than me, about Jodie's age, somewhere in her comfortable forties. She's sipping tea while browsing through a magazine. She looks so calm, so perfect, so... *erudite*. She drops her reading, looks up and smiles at me. I smile back with my mouth full, shrug and struggle to eat as elegantly as a bird.

"They're lovely croissants, aren't they?" she says suddenly.

"Oh, yes, lovely!" Some crumbs come flying out of my mouth and land on George W. Bush's face on the cover of her magazine.

She brushes them off gracefully. "I'm sorry to interrupt you, but I think we can board our flight. You're going to Paris, aren't you?"

I swallow a mouthful and say, "Well, yes, I'm flying to Paris!" As if it was the most obvious thing to do.

"I thought so." She stands and gives me her hand. "Roxanne Green. Nice to meet you."

Roxanne? What a cool name.

"Lynn," I say briefly, controlling a survival impulse to say, *That's Lynn Blanchett, yeah, that's right, the daughter of superfamous Jodie Blanchett, so who's the most glamorous one now?*

"Lynn? Mmm! Nice to meet you, then." She gives me a condescending smile. "Our gate is this way," she says and darts away immediately.

Oh! Should I...

She stops. "Are you coming?"

Yes, yes! I abandon my croissant to catch up with her.

"First visit to Paris?"

Apparently it's tattooed on my forehead.

"Oh, no! I go often," I lie. "What about you?"

"Not as often as I'd like to," she says, but every single Air France attendant is, like, hello, Miss Green, how are you, Miss Green, how nice to see you again, seat 1A as usual, the Chablis is already in the chiller, ha ha ha, have a nice flight.

"What brings you to Paris so often, Lynn? Studying at the Sorbonne?"

Studying!

"Oh, no, no, work mostly."

"Really? Working? What is it that you do, then?"

"I'm a PR…er…person. I work in couture," I hear myself say.

"How interesting! Paris! Couture! At your age! You must lead a very colorful life."

"I can't complain."

"Who are you working for? Dior?" Roxanne giggles.

"Muriel B."

"Oh, you're working for Muriel. That's so funny. I know Muriel very well. Her father is a good friend of mine. You know him? Francis Boutonnière? It's such a small world, isn't it?"

"Oh, yes! Extremely tiny," I agree awkwardly, since I hardly know anything about Muriel B and I've never ever heard about any Francis Boutonnière. "Do you work in the fashion business, too, Roxanne?"

"I'm just an enthusiast. I make my living as a writer."

"Oh…have you written anything I might have heard of?"

She gives me that smile again. "Are you familiar with self-help titles?"

"Boarding pass, please," a flying attendant asks as we're about to board.

Roxanne hesitates a second, but finally snatches mine. "Where are you sitting? Ah! Business," she breathes and looks up at the stewardess. "Would you mind upgrading my good friend Lynn to premiere? Seat 1B. We just didn't realize we were on the same flight."

"That won't be a problem, Miss Green."

Just like that. I follow Roxanne into first class. "These flights are such a drag," she whispers as they serve us two champagne flutes and a tray of canapés to make it just about tolerable. "We'll keep each other company and you can tell me all about your *big job* at Muriel B!" Another laugh escapes her perfectly shaped mouth.

Oh, God!

"And remember to tell Muriel—you only fly losers and sales reps in business." She's about to give me back my boarding pass but takes a better look at it. "Blanchett?" she reads.

I can practically hear the bell of recognition in her head.

"You wouldn't happen to know—"

"Yep," I interrupt. "She's my mother."

You should see the look on Roxanne's face. I thought for a second she was choking on one of the lovely canapés she threw in her mouth. "You're Jodie Blanchett's daughter. But, darling, it's…IMPOSSIBLE!"

I gulp my champagne. I'm Jodie-freaking-Blanchett's daughter. That's just the way it is.

Jodie Blanchett, the designer behind the revival of denim chic.

Jodie Blanchett, the guru of anorexia clothing.

Jodie Blanchett, the worst mother on the entire planet and the one person responsible for putting me on this plane.

"I know Jodie very well and…she never mentioned any daughter!"

Typical Jodie. She always introduces me as *family,* never uses the actual word *daughter.* "I grew up with Dad," I say to clarify the obvious un-Jodieness about me.

"Whose your dad? I must know him!"

"Bill Blanchett."

"Bill Blanchett? Never heard of him."

"Dad is a…" I'm about to say *simple guy,* but that's such a bad way to sum up Dad. He is all that Jodie's not. Caring, loving, there for me. Their marriage lasted less than a week. Jodie once told me she loved the sound of *Jodie Blanchett.* I'm just the by-product of her quest for a flashy name. "Dad worked in a club she used to go to," I explain. "Like centuries ago."

"Well, your mother was a real trouper, wasn't she. Party party party!" Roxanne points a toothpick at me. "She was my absolute idol back in the eighties! Very liberated! Do you know I was one of the very first people to buy her paper clothes?"

The paper collection put Jodie on the map. Then came the perfume and the cosmetics line. The rest is history.

"I used to hang out a lot with her. We were very good friends. You know, back in the days…." Roxanne laughs again and the sound is quickly becoming annoying. "I don't see her at all anymore. It's like she…disappeared."

"She lives a very secluded life," I say.

It's actually a miracle she came out of her lair to drive me to the airport.

I mean, *she* didn't drive me, of course. Her chauffeur did.

"Muriel is all you're not," Jodie had told me during the ride while helping herself to a mineral water from the limo minibar. "She's been an item since she was a child. She's eccentric. Charming. She's a social animal. She knows everybody and everybody knows her. And she also speaks many languages," she concluded to answer her cell phone.

I opened the old copy of *Learn French in 10 Days* she offered me and looked through the first pages while she was having an angry cell-phone conversation about importing fur from Kazakhstan.

Day 1 was fairly easy and all about finding a bus stop. Day 2 was a real challenge as it encompassed buying bread in a French bakery.

Je voudrais une baguette de pain s'il vous plaît. How was that going to help in Paris? I was positive that buying bread wasn't part of my job description. I couldn't fall back on Day 1 either because I was also darn sure Muriel Boutonnière was not going to ask me directions to the next bus stop.

L'arrêt de bus se trouve à coté de la mairie.

Please.

How could anyone ever manage two languages in one head anyway?

Jodie disconnected her cell phone. "Did William give you some spending money?"

Jodie's the only person in the world who calls Dad William. Everyone else calls him Bill.

"I have my credit card."

"I mean real money," she said and took an envelope from her handbag.

I opened it. It contained a large wad of Euros. Jodie is like the mob, she only believes in cash.

"I can't take that," I protested.

She laughed. "Why?"

"It's too much money."

"Don't be so *common!*" She put her shades on, protecting herself from my commonness. "You're Jodie Blanchett's daughter. People will expect you to pay for everything. And you will! I don't want you to seem cheap, it would reflect poorly on me." She tapped on the driver's shoulder as we approached the terminal. "To the Minute-Drop!"

I tried not to make a face, but she looked at me and sighed. "I can't go inside the terminal. Not at this time of day. There are all…those *people.*"

I sat there beside Jodie, uncomfortable as usual, trying to think of something to say or to do that would impress her. Or at least get her attention. But she was already back on her cell phone, this time yelling at her PA and complaining about how U.S. Customs is ruining the fashion industry.

"Thank you, Jodie," I said when I got out of the limousine.

She put her cell phone on the side for a second.

"Thank you?"

"For arranging all this," I said, pointing at the terminal.

And for giving me the chance to show you I can be the kind of girl you'd actually claim as your daughter.

She looked annoyed. She doesn't like thank-yous or goodbyes. It's her excuse to run away from people pronto and without ceremony. "Please, Lynn. Don't turn it into another mess," she said and they immediately drove away.

Step #2:
Remember: The grass could
ALWAYS be greener.

I want this!

I've always wanted this!

To be given a chance!

I look at myself in the mirror. There is such a difference between the person I want to be and this gross image I see. I'm a small chunky girl just out of college trying to look like a fashion guru about to tackle Paris.

I'm nothing like Jodie. Nothing at all.

I know that's exactly what they expect in Paris. That's what they paid for. Jodie II: a younger, kinkier, sexier, thinner version of the genius mother.

And all they're going to get is me.

Untalented!

Inexperienced!

Unqualified!

I sit on the toilet. I hide my face in my hands and refocus. I am Lynn Blanchett.

That's Blanchett with two t's, dammit!

I AM fab! I AM glam! I AM…going to be sick!

Focus focus. FOCUS!

Knock, knock.

"Yes?"

"We're about to take off, miss. You should go back to your seat."

I walk through the first-class cabin. Look at those people. I don't belong here. I'd be better off with the sales reps in Business.

Roxanne looks particularly excited when I get back into my seat. She drops her magazine and whispers in my ear. "Don't look back. Hubert Barclay is coming our way."

Hubert *who?*

"He's been trying to date me forever. Seriously! A womanizer like him. You must know Hubert?"

"Well…"

"He is so low. I wouldn't be surprised if he was hunting in your age group. He's such a disgusting man."

I throw a quick glance in the aisle to see who she's talking about but all I see is a very handsome man walking toward us. Late thirties. Tall. Athletic. Elegant. It can't be the one she's talking about, because…

"Oh, Roxanne! Tsk, tsk! Going to Paris and not telling me, again."

Wait a minute! What's so disgusting about him?

"So sorry, Hubert. Lynn and I are having a girls-only pleasure trip. You know Lynn? Jodie Blanchett's daughter?"

He looks at me and gives me his am-I-supposed-to-know-you smile. He finally makes up his mind and says, "Of course, how are you, Laura?"

"Lynn," I correct him.

"Yeah, right, Lynn. Sorry. How have you been, since… since last time?"

"I've been good, Hubert," I say, trying to keep my breathing at a socially acceptable speed.

"Lynn is working for Muriel Boutonnière, you know, Francis's daughter."

"Muriel, huh? Her father and I, we go way back," he says and the world keeps getting smaller. "Is she still not talking to him?"

How would I know?

"She doesn't…talk about *that* with me."

We all shake our heads. *Damn Shame* is the consensus.

"Anyway, I don't want to spoil your all-girl…*thing*," he says and walks back to his seat for the takeoff.

"Look at him. He owns half the newspapers and magazines published in this country and he is still scared of me. Men are scared of women who reject them…. Men are scared of rejection, period."

I smile but my heart is rushing while I try to look calm and poised. I recognize him now. This is *the* Hubert Barclay, the billionaire, the media mogul, Barclay the Great, and he actually said *Hi, Lynn* (or Laura, but oh who cares!) and *How are you* and *My favorite color is green, just like yours* (I know, I made that one up).

"Can I top you off?" The flight attendant is back with some more champagne as soon as the plane has reached appropriate altitude. She tries to gives us our dinner menus but

Roxanne refuses them knowingly. "We will have the Dover sole and the white-chocolate *thingy*. And Chablis as usual, dear," she decides for the two of us. "Don't tell her I said so, but I think Muriel doesn't deserve to get someone like you. A Blanchett! Imagine! What money can't buy?"

Yeah, imagine.

"That girl always gets what she wants. She wants to become a designer, and voilà! Her father buys her this Muriel B *fantaisie*. And she never had to work for it. Like the French say, the only effort she ever made was to be born." She puts her hand on mine. "Oh, and I don't mean this for you, dear, I'm sure you must have some kind of…talent. Those things often run in the blood. Oh, that reminds me!"

She starts to shuffle in her handbag.

"You must remember to tell your mother I say hi, for old times' sake."

"Sure."

"And you must give her this." Apparently she keeps a small library in there, because she comes out with a tiny hardcover book.

I read the title. *Roxanne Green's 20 Steps to Success.* I recognize Roxanne on the cover. She's dressed in a strict business ensemble. Her arms are crossed firmly against her body. She wears a pair of sunglasses and is leaning against a white stretch limo. It's a very sunny picture and you can even see some thin palm trees in the background.

"The perfect image of success when imagined by losers!" she says through a now nearly nauseating laugh while pointing at the cover.

I open the book.

"It will give Jodie a laugh."

I read the title of the first chapter: "Step #1: Never be ashamed of who you are."

"You could read it, too," she says. "Lynn, can I be so bold to say that you strike me as a nice person."

"Oh! Thank you."

"No, it's that… Well, if you want to survive in a place like Paris, you need to be a bit tougher. Go to the third chapter, you'll see."

I turn to the relevant page.

"Read it," Roxanne commands.

The chapter title says: "Step #3: Everywhere you go, be utterly bored."

"What I mean is, Lynn…you need to be more of a bitch."

Step #3:
Everywhere you go, be utterly bored.

I'm *it!*

I am the real thing!

Lynn Blanchett, daughter of famous mother Jodie Blanchett and genius in the making!

I have picked up my ugly Adidas bag, farewelled Roxanne and, as I cross customs, I find a tall Arab-looking man holding a piece of paper with my name on it.

"I'm Lynn Blanchett," I tell him.

"Ke suis Massoud, et je suis votre chauffeur."

"Do you speak English?

"No no, no English! *Français!*"

"Right! This—" I point at the name "—is me." I point at me.

"Oh!"

He points at himself.

"Moi, Massoud."

We're doing the Tarzan-meets-Jane thing.

"Should we go to the car? The car? *Le car!*" I turn an imaginary steering wheel.

"Car! Yes, yes! *Par là, mademoiselle.*" He walks toward one of the exits.

I follow him outside and we walk toward a stretch lim— No, that's not a limousine at all, that's just a… er…silly-looking car. Like a cross between a hearse and a spaceship. That must be the compact French version of a stretch limo.

He opens the passenger door for me.

Mmm? Cream leather upholstery. A phone. A minibar. A little video monitor for the passengers to enjoy a selection of DVDs.

Not bad at all!

"Vous voulez aller à votre hôtel?"

"Er…"

"You want hotel?" he tries.

"Yes, let's go to my hotel."

"Good!"

We're off and I take my first glance at France. It's not what I expected. It's dawn, but the sky is nothing but mud-brown mash. The airport is located in the middle of grimy fields and lines of dirty highways.

"Paris!"

"Er…"

I open my eyes.

It feels like we have been driving for hours. Horrible traffic jams. I look to my right and all I can see are gray buildings. But…

I turn to my left and I see it, Paris!

Paris, Paris, PARIS!

We exit the highway. *"Trop de bouchons,"* Massoud repeats like a motto as we slide into the city.

Bouchons?

It feels so unfamiliar. The streets are narrow. Everything looks old and hides the dark rainy sky. People are walking along the wet sidewalks, heads down, and dressed in plain boring colors.

There is a feeling of sadness.

Nobody plays the accordion.

There's no Café Terrace with people drinking wine and eating French bread by their parked scooters.

But then, we turn and drive along a lovely little river.

"Is that the Seine?"

"What?"

"La Seine?" I ask, tapping my window.

"No, no, Canal Saint-Martin. Very very beautiful!"

"Oh, yeah, it's *so* beautiful," I repeat excitedly.

Now it looks like the city I have been dreaming of. Romantic, slow paced, vibrant and full of culture.

But before I can take on this perfect image of Paris, we make another turn and we get blocked in a street that might have been in Cairo for all I know. People of all races yell at each other in different languages while carrying racks of clothes, vegetables, meat. Cow carcasses are unloaded from dirty trucks. Animals are hanging upside down above butcher stalls.

I can't believe my eyes. Here I am, in the comfort of my hearse-spaceship combo, and outside, it's mayhem.

We drive along a huge old monumental arc.

"Arc de Triomphe?" I ask.

"No! No! This Porte Saint-Denis. Arc de Triomphe very much big!"

He shows me how big with his hands.

The Arc de Triomphe is much bigger, he tries to explain. Apparently Paris is full of arcs. They have an excess of arcs.

"Ah, Paris," he says happily and winks at me. "Look, look!"

When I look outside, I realize that we are surrounded by an army of prostitutes. Most of them are very old, overweight and wear ridiculously tight Lycra.

Is this Paris according to Massoud?

But before I can make up my mind about that, we change landscape again.

This is not a car, it's a time machine.

"Et voilà, la Seine!" Massoud points. *"Là!"*

Look!

Paris opens up in front of me. And here is the Seine. Two lines of magnificent monumental buildings run alongside this huge river. I don't think I have ever seen anything so beautiful. I would cry if Massoud wasn't checking me constantly in his mirror.

"It's very…beautiful," I say.

"Paris, Paris!" Massoud stars to whistle, turns away from the Seine and stops the car.

Before I realize that we have arrived at my hotel, a porter opens my door and offers his hand to help me out.

"Bonjour, mademoiselle, bienvenu au Georges V."

"Bonjour…"

I look at the hotel. It's magnificent. Way beyond what I expected.

Massoud gets out of the car and passes the porter my ridiculously small luggage.

"Voilà! Goodbye."

"Hey!" I call after him. "Massoud?"

"Oui."

"Merci, Massoud. Thank you!" I give him my best smile, and I must be doing a good job at it because he smiles back and says, *"pas de problème,"* which, I believe, means something like you're welcome.

"This way, *mademoiselle,"* the porter says, carrying my ugly little bag. He whisks me through the revolving doors.

Holy crap! Look at that. I freeze in the middle of the lobby, petrified. It's so…

"This way, this way!"

Er, okay….

The porter drops my bag in front of the reception desk and I hand the man my passport.

"Mademoiselle Blanchett, yes. But of course, we have you in our English Suite."

"Oh, that's great."

"You are very, very lucky."

"Really?"

"Really, you are. You were supposed to have an executive suite but then we found out who you were," he says with a you-know-what-I-mean smile. "We upgraded you, of course! It's a magnificent suite. André will show you."

André, my porter, grabs my card key and I follow him to the elevator. I can't stop staring at him. He is such an elegant creature, with a funny walk. His body remains perfectly still while his legs go wild.

It has to be some kind of professional trick.

"A magnificent suite…" I repeat, trying to imitate the French accent of the receptionist.

"Oh, yes, floor seven. The English Suite. Very beautiful, *mademoiselle,*" André says and does his funny walk all the way to the door to open it for me.

Mama Caramba!

I take my first step into the room. It's clotted with antiques, drapes and fancy material, yet an awesome sense of refinement strikes me through and through.

"That will be fine," I whisper because I want André to go away before I faint.

I find a five-dollar bill in the deepest darkest part of my jacket pocket and pass it to him.

"Merci et bonne journée, mademoiselle." André hands me my card key and closes the door behind me.

I'm still standing in the entrance. I cannot grasp the fact that this is my room. I feel that at any time the real guests will come in and call the police to escort me out.

Because, let's be honest: I don't deserve any of this.

Jodie just said, "I made a couple phone calls. You're going to work in Paris. It will be good professional experience for you. And please, take off that dress. I cannot be seen with you in that dress."

She didn't say anything about being treated like a freaking New York princess.

But then again, that's how Jodie is.

I slide like a ghost toward the bed. It's huge and truly beautiful, but I wouldn't dare touch it. I can see the door to the bathroom. I am like an insect attracted by the light. I push open the door to have a look inside.

I clap a hand over my mouth not to scream. It's so gorgeous! I have never seen anything so beautiful as this bathroom. All the silver and tiles are shining like diamonds. The towels look so warm and cozy. I need to touch them. I approach them. I reach for them. My skin feels the comfort of them. I turn to the mirror.

Ah!

Something is wrong in this bathroom.

It's me.

I see my reflection in the mirror and I am the odd one out. Not only do I look exhausted, I look like an ugly little duckling with a mad hairdo.

I can't believe that I have been seen by all those people dressed like this.

André the porter looks ten times more swish than me. Roxanne must have had a hilarious time with me. I must be her best joke since the invention of the whoopee cushion. She must be talking about me to all her friends—she might even phone Jodie. "Guess who I met on the plane? Your ridiculous daughter. Isn't she common! She was wearing this ugly dress and hideous jacket!"

I am about to leave the bathroom when the sound of an alarm stops me. I look around and locate the source of the noise. There is a phone above the toilet seat.

Wow, you can sit on the toilet and still talk with your friends and family.

Disturbing.

I pick up the phone.

"Hello?"

"Lynn?" a man's voice says.

That's me, so I say, "That's me." No, no, that's not assertive enough. "This is Lynn Blanchett speaking," I say loud and clear.

"Oh, hi! My name is Nicolas Bouchez. I'm the human resources manager at Muriel B," the man says with a slight accent.

Oh, God!

First instinct: hang up, run away.

Second instinct: hide under the bed.

Third instinct: change your dress, don't add disgrace to disillusion!

"Is everything okay? Are you…satisfied with the room?" he asks.

"The room?"

"Muriel wanted to be sure you'd be happy with the room."

"It's…okay."

I have to sit down on the toilet. It's quite comfortable for a chat on the phone.

"Muriel asked me to welcome you. Check on you. I am downstairs, at reception. You must be starving. Should we meet over lunch? Is there anyplace you'd like to go in particular?"

I try to think, but I can't remember any restaurant name from my travel guide.

"Somewhere vegetarian," I say.

Yes, I've just decided to be a vegetarian!

Just like Jodie!

Anything wrong with that?

Step #4:
Silence is your finest conversational tool.

"Vous avez reservé?" the maître d' asks while staring at my mad hairdo and, yes, I also do stink of petrol (I'll come back to this later).

"Une table pour deux, au nom de Bouchez, ou Muriel B," Nicolas answers.

I nod. Whatever those people are saying in French, I'm just going to nod.

"Muriel B, mais bien sûr, une table pour deux." The maître d' is not surprised anymore. The fashion industry is full of crazy-looking, crazy-smelling people just like me.

Nicolas smiles at me. You see, not a problem, he seems to say.

Nicolas takes my jacket and hands it to the maître d'.

Nicolas waits for me to be seated before sitting in turn.

He fills my glass with water before the waiter beats him to it.

Nicolas jumps on the table, gives me an extravagant French kiss and orders our appetizers (yeah, okay, I made up that one, too).

Well, my original plan was to change my dress, meet Nicholas in the lobby and convince him I'm Miss Perfect.

It didn't happen quite this way.

I walked down the monumental staircase and there he was, standing right in the middle of the lobby.

"I am dressed all in black, you can't miss me," he had said on the phone.

He was dressed in a tight black suit all right, tight black shirt and black tie.

Tight, tight, TIGHT!

I mean, even from a distance I could already see how slim and athletic he was.

I walked a few steps closer and all of a sudden, *whoosh,* he turned to me.

Wait a minute!

This was not a regular human resources manager. They sent me…an angel!

He was looking around as if trying to find me. *Which one of these magnificent women is the extraordinary Lynn Blanchett? Surely not this small creature walking straight toward me, with her mouth wide open and drooling.*

I ran through what to say in my mind. "Hi, I'm Lynn Blanchett… Lynn Blanchett… Hello? Ha ha ha!"

That's not going to cut the mustard. I can't deal with people like him. Bright blue eyes, dark blond hair and lips already forming into a gentle smile.

"Nicolas Bouchez?" I asked him.

He smiled some more. Some tiny wrinkles formed around his eyes. Late twenties, maybe early thirties.

"Yes…."

"It's me. I'm Lynn Blanchett."

Disappointed?

"Oh…Lynn! Sure…. How nice to meet you…finally!"

He shook my hand delicately. I looked up into his very large blue pupils and started to melt.

"Are you…"

"Me?"

"Are you hungry? Tired, Lynn?"

No, I'm speechless, and fascinated by you. You are the most beautiful thing I have ever seen! And you are actually talking to me.

"I…" I began to stammer.

"We will take it easy today. Tomorrow starts the real circus!"

"I…"

"I have booked a table at a nice place, Le Club. It's not strictly vegetarian, but they have vegetarian options. Will that do?"

You are perfect! I want to fall on my knees and just look at you.

"I… Perfect," I finally managed to say. "Absolutely, completely perfect."

"I came on my scooter. I'll get a taxi for you. I just got this new BMW model. It's very convenient in Paris."

I followed him out to a sleek scooter like those I'd seen people riding in movies and TV commercials.

"They are very fashionable," he said. "And so much easier to park than a car."

"Can you fit two on them?"

"Well, there is a back seat, but…"

At the rear of the seat is a little space for an attaché case or a Lynn Blanchett.

"So forget the taxi. I'll take a ride with you," I said.

He gave me the are-you-sure-about-that-you-silly-woman look.

Yes, I'm sure. Absolutely sure. Like I've never been sure before. I'm a scooter-riding Parisian!

"I don't have an extra helmet for you."

"That's all right. I don't mind."

I smiled at him. We climbed aboard and for a second there, I was probably the funniest public relations recruit he ever met. As we made the short distance from the hotel to the restaurant on his scooter, I realized I'd found the perfect way to…

1. Keep very close to Nicolas.
2. Get another good look at Paris.
3. Get a mad hairdo.
4. Filter the gas fumes, hence protecting the environment.
5. Get unwanted attention from maître d's.

"Do you need any help?" Nicolas asks once we are seated and have our menus.

His voice is so gentle and sweet. He is always an inch away from a smile or a laugh because angels have a keen and happy nature.

"Sorry, we do have a menu in English," the maître d' says, trying to snatch the French version out of my hands.

But I say, *"Non"* (*Learn French in 10 Days*—Day 1)."French is fine. What vegetarian options would you recommend?"

The maître d' smiles politely."We only have one vegetarian option."

"Good," I say."I'll have that one, then. It looks delicious."

"Would you mind if I order meat?" Nicolas asks.

"You can order whatever you like." I laugh idiotically.

He orders something in French, then asks me, "Some wine?"

"Sure!"

He selects the wine and then we have a long embarrassing silence.

"Do you smoke?" he asks.

"No."

Is that good? Is that bad? Would you like me better if I did?

"Me, neither," he says.

Oh, it's good, then.

We have another embarrassing silence.

"I…"

I can't believe I'm sitting here with a guy like you!

"I…"

Say something clever, Lynn! "I—"

"I'm a great admirer of your mother's work," he cuts in.

Shit!

"The paper collection," he says enigmatically and nods.

Double shit!

Just when I thought my brain was at its emptiest, the simple mention of Jodie's name bleaches it white.

"She's a genius, isn't she?" He digs deeper.

I enter vegetative state.

Say SOMETHING, Lynn!

"Château Haut-Brion, 1997." Too late, the maître d' is back with a bottle of wine. Nicolas tries a drop and says it's perfect. *C'est parfait.*

"Do you like French wine?" he asks.

"I don't… Yeah, sure, I love French wine." I love anything you love, silly!

"Good."

We have another long embarrassing silence.

If I don't speak soon he'll bring up Jodie again.

"I'm very tired, sorry," I apologize for my lack of conversation, my lack of personality, my lack of…everything.

"Of course, it's not a problem."

I try the wine. It tastes weird, like a mixture of dirt, mushroom and mold.

"Perfect," I say again.

"It has aged nicely, hasn't it?"

"Mmm…yes, yes," I approve.

Then he sniffs the wine, takes a sip and makes all kinds of weird noises before swallowing it.

A gurgling angel. How disturbing.

"Une belle robe, quoiqu'un peu riche en tannin."

I nod. *Oui, oui!*

"You seem to know a lot about wine."

That's right. Compliment him till he bursts.

"Oh, not really. But it's one of my hobbies. Food… restaurants…wine. You are very lucky in New York. So many good restaurants. Famous chefs. Amazing bars."

Oh, no, don't start asking me stuff about New York. I moved to Connecticut with Dad years ago. All I ever do when I go to New York is spend time locked up in Jodie's amazing apartment, glued to her giant-screen TV. Ask me about cable and I can talk forever.

"I love going to New York just for the restaurant scene," he continues. "What's your favorite restaurant, Lynn?"

"Restaurant?"

"Yes."

"In New York?"

"Yes."

"I…wouldn't know. I am not very interested in…food," I say. *"Que me nourrit me detruit."*

"That's…the…anorexic motto," he says and smiles cautiously.

Was that humor? Like… Curvy me…anorexic? Ha ha! Damn that French subtlety.

Another embarrassing silence. He smiles but I can tell that I'm making him pretty uncomfortable.

"I'm sorry, I am so tired." I blame everything on the jet-lag again. Oh, God. He must think I'm so dull.

"Your goat's cheese toast on eggplant salad," the maître d' says as he places the plate in front of me.

I can't stand goat's cheese and I hate eggplant.

"Votre filet mignon," he says to Nicolas and places what looks like a delicious piece of beef rolled up in a thin slice of yummy bacon in front of him.

He nods approvingly. Angels are meat eaters, apparently.

As for my salad, I just stare at it as if it were trying to speak Greek to me.

"You're not eating?"

I'm so hungry, I could faint.

"Oh, I'm not hungry anymore."

"I see," he says. "Do you mind if I…" He points at his steak.

"Go for it, I don't mind you eating."

"You know, this place, this restaurant…" He shows me around with the tip of his steak knife. "It's one of the hottest places in Paris right now, and you would hardly get better vegetarian food anywhere else."

"I don't doubt it, Nicolas. But I am perfectly fine."

Come on. Make an effort!

I fork a little piece of goat's cheese and delicately lift it to my lips. I start to chew and the very taste I don't like about goat's cheese explodes in my mouth.

I want to spit it out and scream but I manage to articulate, "Excuse me', stand and walk to the maître d'.

"Toilet!" I bark, trying to keep the cheese in a corner of my mouth and not spit it out on his lovely dark purple tie. He points downstairs.

I walk fast and make it to the toilets. I run into a cubicle and spit out the piece of cheese. I am so pathetic. I'm tired. I haven't slept for the last twenty-four hours. My nerves are about to snap. I'm having lunch with the cutest man I've ever met, and I'm a freak show.

I sit, lock the door and go for it. I just cry. It's a good thing to cry. Men can't stand it when women cry. They think something's wrong. It's quite the opposite sometimes. Like now. It's just a way to release pressure and move on.

When I walk back to the table, Nicolas has finished his steak. He must have hurried while I was away.

The maître d' comes to our table and asks if we have finished.

"Yes, I am finished, thank you," I say.

He exchanges one of *those* looks with Nicolas. Those American women, all nuts, they seem to agree.

"Any dessert?"

"Just coffee," Nicolas says.

"A trim latte, no foam," I ask, and by the dirty look I get from the maître d' it's like I just ordered the murder of his family.

"Trim latte, no foam," Nicolas repeats and smiles.

Oh, look at that smile. I can spend my life ordering foamless lattes if it has this effect on him.

Then I wonder. What if I was to order a decaf nonsteamed soy milk macchiato?

We're back on his scooter.

Only this time I squeeze my arms around his chest. I close my eyes. I feel him breathing. In, out. Can't we just drive like this forever?

"You can let go now."

I open my eyes. We're back at the hotel.

"Oh, sorry…. I was a bit…gone." I let go of him and his scooter.

"See you tomorrow morning at the office, then," he says. "I'll send a cab. Is eight-thirty too early?"

"I never sleep," I hear myself say, because that's exactly what Jodie always tells everybody, even though I've never heard someone snoring louder than her. "Too many things to do! I'll sleep in my next life!"

If only I could be mute.

"Sure…." He makes a weird gesture that doesn't mean much to me. Maybe he just wants to say that I am by far the weirdest, most disturbing person he has ever met.

"See you then," I say, but he is already gone.

★ ★ ★

I fall flat on my bed in my beautiful suite.

I pick up the phone and follow the instructions to make an international call.

"Er…what?" Delia answers.

Delia is my best friend. I hold her partly responsible for my being in Paris. She's the one that said, *Hey, why don't you phone your mother. She can get you a job as a receptionist or something.*

But she didn't know that Jodie doesn't do anything like normal folks.

Like, if you suggest a gym subscription for your birthday, she sends her chauffeur with an Australian personal trainer that you're also supposed to lodge.

"I met someone," I say on the phone.

"What? Lynn?"

"I met someone."

"You… Do you know what time it is?"

I lie on the bed. If only she could see the smile on my face.

"I'm in bed," she protests. "I'm sleeping! The whole freaking city is asleep! Are you crazy?"

"He's the most beautiful man I've ever seen. And he is…so refined. And he…he…"

She finally caves in. "What's his name?"

"Nicolas."

"French?"

"You bet!"

"Mmm…I don't like it. I don't trust those European types. Great sex. Great fun. They even seem to really listen to you. There's definitely something suspicious about them. Are you in love?"

I rock on the bed and play with the phone cord. I'm a teenager again!

"I don't know. I just met him."

"He's French, use a condom."

"Delia!"

"Is he hot?"

"Aaaaaaargh!"

"You lucky thing!"

We laugh.

"Delia… He doesn't like me."

"Of course he likes you. Everybody likes you."

"No, he really doesn't. How could he? He is so handsome and so…and so…everything…and I'm…well, I'm *me*."

"Nonsense! You're hot!"

"I'm so not."

"Miss Blanchett, you listen to me. This guy…this *Nikoooolaz,* he doesn't deserve you."

I don't say a thing.

"Lynn, tell me you will come back."

Silence.

"You're not permanently moving to France for a man, are you?"

Well…I make a quick mental calculation.

I am ugly: -2

I am very poorly dressed: -2

I am exotic and foreign: +1

I am faking anorexia: -2

I drink trim lattes, no foam: +2

I like to ride on the back of his scooter: +2

I get crazy hairdos after riding on his scooter: -1

I feel madly attracted to the most beautiful, most charming Frenchman: +2

Total: 0

Even Steven!

Step #5:
Seduction seduction seduction!

So here is my new plan: coffee.

I look at the clock on my nightstand and it's only six in the morning. I know, I shouldn't leave the sanctuary of my bed when outside there are hundreds of people waiting for me to be just like Jodie, but I must have it. And then I remember the dreams.

I had so many! In some of them, I was being eaten alive by all sorts of fish. But mostly I had the other kind of dream. Not nightmares at all. *Au contraire*. They were more like…well, erotic, I guess. And they involved him (*him, him, him!*), a pair of very large wings and various kinds of animals.

It's crazy what jet lag does to you, huh?

Or maybe it's just the Parisian atmosphere. The air pollution here probably makes every American woman horny.

I slide out of bed and hop to the bathroom. Where to

begin? I start by looking at my body in the mirror. I feel
so… Mmm?

When I can no longer stand to look at myself in the mirror, I throw on some clothes and head out. The lobby is very
quiet. Nobody's at the reception desk. Nobody's in the
restaurant, even though it seems open. "Hello?" I call. "Anybody?"

It's such a beautiful room. It shines like a new coin, but
still brings you back a century or two.

A tired waiter finally comes out of the kitchen and notices me.

"*Bonjour, mademoiselle, une seule personne?*"

"Breakfast," I say defensively.

"Yes, breakfast. *Suivez-moi.*"

He seats me at a charming little table.

"English or continental?"

"I feel very much like a continental girl this morning." I
beam up at him, quite pleased with my own joke.

He shrugs, kind of *whatever,* and brings back a little basket filled with mini Danish pastries and croissants. There are
Barbie pots of jam, honey and butter to play with on my
table. Add to this, toasted French bread and a large coffee
plunger and, that's right, I am in heaven.

Some guests have joined me in the restaurant. I am particularly interested in the women, the professional ones, the
ones who are about to go to an office, just like me.

I need to look like them and I realize that I have chosen
the wrong outfit. I'm wearing a brand-new gray ensemble
that I bought for job interviews. I look like a cheap businesswoman in a commercial for a dandruff shampoo.

The other women are more casual. They wear designer

denims and simple black or white shirts and, even though it's quite dark in the restaurant, some of them hide their faces behind large lightly shaded sunglasses.

I can do that.

Fashion is so easy!

After breakfast, I take the elevator back to my room. Luckily, I have a dirty pair of jeans. I give them the smell test. Mmm… They're a bit stuffy, but I can fix that with a bit of deodorant.

I don't have a white shirt, though. But I have a plain white T-shirt that I wore for my bus trip to New York. I put it through the smell test, too.

Ouch!

Bless deodorant.

There are two little sweat stains under the arms. Not a problem. I just won't lift my arms. How often does one need to lift her arms in an office environment? And as soon as I get a minute, I will go out and buy myself a simple white shirt.

I check out my new outfit in the full-length bathroom mirror. I don't look like the women in the restaurant. It's my jeans. Wrong model. They're too plain. They're not your designer denims.

Maybe if I fold them like so. Yes, it does give them a bit of character.

Shoes?

What about my Japanese flip-flops? Let's do that.

I twist and turn in front of the mirror. I look…experimental…and I still smell of sweat. More deodorant.

Stinky and ugly. That's my fashion statement.

I look at my gray ensemble on the bed. Woman from

dandruff shampoo commercial or smelly scarecrow? What will it be?

Maybe a pair of lightly shaded sunglasses is the missing detail. I don't have that kind, just plain ugly ones. I try them on. I can hardly see my reflection in the mirror. And that's good. I mean, not to be able to see myself. I immediately feel better.

The phone rings, I pick it up in the bathroom. Massoud is waiting for me downstairs.

Panic!

I hurriedly add a last spray of aerosol deodorant. Isn't it too cold to wear nothing but a dirty T-shirt? I'm going to look naked. I grab a light pink pullover and throw it over my shoulders. Perfect! Now I look like a creature from the eighties who escaped after spending the past twenty years in a shoe box.

"Morning, Massoud," I say as get in the car. "Nice to see you again."

He turns and takes a good look at me and his nostrils twitch.

"No English," he reminds me and opens his window. He whispers something. How do you say, *God, the lady in pink really stinks* in Arabic?

I recognize some of the streets from yesterday, mostly because of the herd of old prostitutes. Massoud stops the car and points at a wooden black gate across the street.

"Muriel B," he says and I am not sure if he is talking about a brothel or a fashion company. "*Rue Saint Denis, très, très* hot!"

"Are you sure this is the right place?"

Jodie sent me to Paris to work in fashion not in prostitution. At least, I hope.

I step out of the car to find myself surrounded by people carrying racks of clothes, and prostitutes, lots of prostitutes.

The sight of Nicolas's scooter instantly makes me feel better. I walk to the gate. I have to apologize to a prostitute since she's leaning against the intercom.

"J'étais là la première, dégage!"

She's shooing me away! Does she…? She thinks that I'm the competition!

"I just want to go into this building." I point at the intercom. "I'm working in there."

"I'm working here, too!" She steps away, very annoyed at me. She spits on the ground. That's what she thinks of me.

I ring and the gate buzzes and opens. I pop my head inside, and then step into the courtyard. It's very old-looking, with a little stone bench and a little angel statue in the middle. Behind the statue stands a large three-story building. It's a sort of private house in the middle of Paris.

I walk on the old pavement listening to the sound of my Japanese flip-flops as I climb the marble stairs to the building.

I can see a reception desk past the French doors and a huge Muriel B logo. There's no mistake. I have reached my own private hell.

But I can do this. I can prove to Jodie and everyone else I can fit in.

I open the door. The receptionist looks up at me. Everything is so silent. It seems that there's just me and her in the building.

"Bonjour," she says. *"Je peux vous aider?"*

"Nicolas Bouchez, please."

"Qui dois-je annoncer?"

Oh, God, how long can I hide that I can't speak a word of French? "I'm Lynn Blanchett."

"Oh, but of course, take a seat, please."

I take a seat in the beautiful white salon by the reception area. Everything feels brand new. You can still smell fresh paint. Electric cables are hanging here and there, waiting for the finishing touches.

Yet, the Muriel B office looks astonishing. A mixture of modernity set inside traditional surroundings. And beyond the black gates, past the courtyard, in the street, there is Sodom and Gomorrah. It's so…fashionable!

I hear heavy footsteps coming down the large marble stairs. I'm so scared. Animals must feel this way before being killed and eaten. I put away my ridiculous sunglasses. I look up and see Nicolas walking toward me.

Seeing him is like a kick in the stomach. He looks *that* good.

Just like in my dream from last night. Yeah, that's right, that dream. The one where he runs after me in the hay barn. He catches me and…

Did he make a special effort to look so good today? Or is he just plain cute like this every day?

"Nice to see you again, did you have some rest?" he asks.

I couldn't stop thinking of you and you've even invaded my dreams. Oh, God, did I say that out loud? "I rested plenty, thank you."

"Muriel is looking forward to meeting you."

"Likewise." Two sentences without sounding stupid. I'm on a roll!

"What do you think of our office? Amazing, no?" he asks

as we start to climb toward whatever purgatory is waiting for me upstairs.

"It's very…well, very special."

"I know. It doesn't look like a trendy district. That's Muriel. She wants us to keep our ears to the ground, you know, be where things really happen."

"The concept is good, I like it," I say earnestly. "It can become some kind of motto—Muriel B. Where things really happen. You know what I mean?"

He smiles approvingly. That's the first time he approves of something I say or do, except maybe for the scooter ride.

"You know what I think?" I ask, because all of a sudden I think that it would be great to do a fashion show right there, in the street below, in the middle of this chaos. That would be…

"No, what do you think, Lynn?"

Wait a second. What if my idea sounds completely stupid? How would I know?

"Well… Nothing," I say mysteriously.

"Okay…."

Dull, dull, DULL!

We reach the landing and my heart is beating faster. Noises, voices, the sounds of movement and laughter are coming from behind a huge tall white wooden door.

"*C'est l'Atelier.* The workshop," Nicolas says. "All the offices are located on the second floor. But this is where the real magic takes place."

He pushes open the door and invites me into their world.

It's a huge space, like a ballroom. Groups of people are gathered around different tables.

They chatter away. They scream. It's a zoo.

Most of them are very young, a majority look Asian, maybe Japanese, and dress in contemporary punk style.

Nicolas whisks me through, and I can see lots of facial piercings, tattoos, dreads and multicolored hairdos.

"Here she is," Nicolas says, pointing at a group at the far end of the workshop. "Do you recognize her?"

"Oh, yes," I say, trying to guess which one in this group of teenagers could be Muriel B, and finally decide that it has to be the oldest one, well, I mean a girl about my age, which happens to be the most elegant one, in a classic kind of way.

"Muriel," Nicolas calls, and, yes, the elegant girl turns first, so I walk straight to her, take a large breath of air, shake her hand and give her my million-dollar smile.

"Hello, Muriel, I'm very pleased to meet you."

She shakes my hand, smiles and says, "Françoise Neuton. Pleased to meet you, too."

Shit!

She points at the smallest, youngest kid in the group. "That's Muriel," Françoise Neuton says amused.

Muriel can hardly be more than eighteen years old. Her lips and nose and ears are infested with multiple piercings and studs. A large tribal tattoo goes all around her neck and arms.

Nicolas clears his throat. "Muriel, this is Lynn Blanchett."

"I see," Muriel says, but we don't shake hands. *"C'est un honneur d'avoir une Blanchett parmi nous!"*

Oh, we aren't going to speak English, then?

I nod. It worked so far.

"Tu parles français, j'espère?"

"Oui," I say. *"Je…* Mmm! *Je…"* Nothing French comes out, not even a word about buying bread at the bakery.

They turn to me. The whole workshop staff stops and waits for some sound to come out of my mouth.

Complete silence.

"So…you've already met Françoise." Nicolas comes to my rescue. "She is our *première*. If Muriel is the creative mind, Françoise is her hands."

"That's very poetic, Nicolas. Well done," Muriel says with a cool and exaggerated British accent.

She looks at me more carefully. Everybody looks at me more carefully. They don't dare to think anything before Muriel has given her own verdict.

"I like your…T-shirt. DKNY?"

"No, it's just a…basic one."

"Basic, I've never heard of them. It's really unattractive in a nice way. That *is* fashion though, isn't it?"

The rest of them are now whispering about the quality of a *Basic* white T-shirt.

Stop staring at her tattoos! I scream to myself.

Is she… Yes, she has a huge stud on her tongue. I can't believe that this is actually Muriel B. My future boss? Nicolas's employer? I mean, isn't she supposed to be at school or something?

"We're working on that piece," Muriel says. She shows me a dress. It hangs on a wood model behind the group. Yak! It's sort of…ugly. "What do you think?"

"Oh… It's sort of…"

"Don't you like it?" Muriel asks amusingly.

Silence again.

"To be honest, well…no, I find it kind of…"

Kind of what, you idiot? Outdated? Too short? Too long? Too tight? Too brown? Not enough? What would you know?

"Kind of…ugly."

Did I just say that?

Françoise Neuton looks away. *"C'est tout de même incroyable!"* She whispers. I must be the most annoying person she's ever met.

"She finds it ugly," Muriel laughs out. She thinks I'm very funny. "Everyone, listen up, Blanchett finds it *kind of ugly*."

I turn to Nicolas. He's cupping his chin in his fingers. He needs to take a better look at the dress. Then he looks at me. Me or the dress? Being given the choice, which one would he trash?

"That's exactly what I think, Françoise! This is not what I had in mind. Redo it! *Allez! Comment tu dis, Lynn?* It's…kind of ugly! *Merci."*

More whispers. I feel like I'm surrounded by a sea of hissing snakes.

Françoise looks at me. Her lips are so tight you couldn't slide a needle through.

Muriel comes closer and sniffs the air around me. Sniff sniff! "You're wearing a very strong perfume. Kazo?"

I cannot tell Muriel she's smelling my deodorant.

"No, it's, er…designed just for me!"

"You American women are really getting away with everything. Ridiculous pink colors, horrible white T-shirts and perfectly awful perfumes. I love it."

I smile, deciding that it's her way to give a compliment.

"Une minute tout le monde," Muriel calls, stopping the background murmuring. *"Je vous presente Lynn Blanchett, la fille de Jodie Blanchett!"*

Hisses, lots of hisses.

"Lynn vient de New York, et travaille comme…"

"*Relation publique.*" Nicolas helps her remember why in God's name I'm here if it wasn't for Jodie's name.

"*Bienvenu, Lynn,*" a very effeminate male voice says from the snake pit and, even though I cannot see who said that, for the first time since I left New York, I feel good.

Oh la la!

Muriel acts as if I've already been working for her for hundreds of years. She thinks I'm all clued up.

She drags me around in the office and tells me about what *we're* going to do to bring *our* company to the top and how *my* work is essential for making *us* the newest, funkiest brand on the market.

"But we need money, Lynn. Lots of money. And you're going to help me get it."

She laughs.

I laugh along, without knowing exactly why.

"You will talk to *them.* Once they realize we've got somebody like you on board, they will give me all the money I need. Imagine, a Blanchett working at Muriel B! Won't they buy into that, huh? Nicolas?"

"Mmm…" That's what Nicolas thinks about me.

I am just very "Mmm."

Back home, I imagined Muriel B to be a mature woman, elegant, well traveled, drinking champagne like I drink water. Somehow, I imagined her like Roxanne Green.

And look what I get.

A teenager with tribal tattoos and delusions of grandeur. She doesn't drink champagne. Instead, she opens one can of sugar-free Red Bull after the next and never misses an occasion to burp. Her hair has been fashioned into a set of well-defined short black spikes. She looks very sexy but at the same time very dangerous and free spirited.

"That's my office. That's the only place where I can get some peace. You like it?"

Her office is a large room, very bright, with high windows and ceiling. It's amazing. It's stripped of any furniture but for a low floor table, on top of which is a streamlined portable computer, some documents and a few electronic gizmos. Behind the table is a huge Buddha statue, suspended against the wall. His eyes are closed and he holds up his hands, pointing to Nirvana.

"It's very…Zen. I love it."

There are no chairs. She sits on the wooden floor, in front of the table, and invites us to join her.

"We need to talk to *Him*, Nicolas. Get *Him* on the phone."

Nicolas looks at his watch. "Catherine has arranged a phone conference. It starts in only five minutes."

"Did you explain to Lynn what's going on?"

"Well, we need to talk to the bank now and, er, we… Maybe Lynn doesn't need to know everything right now, Muriel."

Muriel shakes her head. "You didn't tell her, did you?"

Tell me what?

Nicolas sighs. "We're broke, Lynn."

"And you are our last hope," Muriel explains.

Me? But…I don't have any money! Alarm bells sound in my head.

"Bonjour! Muriel? Tu m'entends?"

A voice has just come out of a weird triangular black object in the center of the table.

"Pierre?" Muriel asks. "Can we make this conversation in

English, because we have Lynn Blanchett from New York with us."

"*Pas de problème,* I mean, yes, Muriel."

She presses a button on the gizmo.

"Pierre can't hear us now. Pierre is the financial manager of Crédit de la Cité."

"It's our bank," Nicolas explains.

"It's my father's bank. I mean, my father owns the bank and every cent in it," Muriel clarifies.

"We've asked them for a lot of money," Nicolas whispers even though the phone is on mute.

"And you are going to help us get it." Muriel releases the button and I feel like I am falling into a bottomless hole.

"Muriel?"

"We're back, Pierre. Sorry, we had to go to another conference room."

She presses the silence button again.

"Ah! And, by the way, Pierre is my brother, and we can't stand each other."

Brother? But…he speaks with a French accent.

"I heard that, Muriel," the triangle says. "Ha ha ha! Don't listen to her, we love each other. Who is with you?"

"Nicolas Bouchez, Lynn and me. Lynn is our new recruit and she is a major asset for the company. She's Jodie Blanchett's daughter, you know!"

I am money in the bank.

"Hi, Lynn. Nice talking to you. So go for it, Muriel. Pitch me, because here, we're not very happy with the last business plan you have sent in. It's very…em…*naïf*…questionable."

"Well…I believe Lynn would be the best person to talk

to. She has lots of brilliants ideas! Lots! She's…you know…has all those brilliant ideas about…new business strategies, exactly." Muriel turns to me and rolls her hand to invite me to speak to the triangle. "Lynn?"

Who are these people? What do they want from me? I don't know anything about their business strategies! So what does she want me to say?

"Lynn?" the triangle asks. "Can you hear me? I can't hear you. I think we've been disconnected!"

Muriel points at the triangle. I need to talk to the triangle and say something brilliant to convince it to spit out millions of euros. So I bend over the gizmo and mutter, "*Bonjour,* Pierre. It's nice talking to you, too."

There is a silence on the other end of the line. Apparently I need to say more. But I have no idea what I should say to the triangle and the silence only becomes heavier.

"Muriel?" Pierre snaps and cuts me from the conversation.

Muriel gives me a dark look, as if I have just missed an obvious opportunity.

"Yes, Pierre."

"Georges from Finance is sitting here with me. He went through your accounts. You're spending too much, and we can't see you making any sort of income in the near future."

"Building a name takes courage, Pierre. You know…it takes balls. And Lynn Blanchett will help us now. I'll forward her CV. She is quite amazing."

"Yeah, do that. Send me her CV and my people will check her out."

Check me out? Oh, God!

"Pierre. I need the money. You know it. We've come too far to stop now."

"We all need money. Listen, I've got to go and… Well, it was nice to talk to you, Lynn. I'm, er, a big admirer of your mother."

They start to speak in French. I just listen to the melody and keep nodding.

I can feel cold sweat running along my spine. Check my CV? What CV? Nobody ever asked me for a CV. Jodie didn't mention any CV! She just said, "Try to look like you know what you're doing," or something like that.

Muriel presses a button on the triangle and it dies.

She looks at Nicolas and shakes her head. Then she looks at me.

"So, that's all you had to say to him? Thank you for your help, Lynn."

"Lynn might need more preparation." Nicolas comes to my rescue again.

"Preparation! We have no time for preparation! We are broke, Nicolas! Broke!"

"I know. But we'll find solutions. We always do." He looks confident and calm but in a super-sexy kind of way.

She stares at him. She is about to eat him alive, bones and clothes included.

"Listen, Muriel," I say hesitantly. "I didn't come here to convince your brother to give you some money. I didn't even know you were broke."

That's it, Lynn, swap responsibilities.

"Well, why don't you explain to me why you *are* here!"

What? Is she serious?

"But…you're the one who made me come here," I stammer.

"She's right," Nicolas says and looks at me as if I was some sort of doom she had forced upon them. "Inviting Lynn was your call," he reminds her, making it obvious he never wanted me here in the first place.

I feel the need to defend myself. "I came here to…"

To *what?*

"To…help you," I try.

"Help me?" Muriel nearly shouts.

Think, Lynn. What do you mean by *help* her? How does she need your help? Remember what Roxanne said.

"Well, we all know…that…you're just spending your father's money for this…*fantaisie*…right?"

Oho, don't go this way, Lynn! But it's too late. I already am.

"And…this is just, like, a rich-dad-financing-his-daughter thing. Nobody really believes that you're for real. So…I came here…to make people believe that you're for real."

Bravo moi!

They both look at me. Then they look at each other. It's clear that she hasn't been addressed like this…ever!

She is going to kill me. They are all going to kill me. She is going to press the 'kill the ugly American bitch' button on her intercom and a herd of gay Asian designers will pour into the office to crush me!

"Mais de quoi elle parle, celle la?" she yells out. "Do you listen to yourself?" She grabs the triangular gizmo and throws it at the poor Buddha.

"Muriel, calm down," Nicolas says. "This is not the right time or the right place for one of your tantrums!"

He looks perfectly used to this. She yells. He hushes. She breaks. He fixes.

"Nicolas, tais toi!" She points at me. "You, you are coming with me!"

I must have hit a sensitive spot. She stands and leaves her office in a fury. I look up at the Buddha. I just want to check if he has opened his eyes, but no, he still pretends that he can meditate amidst such mayhem. I turn to Nicolas for an explanation but he just shrugs.

"I guess you better follow her. And, Lynn…"

"Yes?"

"I'll need a copy of your CV, you know, for Pierre."

Shit.

"Lynn!" Muriel yells all the way from the reception area.

I just want to go back to the hotel, take a last shower and return to the airport to catch the next plane home.

Paris. The city of love. Yeah right. It's the city of people going bonkers!

I'll just tell Jodie I caught the flu.

Or dysentery.

Jodie's so scared of microbes, she'll forgive me for giving up so fast.

I have no idea where we're going. I have to run after Muriel and she makes a point of walking a few steps ahead, but then, all of a sudden, she stops and turns to me.

"I am not just spending my father's money. I have been in this business for five years. I have talent! Everyone says that I have talent. So who are you to talk to me like that?"

I swear, she is about to cry. Just like the silly little teenage girl that she tries not to be.

"Muriel, I don't want to play this game with you, we're both too old."

"What game?"

"The little-spoiled-girls game."

"I'm not like this! I'm... I am just so stressed. *Merde, tout va mal!*"

She walks away. We're on the run again, only this time I grab her wrist and stop her.

"Things are never as bad as they seem."

"You're wrong, Confucius! Things are generally much worse."

Confucius?

I smile at her. I like her. She is wild but I like her. And she smiles back at me. She's cute when she smiles.

"What is there to smile about?" she asks.

"You. You're funny. Confucius!"

"Are you always like this?"

"Like what?" I ask.

"Saying whatever pops into your head?"

Please. She should take a peek in my head! So far, this is nothing.

"You're weird," she says and resumes the chase, sliding among the tourists and passersby to disappear inside a coffee shop. Only, it's not a coffee shop, and once I follow her into the place I immediately understand a thing or two about Muriel B.

The coffee shop is a tiny secluded bar. It's full of women. Tall women. Short women. Fat women. Thin women. Young. Old. Dark. Blond. Women only.

Muriel is at home in here. She kisses the barmaid on the lips.

"*C'est ta nouvelle copine?*" the barmaid asks.

"She thinks you're my girlfriend. Do you think we would be a nice match?" Muriel says, smiling at me over her shoulder.

Oh, God!

"She is not my girlfriend. Lynn is from New York." She explains to the barmaid.

"*Quoi? J'parle pas anglais, moi.*"

"Do you mind talking in French, Lynn?"

Shit!

"*Non,*" I say.

The barmaid asks me something in French, so I just smile mysteriously. I do a smile that's neither yes nor no. A kind of undecided smile. She asks me again, and looks at Muriel, seeking an explanation.

I decide to say *oui,* and they laugh. I laugh with them. And I nod, of course.

"So? What do you want to drink then?" Muriel asks.

Oh, I see.

"Just a coffee. A trim latte. Something like that."

The barmaid looks at me as if I had just landed from outer space.

"*Donne lui un café.*"

That grants me a horrible short-black and a disapproving face. It's 11:30 a.m. Coffee time is over. Muriel orders a *perroquet.* It's like a strange anise cocktail with mint syrup. The barmaid takes the same thing but without the syrup. She doesn't take it *too sweet.*

"*Ça fait combien de temps que tu es à Paris?*"

"Muriel, we need to talk. In private." I take her glass and walk to a booth far away from the bar. I want to take her away from the barmaid and all this maddening French language.

She caresses the barmaid's face and comes to sit with me.

"Do you like it in here?" she asks.

Two Japanese girls have just entered. They are dressed in

school uniforms, only their skirts are far too short and reveal their underwear. Their faces are covered in colorful makeup. They look like two little porcelain dolls out of an sleazy old man's fantasy.

"The place has character," I lie. I feel so inappropriate. Hell, I've never been in a place like this before.

Once, with Delia, we went into a sauna parlor, but apparently they didn't even have any real saunas and their masseuses were not really masseuses either. But that was an *accident!*

And I don't want to judge anyone. Damn, I just feel very uncomfortable watching girls engaged in passionate kissing at lunchtime.

"Is this your kind of place?"

"Well…"

"See those two Japanese girls?"

I nod. They're sitting right behind us, sharing a pink milk shake with two straws. "Yes, I noticed them."

"Those two are really sick. They like weird games. They enjoy pain. I played with them last New Year's Eve. I couldn't sit for a week without shrieking."

She smiles at me.

"Do I shock you?"

"Muriel, I *am* from New York," I lie again.

In fact, I don't know anyone like Muriel and yes, I am shocked and uneasy. Why did I think that all successful people should be elegant and refined like cheese crackers? Instead, I find myself with crazy young punks and unbalanced teenagers.

"Can we talk about the job? That's why you flew me to Paris, isn't it?"

"American women! Business! Business! Is there anything

else that counts but your careers? Business was back there, when we talked to Pierre and you blew it. Now it's time for something else."

Like kissing sadomasochist lesbian Japanese girls dressed in school uniforms?

"It seems…" I start again.

Oh, just say it, Lynn!

"It seems that Nicolas wasn't too keen on having me in Paris."

"Nicolas! He has lots of neuroses, that boy. His mind is full of *no, no, no!* My mind is all *yes, yes, yes!*" She laughs like a hyena and the two Japanese girls turn to check what she's drinking and order two of the same.

"I wanted to get a big name from New York," Muriel continues. "A person that everybody would know in the business. Just like you."

"Just like me? Muriel, nobody knows me."

"Your name, Lynn, everybody knows your name. Your name is going to open all the doors. And I spent a fortune getting you here. So now you need to convince me that you were a good investment and that Nicolas was wrong."

"Wrong?"

"To think you were a waste of our time and money."

She drinks her *perroquet* with a large smile on her face. She really enjoys toying with me.

"After talking to your brother, it's rather odd that you would try to convince me to stay, Muriel. It looks like you're broke. And by the way, how come he talks with a French accent?"

"He grew up with Dad in Paris. I grew up with Mum, in London. Mum was a model."

"That's…very nice."

"No, they're horrible parents."

"Oh…"

"Lynn, we're not here to discuss my parents. We're here to talk about me! Me! Me! Me! You see, I'm going to take off. I know it. It's my destiny. I am the next Coco Chanel."

That or locked up in a mental ward.

"I am not a businesswoman. I am an artist. I am crazy. I want to be crazy. And my company should reflect my personality. That's why I need people like you. An American businesswoman with a big name that can help me reach the top."

"I'm not sure that I'm the person you are looking for, Muriel."

"Your mother vouched for you. Your mother is a genius."

I have this picture of Jodie working in her little workshop when she was still unknown and broke. I was very young but I remember her hard face looking down at me, snatching the fabrics away from my hands. "I told you not to touch! You're going to mess everything up again!"

Suddenly, someone's singing a catchy French tune in Muriel's pocket. She fishes out a sleek-looking cell phone. "Nicolas," she sneers. "Work, work, work!" She throws the phone on the table.

"Aren't you going to answer it?"

"He probably needs me to go back to the office and help him with *something*." She finishes her *perroquet* shaking her head.

Actually, *I* would love to help Nicolas with something, like…anything. "Let's go back to the office," I say when the phone is done singing.

"Oh, no! We did enough work for today. Let's go to my place. We can talk some more at my place."

"What about Nicolas?" I ask, nodding toward the phone as if he was trapped inside and needed immediate attention.

"We'll phone him back. We can meet him at my place. Nicolas loves my place."

Mmm? Nicolas loves her place. I didn't think of that. Nicolas and Muriel? She has such short hair. That's definitely an advantage over me when taking a ride on his scooter.

I love privacy.

Being inside your home is like being inside a safe nest. You close the door and you can recuperate from the mad and stressful goings-on of the real world. Your home is your only chance to get peace and quiet. I love my home.

Muriel is completely different. Her home is like a train station at rush hour. It's full of people from various walks of life, some of them she doesn't even know by name.

Muriel lives in a huge modern flat not too far from the office. I swear, the minute she opened the door, it seemed more busy and hectic inside than on the streets below.

There is this guy from Spain. He wants Muriel to fix a meeting for him with Fjord Model Agency. Muriel met him in a club in Paris and doesn't even remember his name anymore. She told him that she could help him become a model or, eventually, get him a part in a porn film. She introduces him to me as her beautiful Spanish Stallion.

He sleeps on her sofa.

"You are Fjord Agency?" he asks me.

"No, I'm Lynn Blanchett."

Sprawled out in front of the giant TV screen are the Fat

Breeders, a band from London. The whole band is crashing in Muriel's apartment. From the drummer to the backup singers.

According to Muriel, they've been here for two weeks. By the looks of it, they'll never move out.

"Lynn is from New York, she's Jodie Blanchett's daughter," Muriel presents me proudly.

"Hi," they say lazily, as if they didn't really give a damn, or were already *so* used to meeting all kinds of *real* celebrities.

In the kitchen, two girls are sharing a frozen yogurt. They look like twins. They both have long blond hair in a tight ponytail and wear identical sweatpants and T-shirts. And, of course, they have bodies to die for.

"You must know Irena and Jacky. They're from New York, too."

Irena and Jacky are dancers, temporarily making their living in Paris as topless waitresses. Muriel forgot how they came to live in her apartment.

"They've been here forever. I am not even sure they're really gay. They bring all kind of weird men in here. Macho types. They're very, very loose girls."

In Muriel's bedroom, we need to whisper. Carolina is asleep in her bed. She has just arrived from Nigeria and models for Elite. Carolina is not her real name. Her real name is too hard to pronounce and sounds vaguely like Carolina.

"I like her. We're not very serious about each other yet, but I could fall in love with her. She has the potential to become big. Who knows? She's so young."

We bend over her like two fairies watching over the little sleeping princess, planning her bright future. Muriel pushes me into her private office.

Only, it's not private—or an office—at all. There is a sofa, clearly being used as a bed, and a horribly messy desk. Seated behind the desk is a very thin man of indefinite age. He's typing on a laptop computer. He finally stops and takes a look at us. We are part of another world to him, like he really can't see us, but merely feels our presence.

"Bonjour," he says.

"That's Stephan. He's my favorite writer."

Stephan lives in the apartment, too. He never ever leaves it, apparently. He is the only French person in here. He has been writing for years and, in the opinion of all the editors he has sent his prose to, he is the most untalented writer of his generation.

"That's exactly why I love him. He doesn't compromise."

Stephan's skin is yellow, turning green, like his eyes. He looks sick.

"He never eats. That's worrying," Muriel says, sighing in a maternal way. Or at least as maternal as someone like Muriel can get.

He wears nothing but an old, very dirty bathrobe, and his skinny limbs coming out of it make him look like a dying insect.

"Lynn is from New York," Muriel tells him. She speaks slowly and loudly as if he were her deaf grandfather.

"New York! Yeah! Bagels!" That's all he has to say about New York before resuming the frenetic typing.

"He doesn't do drugs. He is naturally like that. Isn't he great?"

"He is fantastic," I say and I look around the office. I have been looking for traces of Nicolas's presence. The apartment is in such a mess that it would be hard to say who lives here and who doesn't. It should get mentioned in travel guides: If you are in Paris, look cool and are searching for a free place to stay, just move to Muriel B's flat. All welcome!

"The flat used to belong to my grandmother. They gave it to me when she died. She had such terrible taste. Very *bourgeois*."

"Shouldn't we call Nicolas?"

"Relax, Lynn. One thing at a time. Today, we're getting to know each other. Tomorrow, we can talk business and money."

By now, I have learned quite a few things about Muriel B. She frequents lesbian bars, runs a crazy bankrupt company and lives in an even crazier apartment. She still knows nothing about me but assumes that I can help her.

We're back in the living room. The Fat Breeders have found something more interesting to watch than MTV. Carolina has gotten out of bed wearing nothing but a tiny electric-blue G-string, hiding absolutely nothing of her long, beautiful, ebony body.

She stretches and rubs her sleepy eyes and smiles when she sees Muriel. She does a few joyful leaps to take her in her arms. You would swear she still believes she is eight years old and doesn't yet notice that she has a pair of amazing breasts.

"Hello, darling!"

"Pourquoi tu me parles en anglais?"

"This is Lynn. I told you about her. She's Jodie Blanchett's daughter."

Carolina doesn't need more information. She bends over

me and gives me a big kiss on the lips. And yes, I feel her naked breast against own less perky ones. I can feel the blood coming to my cheeks and I am sure that I am red as a tomato.

"J'ai faim!" Carolina yells and leaps happily toward the huge stainless-steel fridge.

Muriel shrugs her shoulders. "She's hungry all the time. And she stays so thin. She's lucky."

Carolina comes back with Irena and Jacky's frozen yogurt. She dips a spoon in it and sucks it provocatively. Muriel pats her bum.

"Where does she put it?" Muriel says.

"One wonders," I mutter.

The Fat Breeders must love it here. I'm sure that they are going to write songs about Carolina's butt.

Muriel pushes Carolina playfully. "Go take a shower. You smell! I need to talk to Lynn."

"I don't smell. It's her that smells," Carolina says, pointing her spoon at me. She realizes she might have been a bit too rude so she's back licking the spoon provocatively to make me like her again.

Abruptly Muriel takes my hand and drags me to the bedroom.

She closes the door behind us. She leaves the heavy curtains closed and switches on the bed-top lights.

The room smells of sweat. I can actually feel the lack of oxygen. I am very uncomfortable.

Muriel sits on the corner of the huge bed. She pats the space beside her to invite me to sit.

"Are you hungry?"

Actually I am starving. I am so hungry that I feel light-headed. Add to this the caffeine and the stress, and I am about to burst.

"No, I am fine."

I sit very cautiously beside her. She makes a slight hop to get closer.

"For what it's worth, I like you."

"So you said."

"I mean I really like you. I feel…you are like…my big sister."

She gets even closer. I don't believe sisters look at each other that way!

"I think we could work together." She hops even closer.

I try to move away slightly, but she puts her hands on my leg. "You, me, Nicolas. We can be a great team. Do you like Nicolas?"

I can feel the weight of her hand on my knee. It's sliding up now. I close my eyes. "He idolizes me. It's very flattering." She tickles my thigh with the tips of her fingers. "He is so cute, isn't he?" I hear her say.

I grab her hand and put it back on her own lap.

"He is rather cute," I confirm clumsily.

"Pity he is gay." She puts her hand back on my knee.

Gay!

"Gay?"

"Gay! *Comme un phoque!*"

She looks up at me. She caught me by surprise and it excites her.

"Of course he is gay. Everybody is gay."

She takes advantage of my stupor and goes for the kiss, only she stops when the door opens. We look like two lovers caught by the husband—or the wife—who knows?

"Ah, quelle salope!"

Carolina drops her yogurt pot and runs to the bed. Before I can explain that it's not what it looks like, she jumps on Muriel and throws a couple of punches. But instead of fighting back, Muriel laughs her head off.

Oh, God!

I stand and step away from the bed.

"I…I need to go back to the hotel."

They don't listen. They just fight on the bed, and now Carolina is laughing, too. They find everything hilarious.

I walk out of the room. The Fat Breeders are watching them fighting. They are in heaven.

I walk to the door. As I pass in front of the office I can hear Stephan, the worst writer of his generation, yelling, *"Bagels!"*

I put up the Do Not Disturb sign and lock the door to my room. I don't ever want to go out again. Here, in the room it's safe and comfortable. Out there is madness. Crazy Japanese girls, Pierre the banker, frozen-yogurt Carolina and the Fat Breeders.

And Nicolas!

He betrayed me!

Somehow… Okay, so I haven't quite figured that part out yet.

But come on. He took me on his scooter. Everyone knows a scooter ride means something. It's like a secret bond. You cannot seduce a girl with your scooter and then tell her that you are gay.

Bastard! Oh, I hate him.

I sit at the desk. I see the Air France flight coupon and

my passport. I can leave…whenever. And now would be a good time.

This job, this place, these people, it's all way out of my league. It's not at all the way I pictured it, not even in my worst nightmare.

I pick up the flight coupon. I see Roxanne Green's bible: *20 Steps to Success.*

I open the book. Roxanne wrote a phone number on the first page. "You can phone me in case of emergency," she said.

I dial and I recognize Roxanne's voice.

"Who's that?"

"It's…Lynn. You know? We met on the plane."

"Mmm?"

"Jodie Blanchett's daughter."

"Yes, I know. Listen, I'm in the middle of something, darling."

"It's an emergency, like you said."

"Did they fire you already?"

"No, it's much worse than that."

I am about to cry. I don't want to cry. That would only annoy her more and she would hang up.

"Are you crying?" she asks.

No wonder her books are such hits. She reads people's minds.

"Listen to me, darling. Remember what I told you? Step #6."

I remember how good and easy it felt in the plane, listening to Roxanne going through the different steps. And how miserable I feel now. I start to cry. I can't help it. Please don't hang up. Please!

"Can you read step #6 for me?"

"Yes," I sob. I turn the pages to the sixth chapter. "Step #6. Sometimes it's hard to be successful."

Step #6:
Sometimes it's hard to be successful.

I'm eating my fourth croissant, drinking my fifth coffee and I'm pretending to read the same French newspaper for the gazillionth time and there is still no sign of Massoud.

"Can I have another pot of coffee?"

"Sorry, breakfast service is actually closed."

How rude!

I look at my watch. I'm the last guest in the restaurant and I'm getting on the waiter's nerves. I decide to take another look in the lobby.

"Have a good day, *mademoiselle,*" the waiter says. Trust me, he really means *good riddance.*

I check myself once more before I enter the lobby. Look at this gorgeous young woman. It's Blanchett's springtime, I'm blooming. After talking to Roxanne, I went on a shopping spree. The funny thing is, I *did* find a shop called Basic selling Basic T-shirts.

I am dressed in the same fashion as yesterday, but with a brand-new pair of Diesel jeans (175 euros), a simple white Basic T-shirt (39,90 euros) and I have a pink H&M scarf (9,90 euros) on my shoulders. I even splashed myself with some Kazo cologne (80ml/39,95 euros). "We American women can get away with everything!"

Where is everybody? Where is Massoud? How unprofessional of him. I try reception again.

"No, Mademoiselle Blanchett, there are no new messages."

"Phone calls?"

"No phone calls."

Aren't they supposed to be worried about me? I feel like the ugly little duckling, you know, the smelly little girl that nobody wants to play with.

"Can I make a phone call from here?"

The desk clerk points at the phone booth across the lobby. He doesn't even bother talking to me. What happened last night? Did I get disgraced while I was asleep, and all of a sudden everybody knows that it's okay to be rude to me?

I walk to the phone booth and place my call.

"Muriel B, *bonjour!*" says a voice at the other end of the line.

"This is Lynn Blanchett," I snap.

"Who?"

Is she joking?

"Lynn Blanchett. From New York. Can I speak with Nicolas, please."

"Mr. Bouchez is not in the office."

"Let me speak to Muriel, then."

"Mademoiselle Boutonnière is not in the office either…I'm sorry."

"Is anybody else but you in the office?"

Silence.

"Goodbye, then."

I hang up. I'm so frustrated. I imagine Muriel and Nicolas locked in their offices, shaking their heads. No, no, no! We don't want to speak to any Lynn Blanchett. She's an ugly little duckling. Shoo, shoo!

"Can you get me a taxi?" I ask the concierge.

"Certainly. Where will you be going?"

"Muriel B. Office. It's somewhere…" I point toward what I believe is the direction to the office. "This way."

"I am sure we can manage to find the address for you."

He smiles. Or is that a smirk?

I'm furious. They took me away from home. They flew me across the Atlantic. For what? To forget about me like yesterday's favorite flavor?

And Nicolas? Mr. Backstabbing-Bouchez! Does he think that it's all right to flash his pretty looks, his charm and his suave accent right in my face, just like that?

Mademoizelle Blanchett, yu are zooo delicioze, I wanta iit yu!

And now that I'm really dazzled and want a taste of it, too, it turns out he thinks I'm a waste of time and he's gay! I am going to strangle him with his tie.

The taxi drops me off in front of the office.

"Just move, all right!" I say to the prostitute. It's the same girl. She must be leasing this spot. She doesn't dare to spit today. She feels I'm about to blow and she's not willing to pay for it.

I press the intercom and cross the courtyard. I'm not impressed anymore. I'm not this ridiculous American girl that can't handle the glitz and glamour of it all. I'm Lynn

Blanchett, heir of the Blanchett empire! Lynn Blanchett, daughter of a genius! I am a complete bitch with a new wardrobe who is about to OD on caffeine!

I walk straight to the receptionist. I don't say hello, I don't say please, I don't say sorry, I don't say anything but "Nicolas Bouchez! Now!"

"Oh, he is out of the office."

"Like hell he is!"

I don't wait for more lies. I head upstairs and make my way to his office.

"Mademoiselle Blanchett! Please!"

I open the door to his office. It's empty. "Nicolas," I call. He's hiding. Coward! I walk to Muriel's office. It's empty too.

I make my way to the workshop. I push the door. Where is everybody? Where are all the punks?

Back in Japan?

Françoise Neuton looks up at me. She's working on a new version of the dress that I trashed yesterday.

"Can I help you?"

She's alone in the workshop and something's up, because she seems too happy to see me.

"Where is everybody?"

"Is it any of your business?"

"Oh, believe me. I'll make it my business."

She takes off her glasses. She wants to take a better look at me.

"I talked to Muriel this morning. You're over, Mademoiselle Blanchett."

What?

"Didn't they tell you yet? Mmm?" She brushes the dress with her hand. "Do you like it better now?"

"Where is Nicolas?"

"Oh… He will be out all day, at the Carrousel du Louvres."

"Where?" He didn't even bother contacting me. He just discarded me as if I didn't exist anymore.

"I'm sure that you can meet him there. After all, it's his job to tell you you're out."

I don't find the strength to strike back. I turn my back to her and focus on breathing.

"It was nice meeting you, anyway," she says. "I've always admired your mother."

I crawl back downstairs.

"You were right, nobody's here," I say to the receptionist. "Can you get me Nicolas on his cell phone?"

"Sure." She dials and passes me the phone.

"Oui?"

"Nicolas? How are you, darling? Lynn Blanchett talking here. You remember me?"

"Yes, Lynn. I remember you."

"Guess what? I'm at the office. And guess what else? Nobody's here but me."

"I know. I'm sorry. I should have phoned you."

"How thoughtful of you!"

How do you say *fucking bastard* in French!

"Listen…" Nicolas tries to sound consoling. "Why don't you go back to your hotel, and I'll come as soon as I'm finished. We'll talk."

"No, don't bother. I'm coming to see you. Right now."

"Lynn, wait."

"I'll see you in a minute."

"Lynn!"

I hang up. "Gosh, I forgot," I say to the receptionist. "They were waiting for me at the Carouzal Louvres."

"Le Carrousel du Louvres," she corrects and gives me the I'm-so-sorry-for-you look.

"Can you get me a taxi?"

The Carrousel stuff is like a shopping mall right under Le Louvres. And Le Louvres is…oh, you know what Le Louvres is. Isn't that crazy? They have so many castles over here that they have shopping malls under them. Imagine that. Upstairs, their kings used to carry on their despotic businesses, while now, downstairs, there are gift shops, tourists and the mixed smells of French fries and cinnamon buns.

I'm sure I'm in the right place, it's like Fashionworld down here. They have dresses and fashion displays hanging all over the place. Dior. Chanel. Gucci. Gaultier. Christian Lacroix.

I take a closer look at the Christian Lacroix dress. It looks like something from the distant past, but at the same time, it feels real. Not like a theater costume, but like a real thing. I love it!

I walk faster to the showrooms. I want to keep this feeling. Cinnamon buns and Christian Lacroix. It will give me some strength to confront Nicolas. I walk to the two men guarding the entrance to the showrooms.

"Hi, I'm with the Muriel B group."

"Sure."

They don't need any other form of credential. They open the red velvet rope and let me in.

I walk into the first showroom. It smells of wood dust and glue. All kinds of technicians are playing around with wires.

Carpenters are building wooden structures. Everybody looks very busy and I'm walking in the middle of it all, unwelcome and purposeless.

I…I can't do it. I just saw Nicolas, and I immediately stopped breathing.

I have no defense mechanism against a guy like him.

He stands among a group of Muriel B's finest Asian punks, talking with a little man with short gray hair and a beard. Oh, and he's dressed like a catholic priest.

Muriel's with him and whatever happened before I arrived, it took the jam out of her doughnut.

"Muriel, dear, there are no two ways about it," the priest says with a strong British accent. "You won't get the afternoon spot. It's already booked for Dior! You can't compete with Dior, darling."

"Hi," I whisper, but nobody notices me.

"The nine o'clock spot is very nice anyway. People are fresh at nine o'clock."

"So why don't you give it to Galliano, huh?"

I clear my throat. "Hi," I try again.

Muriel turns to me. "Lynn…I thought we were not supposed to see you again," she snaps sharply. She turns to Nicolas. "Wasn't she supposed to be on a plane or something?"

"I…"

Nicolas puts his hand on my arm. "Let's go somewhere quiet." He doesn't seem upset to see me. Worse, he doesn't seem guilty!

Instead, I'm the one about to have a cardiac arrest while he looks calm and in control. Can't he stop being perfect for one single second?

He pushes aside a black drape, walks me through and we

find ourselves alone under a grandstand. I normally love to go under a grandstand. It always reminds me of high school and first kisses.

Only, I'm quite sure Nicolas didn't drag me here to give me a French kiss.

"I am really sorry, Lynn," he kicks off. "I didn't want to call you. I wanted to do this face-to-face."

Oh, God! My back bones melt and my body is turning into a deflated balloon. I close my eyes and ask myself what Roxanne would do if she were here.

"I need more than an apology, Nicolas. I need an explanation." I hope my voice sounds as strong as I intended it to.

"We…we'd love to have you working for us. But…"

But is such a horrible word.

"Muriel and I talked yesterday night. And…she doesn't feel the vibes between you two."

Vibes? There're so many good reasons for me not to be here. But *vibes!*

"You must be joking, Nicolas!"

"I know. It sounds, well, a bit crazy."

I'm not going to cry, I swear, I'm not.

"What about your own *vibes?*"

"What do you mean?"

"I know you didn't want me to be here in the first place. Admit it."

"It was Muriel's decision."

"But you convinced her to send me back, didn't you?"

"Lynn, Muriel has big expectations and big ideas. But we simply don't have the money to back them up."

"Just say it—you don't like me."

"I'm sorry, Lynn, I know it sounds unfair."

I sigh. "It's more than unfair, Nicolas. It's revolting! You were not with us yesterday. You didn't see what I saw. The reason Muriel doesn't feel the vibes is that I refused to kiss her."

"Oh, don't say that. Muriel's not like that."

"Like hell she's not! I don't kiss, I don't get the job. That's how simple it is."

"It doesn't work that way, you're wrong."

"Really?"

Let's give it a try, then. I put my hand on his arms. I feel his muscles tensing. I take one step forward. I lift myself on my toes and land a kiss on his lips. Yes, that's right. I steal the kiss that I didn't give to Muriel yesterday.

I let him go. He wasn't very responsive, but he didn't fight it too much, either.

"So?" I ask. "Can I get my job back now?"

"Lynn, this is completely absurd."

"Absurd, huh?"

Okay. He makes the rules. I go again. I'm back on my toes and on his lips. I'm right against him. I feel him. I feel how tense he is.

"So?" I ask again.

"This is crazy."

"Well, that's Muriel B's style. I'm just like her, getting the vibes."

"I'm…so sorry." He steps away from me. He doesn't want me to go for a third. "I need…you know…" He points toward Muriel and the group. "We'll arrange your trip back and, well, we're broke but we will…pay for everything. That's…"

I nod. "Just go, Nicolas."

"I'm sorry, Lynn."

"Yeah, right."

I want him to go away before I fall apart. He gives me some kind of sad smile and leaves me there.

I fall down on a wooden box. It's covered by some sort of white dust. That's going to stain for good.

I feel so lonely and lost. I am in Paris, far away from home, surrounded by strangers, hiding under a stand with the souvenir of a hopeless kiss.

"That's the best I can do," I hear the priest say. "And honestly, Muriel, I don't have all morning to argue with you."

"It's a fucking joke! I'll sue!"

"You'll sue? Ha! Do you realize that I booked you here only as a favor to your father?"

I can see them from where I sit. I can see the catwalk. I could hide here for the day and enjoy the shows. Nicolas looks so confused.

Is he still thinking of me?

"Maybe we can make it…a breakfast event. With coffee and croissants…and…I don't know…" Nicolas says clumsily.

Muriel takes a better look at him. "What's wrong with you?"

Is it me, or does he looks extra pale?

"This is fashion, Nicolas! Fashion doesn't wake up at seven in the morning. Fashion doesn't wake up before noon."

Why bother discussing this with the priest? They should have the show in the street. That's the very first thing that crossed my mind when I walked into Muriel B's office. Set it among the prostitutes. Hell, if they could shake off a pound or two, you could even use them as models.

I stand. I get out. I don't have anything to lose. I don't care if I'm going to sound ridiculous. I walk over to their group.

"Do it in the street," I say.

"What?" Muriel barks at me.

"Muriel B belongs to the street. It's young. It's provocative. It's different. Just set a stage in front of the office and do the show in the street."

"Who are you?" the priest asks.

"This is Lynn Blanchett," Nicolas says. "She is...*was* our PR...consultant."

"Everybody will talk about it," I continue. "That's the spirit of Muriel B. Free Fashion. Street Fashion."

"In the street," Muriel repeats.

Nobody dares to say anything.

They wait.

She looks at my butt. "Look at you!"

She slaps it gently and brushes off the white dust, and when she is finished brushing my ass she just says, "I like it."

"You must be out of your mind!" the priest blasts.

"Forget about our booking. Give it to Galliano. We're doing my show in the street. How did you put it, Lynn? Free Fashion. Street Fashion. I love it."

The priest rises and shakes his hands in a kind of a *I wash my hands of all your madness* gesture and walks away.

"I love this girl, she's a genius," Muriel shouts, and embraces me. "Nicolas! We have to change everything. The show will take place in the street. Phone everybody, absolutely everybody. You have to work closely with Lynn. Let her know everything you're doing."

She walks away, followed by her entourage, leaving me behind with Nicolas.

"*Bien joué,* Lynn."

"What?"

"That was…very *inspired,*" he says.

What? The kisses? Say it! Say you liked it.

"Your idea to do the show in the street is a surprisingly good idea."

"Sure."

Coward, coward, COWARD!

Step #7:
Mingle, Snuggle and Connect

I am a star! Look at me in my Basic clothing! I'm the best thing that has happened in this town since...I don't know...Napoleon?

"This party must be *so* boring for you."

"Not at all, it's amazing. Look at this place," I say.

"Americans are *so* ignorant but so entertaining. While we French, we are very cultured but very boring."

Is that a compliment?

"Oh, I see you as the nasty kind..." He moves his hand in the air. It's a dancing-puppet version of me. "A nasty little party girl! Just like your mother!"

"Not at all, Jean-André," I say. Jean-André is an aging gay Frenchman who, apparently, knows everyone. "I am a very boring American, in a French kind of way, and I am *so* over the going-out thing," I hear myself say.

"No, no, no, darling. You're a New Yorker. New Yorkers

are not Americans. We have been there recently with Kazo, you know…."

He whispers the name and pauses. He wants to give everyone enough time to realize that he is talking about *the* Kazo, the famous Japanese designer.

"We were in New York for leisure because Kazo, you know, loves New York, but everybody was making a point of being so *boring*. They don't drink, they don't smoke and of course they don't fuck."

"Fun is not fun anymore," I say to the laughing little man. I don't even think Jean-André is his real name.

"Fun is not fun! *Vous êtes irrésistible, ma chère!*"

We're enjoying a warm evening in the garden. Fiber-optic cables provide a gentle light. Artificial streams of blue-colored water run along moss and bonsai trees. Oriental New Age music plays in the background. We feel Zen sipping our Bloody Marys and chewing celery.

In the middle of this Japanese garden lies a huge condo that seems to be built out of rice paper and wood. All this is perfectly mind-blowing, of course, because we're actually in the middle of Paris and on the property of the famous Japanese designer Kazo, you know….

"Kazo, you know…spends most of his time in Paris. This house is a reflection of his creative madness. *Sa folie!*" Jean-André explained to me.

Kazo's not here. Kazo is drinking his own Bloody Marys in Los Angeles and, like us, celebrating the twenty-year anniversary of Kazo Fashion.

Amazing dresses and garments are suspended in the air all around the garden. Tall beautiful models are drinking pink, red and blue cocktails while sucking sushi canapés passed around by hunky waiters.

"Hey, I love your dress," a tall blond girl passing by says out of the blue. "Calvin Klein?"

"Jodie Blanchett," I say.

I never thought I could ever put on one of Jodie's garments. But I've been so malnourished since my arrival in Paris that I slid into this one like a wet piece of soap.

"Very cute!"

She smiles at me. She's extremely cute, too. God, is she flirting with me? Is everyone in this business so sexually ambiguous, or is it just me?

"You must know Clarice, everybody knows Clarice," Muriel says. Out of nowhere Muriel has materialized at my side.

"I'm Clarice Kleron." The tall blonde gives me her hand and giggles.

"This is Lynn," Muriel presents me. *"Lynn est une perle."*

I am a pearl. That's how Muriel presents me to everybody. I'm the pearl that she found in New York and dragged back to Paris.

"Yeah, I've heard about you," Clarice says to me. "You're Jodie Blanchett's daughter."

"When did you hear about me?"

"Well, tonight. I'm going to the Gucci party after, would you like to come?"

I'm getting picked up by a beautiful blonde!

"Not tonight, sorry," I say. "I have to work tomorrow."

"Pity," she whispers and walks away.

"American women are going to conquer the world,"

Jean-André laughs out. "They can't cook, they can't fuck, but they conduct business better than any man."

Is that a compliment? No time to ask because Jean-André keeps talking.

"Kazo, you know…thinks that the next American president will be a woman. Somebody just like you, Lynn. A pearl."

"Would you excuse me, Jean-André?" Muriel interrupts. "You might pass on Clarice," she whispers to me, "but I want to go to the Gucci party with her." She walks away and goes after my girl.

"Alone at last," Jean-André says. "I know somebody that's dying to meet you."

Kazo?

"I know what you're thinking. No, it's not Kazo, you know…. You will meet him one day, don't worry. Kazo, you know…loves to meet talented people like you."

Jean-André walks me inside the condo. He pushes one of the sliding walls and invites me to walk inside a secluded room.

"Sit, Lynn, sit."

There's no chair, of course. If your business is to manufacture and sell chairs, forget about Paris. They all sit on the floor and pretend to be Japanese these days.

Jean-André slides the wall shut and I find myself face-to-face with a very fat man, lying on the floor like some Roman emperor, picking on a food platter laid in front of him.

"This is Xavier Urbain, you know, the founder of Xu."

"Of course," I say, but I have absolutely no idea what Xu is.

"I am pleased to meet you, Lynn. We heard a lot about you," the fat man says with a French accent, swallowing a stuffed grape. "And your mother is…a goddess!"

"So, you're working for Muriel B, you poor thing," a very elegant woman sitting beside him says. She reminds me of Roxanne. Same age, same style, same elegance.

"Lynn, you must know Chloe Destouches."

Who?

"Er…surprisingly not," I say, shaking, well, rather touching her hands.

"Where have you been hiding, dear? Chloe is the black queen of fashion! No, no, Chloe, no false modesty, that's all true! You can read her ruthless prose in the pages of *Marie Claire*."

"Ah! Sure, yes!"

The cutest of all the waiters stands quietly behind them. Jean-André snaps his fingers at him.

"Get Lynn another Bloody Mary."

"And some more stuffed grapes. They're disgustingly good," Xavier Urbain says, then sucks in another one. "How are things at Muriel B? Chaotic, I imagine. It must be so exciting to work in chaos!"

"I'm still settling in."

"I heard that you're doing wonders."

"'Muriel B belongs to the street,'" Jean-André quotes me. "Everybody talks about it. It's brilliant, Lynn."

"Pity that the talent of a Blanchett is wasted on someone like Muriel," Xavier spits out along with some grape seeds.

"Oh, but no, Xavier! You're cruel with the young Muriel," Jean-André protests. "Fashion's such a difficult business and it's so hard to go on pretending you're a genius for so long."

"Ha! Muriel will never be mistaken for a genius."

I have a feeling that I shouldn't be here.

"She has a rich father, and that's all there is to it," Chloe chimes in.

"She has no idea what she is doing." Xavier pops another grape.

"She's a joke."

"Not even a funny joke, Chloe," Xavier says.

"She's the proof you can buy your way in this business." Clearly Chloe enjoys her ruthless reputation.

"She's a fake, didn't I tell you that before?" Jean-André forces himself back into the conversation. "She has no talent! No talent at all!"

"She'll be over in six months," Chloe concludes, picking out the stuffing and skinning the grape before eating it. "It's a cruel world out there, isn't it, Lynn?"

Jean-André puts his hand on mine. "You're very young yourself, you wouldn't know."

"Those kids want the fame, but they don't want to do the real work for it. And they think that you can get famous just like that…." Xavier snaps his fingers as the waiter walks in with my Bloody Mary.

"Look at him…." Xavier snaps his finger again. "He appears and disappears at will."

They laugh and the poor guy has no choice but to smile and become invisible again.

"I wonder what makes somebody like you decide to waste time with a company like Muriel B." Another grape disappears into Xavier's gigantic mouth. "Francis Boutonnière is actually fed up with paying the bills. Do you know that they're broke?"

"I'm sure that Lynn knows what she's doing," Jean-André says. "She is like Kazo, you know…she is very impulsive and follows her feelings rather than reason. Geniuses and crazy people are like that."

Help me! Is that a compliment or an insult?

"I really would like to talk to you later," Chloe says. "Maybe we can make a feature on you for *Marie Claire.* 'American Girl takes risks in Paris.' The thing is…"

She looks at Xavier and back at me. She needed those few seconds to think of something nasty to say. "I know your mother very well but I never heard a single word about you."

Join the club, Chloe, I think to myself. But tonight I refuse to let Jodie's lifelong disappointment in me ruin my good time. They think I'm brilliant. So instead of sinking into myself I smile and say, "Someone like me should always remain in the shadows."

"Modesty. Is that another one of your flaws? Mmm?"

Oh, this time, I know! This wasn't a compliment at all. Chloe is much more obvious than Jean-André.

"I have to go back to Muriel, you know…working for her and all."

An embarrassing silence follows. I know exactly what they're all thinking: how could I prefer to go back to Muriel when I could stay with such fabulous people?

"We'll catch up later then," Chloe says, which sounds like something a toreador says to a bull before a fight. "And ask your assistant to send me your bio."

"Sure!"

"It's nice to see passionate people back in this business. Fresh and innocent!" Xavier says and then ignores me as if I had already left the room.

Jean-André makes a silly gesture with his hand. Somehow, I have disappointed him.

Muriel is still chatting up Clarice. She is very sexual, touching and caressing her. I haven't decided yet if I should tell her about my encounter with Chloe and Xavier. Before I have a chance to say a thing, however, Muriel squeals, "Oh, look who's here!"

Nicolas passes the garden gates. Blood rushes to my cheeks. I don't want to see him. Not after what has happened. Not after…

"Are you sure he's gay?" I ask before he can hear us.

"I don't know, ask him." Muriel laughs out loud.

Too loud.

Maybe bisexual? I can live with that. Think about it. He would bring home gorgeous angels just like him…. Mmm….

"Lynn, you look fantastic," Nicolas says when he reaches Muriel, Clarice and me.

"Jodie Blanchett."

"What?"

"The dress." I explain.

He looks amazing, too. He wears a stylish gray suit with a simple tight black T-shirt. Why are gay people so hot? It's like being teased with a cream cake that turns out to be plastic. It's so unfair.

"Can I get you another one of those," he says, taking my empty glass.

"Oh, why not? Bloody Mary."

Why not, huh? Well, how about because you're getting drunk?

"Wait! I might take something nonalcoholic." That's it. I

am a sensible woman. I am in control of myself and I am not a greedy drunk like my uncle Ted.

We cross the garden together toward a lovely bar covered with food and prepoured drinks.

"Is that orange juice?" I ask the waiter.

"No, it's…" He says what it is but I don't understand. It looks like juice so I take it. I sip and it's horribly bitter and peppery but very fashionable.

"I think it's a ginger juice." Nicolas goes for a Bloody Mary. "They are Kazo's favorite. It's his special recipe, invented by his caterer. Do you like sushi?"

"Yeah, once it's cooked."

Nicolas gives an apologetic smile to the waiter. The you-know-she's-American kind of smile.

"I wanted to talk to you. First, I want to apologize for the way you've been treated," Nicolas says.

"Apology accepted." I'm so easy.

"Then… Well, I don't know how to tell you this, but at some point, yesterday, we lost faith in you."

"Mmm, hmm."

"There were bad vibes."

"Mmm, hmm."

"Now, everything is better."

"Mmm, hmm."

"The problem is—"

"Listen, about the kiss," I break in. "It was just—"

"I know, don't worry. It didn't mean anything to me, either."

Oh!

"You just wanted retribution and there we were. But that's not what I wanted to talk about."

He drinks a mouthful of his Bloody Mary. He looks so manly. I can't stop staring at his strong hand holding the tumbler.

"Well, Lynn, before you came to Paris, we were fishing for someone else to take the job."

"We?"

"Well, I mean *I've* been fishing behind Muriel's back."

"I changed my mind," I said to the waiter, giving him my glass of ginger juice and grabbing a Bloody Mary.

"I know it sounds awful." He really looks embarrassed. "And there's something else."

What? You've hired someone to kill me?

"I did find someone. Fran Wellish," he says like I should know who he is talking about.

"We thought, well, *I* thought we needed an alternative. Muriel is crazy about your mother. So I figured your mother's former PR manager would be a perfect catch."

Holy fucking crap!

"Oh, *that* Fran!" I say and push down half of the Bloody Mary. Jodie never ever introduces me to any of her colleagues. I have never heard about any *Fran Wellish.* And I'm damn sure that she never heard of me. Or if she did, all she'll know is that Jodie despises me and has been trying to hide me in a box for the past twenty years.

"Yesterday, I convinced Muriel to bring her in for a formal job interview."

"And when is she coming, exactly?"

"We've scheduled to fly her over tomorrow. I know. It might sound rude to put you into a competition like that. But trust me, Muriel has made her choice already. And it's just too late to stop Fran from coming."

"Fran Wellish, yeah, she is good," I say.

I'll never be up to the challenge. Jodie only surrounds herself with top people.

"Have you worked together, then?"

"Oh, we've crossed each other's paths," I lie.

"You don't sound too keen on her."

"You know. We had this…*thing*. Jodie had a bit of a protégé *thing* going on for me. Fran was…you know…so mad about…that *thing*."

Stop talking, Lynn. Just run away.

"Did you tell Fran that I was here, too?" I ask.

"Not yet. Well, we thought that you'd be…"

"Gone?"

"I'm so sorry, Lynn. Everything is different now. Muriel is crazy about you. Your idea was—"

"Fucking brilliant!" Muriel breaks in. "You told her, didn't you? Don't worry, Lynn. I am sure you're not too scared about a bit of competition."

"Lynn knows Fran Wellish well. They've worked together."

"Good. So you probably also know why I should hire you instead of her. Ha ha ha! I have to tell you, she comes highly recommended."

"Yeah, so I've heard."

So, this is it. No matter what I do, I will finish against the wall. A certain Fran Wellish is coming tomorrow, and she will say that she never met me before in her life. That my own mother doesn't even dare introduce me to her closest collaborators. They are going to confront me and I am going to die of shame.

"Who knows—" Muriel blinks gently at me "—I might

hire both of you and you would be like the Blanchett gang in Paris."

"Yeah, who knows?"

I should be crying.

But I'm laughing instead.

I'm laughing because hot air is being blown on my bare bum.

I am sitting on the most amazing toilet. There is no toilet paper. You follow the instructions engraved on the wall. You flush by passing your hand in front of an infrared sensor. It doesn't just flush. No, no, no. You stay put on the toilet and high-pressure water comes straight up your butt! And then, hot air is blown up to dry you and it tickles like hell. There is nothing like a dreadful situation in Paris and hot air up my ass to crack me up!

But listen, that's not all. The toilet seat appears and disappears. You pass your hand in front of another sensor and a trap opens in the wall. *Pouf!* The toilet's gone. The trap closes like it was never there.

Too much!

God, it's good to laugh. I pass some cold water over my face and look in the mirror. I don't look that bad. I latch on to the joy this futuristic bathroom has brought me and give myself a mini pep talk. I am in Paris on a kind of paid holiday. Instead of being in some filthy backpackers' hostel catching crabs, I am standing in Kazo's bathroom, feeling rejuvenated after some hot air up my bum.

They can't take this away from me.

The bathroom door is also automated. It slides open. It's

so very fashionable. There is a tall blond model waiting outside. Also very fashionable.

"You're going to love this," I tell her. She doesn't react. She doesn't even blink. I bet all the fashion people are used to having their bums blown. She disappears into the toilet.

Kazo's house is as impressive as his garden and his toilet. All the walls seem to slide. You can change the geometry within a minute. There is very little furniture, no chairs, of course, and you have to take off your shoes to come in.

I'm starving. I walk to the indoor buffet.

More raw fish. Dammit! I am in Paris and I am permanently starving. Isn't France the country of good food and wine? Ah, there is some dessert on this buffet. It looks like some creamy light chocolate mousse in a shot glass.

"What is that?" I ask the hunky waiter.

"C'est du foie gras de canard cru dans une crème de châtaigne."

"Oh…"

Whatever.

I take one of the glasses and drink it. The stuff refuses to go down. It's revolting! It's not a dessert. It's some salty creamy goo. It tastes like rotten guts. Oh, God! My stomach sends it all back into my mouth.

I must get rid of it. Where? I turn away and spit it back into the shot glass, spreading some on my hand and—oh my oh my—on the floor.

I hope nobody…shit! Nicolas!

"Er, you don't like it, do you?"

"It's…not…sweet!"

"Well, I don't think it's supposed to be sweet. It's raw duck liver with chestnut cream. It's not vegetarian either."

Oh, that explains the rotten gory aftertaste.

"Raw fish. Raw liver. What's the problem with the caterer? Saving on gas and electricity?"

"Sushi is always on the menu at these parties. No cooked food—too passé. And absolutely no garlic. It's all about fashion, Lynn."

No garlic? I get it. They're vampires. It all makes sense. Look at them. Dressed in black, sucking each other's blood. Torturing themselves in the name of success. They eat revolting food (raw, because vampires only eat raw food). They grow too tall and too beautiful. They dress to kill. And people like Nicolas, so clever, so kind. They become slaves to rude spoiled monsters like Muriel. God, it's so…creepy!

"Nicolas, can I ask you something?"

"But of course, Lynn."

"Why do you dislike me?"

Ha! I caught him off guard and straight in the jaw. He smiles clumsily. "You're wrong. I don't dislike you."

"You act like I'm the plague descending on Paris!"

"I'm trying to protect Muriel's interests."

"You really think I'm that bad?"

"Actually…" Suddenly, there's something warmer about his smile. "I don't know anymore. You have…good ideas."

That's it, Lynn! That's it, keep it going.

"You know, we should talk," I propose.

"We should. You're right."

"I mean, now."

"Now?"

"Take me away from here."

"You're not enjoying yourself?"

"Why, are you?"

"Well," he said mysteriously. "I know a place…."

Step #8:
Never put love in the equation for success.
Love is a freak number.

Nothing happened!

Not a thing.

Nada!

Not even a kiss.

Because…

Mmm? He doesn't like me?

And, oh look, the sun's rising. It's so… God! I can still hear the music in my head and I want to dance, all alone in my suite.

I feel so giddy, and for no reason at all, because nothing happened! And nothing will ever happen, unfortunately.

So, what is it? Can you explain that to me? What is the nature of this magic spark? One minute, I'm like, life is good, Nicolas is gorgeous, I could totally do him, no big deal. And a minute later, I'm lying all alone on my bed, feeling

like I want to destroy my entire room. I want to throw the
TV set through the window and then jump to ease the pain.

Argh!

As if things were not complicated enough.

I can't keep up.

Be logical!

Act your age!

Hmm…maybe instead of doing that I'll just phone room
service and ask for a nice cup of relaxing herbal tea and a BLT.

Breathe in, breathe out.

Oh, Nicolas, Nicolas, NICOLAS! What have you done
to me? I'm thirteen again. I'm going through the biggest
crush of my entire life. I want to write about it in my secret
journal, if I had a secret journal. I want to write your name,
surround it with little hearts and hide it under my bed.

I want to dress up for you.

I want you to look at me.

I want you to listen to a love song and think of me.

I want to talk to you. I want to tell you everything about
me.

I want to leave silly messages on your answering machine.

I want to stalk you.

I want to kidnap you.

I want to tie you up in my bedroom and then I want to…I
want to…

That's it! Screw room service. I'm jumping through the
window.

Oh, but wait! Before I do that, I need to tell you about
last night.

We escaped Kazo's (you know…) together.

"I know a place…" he said mysteriously.

"What kind of place?"

"You know, a place where we should go. A very special place, for me."

"Your favorite place?"

"Yeah, something like that."

"I'd love to see your favorite place," I said.

"It's a quiet place. Nothing fancy. We can take a taxi."

"Can't we walk?"

He smiles. "Walking is fine. I used to love walking." He told me he used to cross Paris, dreaming of the future.

I told him I had been a keen walker, too, but didn't tell him that I still take those long walks to the Riverdale Dam on Sundays, or that I still gaze at the waterfall and dream of the future just like he did.

"Everything was so easy when I was young," Nicolas said. I think he was a bit drunk, or just very tired. Whatever it was, I felt as if we could open up to each other.

We discovered that we have a lot in common.

1. He liked to walk and I like to walk. (As I already mentioned.)
2. Breakfast is definitely our favorite meal.
3. We both love Christmas but (4. we always get disappointed once we've opened our gifts.)
5. We want to be Buddhists but (6. we don't know how to start.)
7. We prefer the mountains to the sea.
8. Apple and cinnamon is the best flavor for a muffin. Well…muffins are not very popular in France, but we agreed that (9. the best dessert ever is an apple-and-cinnamon pie.)

10. We prefer red wine to white,
11. coffee to tea,
12. morning to evening,
13. sweet to salted,
14. green to blue,
15. "Mary's in India" is the best Dido song.

Oops! Wait a minute! A guy that likes Dido has to be gay, hasn't he?

"Is it true that you're…"

"What?"

"Well, you know, gay?"

"Who told you that?"

"Not that I'm judging you. It's perfectly all right to be gay. Gay is normal. Gay is even more normal than not gay, if you see what I mean. Aren't we all gay, anyway?"

"*Aren't we all gay?* That sounds like somebody I know. Did Muriel tell you that I was gay?"

"She might have mentioned something along those lines."

"Do I look gay to you?"

"No! I mean, yes, you know. Nicolas…whatever you are, just be yourself." I sounded like an ad for running shoes.

"Not everybody is gay, Lynn."

What did he mean? I needed to know. I stopped walking.

"I'm not gay, all right?" he says.

"Really?"

So…I needed more clarification.

"Do you mean not gay in a French way?"

"No, I mean not gay in an international way!" Nicolas looked a little pissed.

"Oh… Not that I thought that you looked gay, anyway," I offered feebly.

We live in such confusing times.

Nicolas rolled his eyes. "Here we are," he said as we arrived at a small canal.

I immediately recognized the place. Massoud drove past here. It's the romantic version of Paris I liked so much and it's also Nicolas's favorite place. That's one more thing!

16. The canal is our favorite place in Paris.

"I grew up here," Nicolas tells me. "It still feels very special for me."

It's so romantic to walk along the river. It smells of spring. The deep dark water runs quietly. Small café terraces are packed with young people. There is a light atmosphere and lots of music.

Well, that's the Paris you dream about. The way I dreamed about it anyway. The city of love. I felt like joining the crowd of one of the cafés. I told him.

"First, I'm taking you to my special place."

We stopped in front of a tiny restaurant set in a very old house trapped between two huge modern buildings. It looked strange. It looked like a piece of the past trying to resist being squashed by the present.

"Look at that, Restaurant l'Escargot." Nicolas smiled proudly.

I had no idea why he brought me there, because the restaurant was closed and it looked as if it had been abandoned for a long time.

He invited me to take a peek inside. We stuck our faces to the windows and I could see a very cozy little space.

"It's been closed for three years now," Nicolas explained.

"You thought they would reopen it just for us?"

"No, of course not. That's where I grew up. In that restaurant."

He sounded very emotional.

"My parents used to run it."

"Oh…"

"I know, it's very *unfashionable*."

"No, no, Nicolas. It's…it's great."

I tried to sound earnest, but I must have come across as sarcastic because he looked really disappointed.

"Nicolas, I'm so happy that you brought me here."

"Yeah, right."

"Hey, look at me. It's a very nice place." I wanted him to know I meant what I was saying.

"It's all right, Lynn. It's not like I'm ashamed of it. I love this place."

"Why should you be ashamed?"

"It's something I tend to keep to myself. People in this business can be quite…pretentious."

Did I sound pretentious? He brought me to his special place and I made him feel awkward about it.

"I don't judge you, Nicolas. You know…everyone has their own secrets. I do."

"Really? Like what?"

Like…you were right, I don't deserve to be here. No, can't say that. Better to stay mysterious.

"Oh, Nicolas, a woman's secrets are very personal," I said, and gave what I hoped was a sly smile.

He pointed at L'Escargot.

"I showed you one of my secrets. Now you show me yours."

So much for mysterious. Okay, what can I say? "Well, I didn't really grow up in New York."

He looks at me blankly. He needs more.

"I grew up in a place called Red Hill, Connecticut, with my dad, and if you repeat it to anybody, I'll kill you."

"So we're both trying to hide our past, in a way."

17. We both try to hide our past.

He pulled the restaurant door, as if routinely checking it was well locked. "My parents still want me to take over the business. They haven't given up on me yet."

"They must be proud of you. You have such an amazing job at Muriel B."

"No, they're actually not proud at all. They think that one day I will give up this fashion nonsense and take over the restaurant. That's why they haven't sold it yet."

18. We're big disappointments to our parents.

"It's a nice place," I tell him. And I mean it.

"You think so?"

"It needs a serious cleanup."

"Running a restaurant is hard work."

"I'm sure you'd be a great restaurateur."

Hey, as far as I'm concerned, he'd be a great anything.

We settled in a tiny bar just beside l'Escargot. A brass band was playing engaging old tunes. We drank red wine out of tumblers. The walls were covered in old posters advertising concerts that took place years and years ago. Everything was protected by a thick layer of mixed brown fat and dust.

I didn't mention it, but I saw a huge beetle doing its daily slalom exercise between the glasses and disappearing under one of the tables.

The bar was crowded with young French people. Everybody was drunk or getting drunk and their lips were all blue and purple from the liters of cheap red wine being gulped down.

Nicolas's lips turned purple red, too. Who would have thought that would make them look even better.

"When I was in that kitchen," he said, "helping my dad, I thought, when I grow up, I'll never peel a potato again." He laughed. "Now all I remember is how simple and nice life was in that kitchen."

"And how everything became complicated and disturbing. I know the feeling," I said.

19. We long for the simplicity of the past.

Suddenly a disturbing thought popped into my head. "You love her, don't you?" I said suddenly.

"Who? Muriel?"

"You're so…" I made a face to show how completely fascinated he looked. Why else would he go against his parents if not for love?

"I don't love her. I admire her," he admitted. "She's impossible sometimes. Most of the time. But she's something special."

He suddenly looked all dreamy and distant, as if she was so special to him it actually called for more wine and introspection. If he didn't love her, he truly cared for her, far beyond his job description.

"What about you, Lynn?" he asked, coming back from his own little world.

"What about me?"

"Why did you come to work for her?"

I shrug. "Paris. Fashion. Fame. You know, the usual."

"I don't believe there is anything usual about you," he said.

"And exactly what do you mean by that?"

"You know, the way you handle things."

"Like?"

He looked very embarrassed. He drank some more wine and said, "Like that kiss."

That kiss. I stare at him blankly, unable to think of something clever to say.

"The kiss! The one you gave me."

"Ah! *That* kiss! Which one? There were…two, I think." My power of speech had returned.

"Both, really."

"Well, you've clearly established that they were meaningless." I smiled at him.

"Were they?"

"Why? Did you think about them?" This time I was the one needing some more wine.

"Maybe," he said thoughtfully.

"Did you think about them a lot?"

"Could have."

"And what did you think about them?"

"I…don't know. It was confusing."

"Confusing?"

"And intriguing."

"Definitely intriguing." I could feel the blush rushing to my cheeks. Please, God, let him think it's the wine.

"It made me wonder…"

"What?"

"If—"

"*Êtes-vous américains?*" the lady sitting next to me interrupted.

Damn!

I turned and realized that she was no lady. She had huge hands and she seriously needed a shave. She would always need a shave.

"No, I'm American," I said. "He is French."

"*Êtes-vous des amoureux? Elle comprend pas, hein?* Lovers?"

"*Non, non, seulement des collègues,*" Nicolas answered her— I mean him.

"You look like lovers," he/she pronounced.

I blushed so much that the room turned red with the glow from my face. The drag queen leaned over to speak into my ear.

"The young man, he is in love with you," and he/she blinked at me as if it was a done deal. "And you are a lucky girl, because he is like an angel. *Comme un ange!*"

God, don't I know!

"What did *she* say?" Nicolas asked when the drag queen went back to her own conversation.

"She said…she said we make a handsome couple. Ha ha ha!"

He blushed, too, I swear, he blushed!

★ ★ ★

We were the last ones to leave the bar. I asked if we could walk back to the hotel. Nicolas said that it would be quite a long walk, but that was exactly what I was after. Quite a long walk. A long, long, long walk. A walk that would take us forever.

I told him about my childhood. I told him about growing up away from Jodie. And it felt good to talk about the real me, the girl that used to hold daisies under her chin, and if they shone yellow on your skin, it meant that you were in love.

The girl that used to hide in Jodie's room and pretend to be locked into the tower of a castle, waiting for Prince Charming to come and free her.

But the prince never came, no matter how long she waited. He was too busy playing video games at the mall, I guess.

We fell silent. We were getting closer to my hotel and I was getting anxious. Should we part? Should I ask him to come up to share a bag of peanuts from the minibar, and a bottle of champagne and my bed?

We stopped in front of the Georges V.

I was about to say something, but he stopped me.

"I want to tell you…"

Yes, yes!

"I was wrong and I'm sorry. I think you are great."

Mmm?

"You're great for Muriel B, I mean. And…"

And?

"I think we all made up our minds about you. And…"

Okay… And?

We looked at each other. Oh, yes, we were getting closer.

My lips were almost reaching their ultimate goal when…he kissed me. On one cheek and then the other. Like a brother or my best gay friend.

That was so…gay.

Then he made a funny face, turned his back to me and walked away. That was it. All I ended up with was a lousy pair of kisses on the cheek and red-purple lips from cheap wine.

"Hey, it's Lynn," I say on the phone.

"What's wrong with you? Do they ever sleep in freaking Paris?"

"We kissed!"

"Goddamn it!" Delia wakes up in a flash. "Is he a good kisser? It's very important that he be a good kisser."

"It's hard to say, I kind of stole our first kiss. But we just spent the night together."

"God, you're fast!"

"I mean, we went on a date. Nothing definite happened!" Okay, maybe it wasn't exactly a date in the traditional sense, but it still counts.

"Oh. False alarm, then. I'll go back to sleep and you call me back after you do him!"

"Delia!"

She sighed but I could hear the squeak of her bed as she sat up. "Okay! A date! Did he walk you home?"

"Yes."

"Did he kiss you?"

"Yes…"

"No, no, no! You don't sound right. Where did he kiss you?"

Delia knows me too well.

"On the cheek. But it was quite close to my lips."

"Uh-huh…"

"Delia! I said *almost on my lips!* A very, very erotic cheek kiss!"

"Yeah…anything else?"

Sometimes I forget why I'm friends with Delia.

"No!"

"I thought all those French guys were sex maniacs."

"No, he's not a maniac, he is…charming. Yeah, he is *so-o* fucking charming."

I spent my childhood waiting for a guy just like him. Now I knew why he couldn't come: he was busy peeling potatoes in l'Escargot.

"Do you think he could be the One?" I hear Delia ask.

I look through the window. It's so calm out there. No way I'm going to jump. I'm far too tired for that.

"I don't know," I say as I collect all the pillows around me. I squeeze them. I squeeze them and wish I was squeezing Nicolas instead.

Step #9:
There are two kinds of people: those who
have their names in the papers, and those
who don't.

I'm not available.

I'm not here.

I'm not in Paris.

I'm not coming out from under my blanket.

I'm supposed to meet Muriel and Nicolas to discuss my contract, but I can't bring myself to go.

I'll stay right here, in my suite, until the police pick me up and put me in jail.

Only, I'll be at the airport before they show up. I'll be on my way home. And then, I'll dig a big hole in Dad's backyard and bury myself so they'll never find me!

It's not my fault everybody is so incompetent at Muriel B. Any other *normal* company would have asked more than just my name before relocating me to Paris.

Oh, but not at Muriel B. No, no. At Muriel B, nothing's done the right way. My company, after all, should reflect my personality.

So why do I feel so guilty? Why do I feel like a stink? Why do I feel like I did something wrong?

Because I'm the biggest freaking fraud in the history of fashion! And Fran Wellish is about to arrive and expose me.

The phone's ringing. It has to be the police.

Too bad! I'm not answering.

I wait until it stops and the message light flickers. I pick it up, thinking I'm safe, but instead of getting my message, I hear Nicolas's voice, "Er…Lynn?"

The phone tricked me!

"Lynn, can you hear me?"

"Yes, Nicolas. I hear you. But I'm busy. I have another very important call on hold."

"Wait…I wanted to—"

"I'll call you back."

I hang up before he can say that he has met Fran Wellish and that she said Jodie never mentioned anything about a daughter.

I press my messages button. First I'm going to check who phoned. Then I plan to disconnect the phone and start packing my things.

"*A-allo*. This is Chloe Destouches. We met yesterday at Kazo's. I meant to call you. I just talked with my chief editor, and, well, we would love to do a piece on you. It would be a feature. Three thousand words plus. 'An American Girl in Paris.' Or 'Jodie Blanchett's Daughter Takes Over Paris.' Or 'Lynn Blanchett does Paris.' Something like that, *anyway*. It would be just wonderful. Phone me at…"

God! A feature on me in *Marie Claire?*

Can I do the star-makeover segment, too? "Lynn Blanchett: From Swamp Thing to American Princess."

I force myself to swallow my excitement and think logically for a moment. Don't do it, Lynn, you're not up to this. Don't pick up the phone.

I pick up the phone and dial.

"Yes?"

"Chloe? This is Lynn Blanchett."

"Oh, wonderful!"

"Are you serious about the article? I mean, who would be interested? It might be boring for your readers."

"*Au contraire.* You are a very interesting subject. You are the dream come true. The glamorous heir of a fashion empire, conquering Paris. We could turn it into a series."

A series about me?

"We can follow your career. We would show your character easing into French high society… Mmm? I think we can do something great with you. What do you say?"

All those years, I've been wondering what it would feel like to be one of those celebrities. You know, to be like Jodie, to have stories written about me and my picture taken in a fabulous house in Italy or anywhere sunny and sophisticated.

And now my chance is here. All I have to do is say yes.

"That sounds great."

"Let's meet in the Quartier Latin. What about now? We can have breakfast together. I believe this would be the perfect atmosphere."

"Perfect," I say. Suddenly I'm excited to leave the safety of my bed.

"I'll arrange a photographer. But be casual, we want our

readers to see the real Lynn, and it's *so-o* easy to correct your imperfections with digital imaging."

I write down the address of her hotel and hang up, when the phone rings again.

"Lynn? Don't hang up. We need to talk!" Nicolas says.

He really sounds worried.

"Ah! Nicolas, I can't talk with you right now. I have a very important meeting with Chloe Destouches."

What a perfect excuse not to meet him.

"I know and I want to advise you not to go to that meeting."

"How do you know?" I can't believe that once again I'm the last to hear the latest gossip about myself.

"Lynn, listen to me. I can't talk right now but I don't want you to go."

Is he scared that I'm going to do a disastrous interview? Or...

"Did you talk with Fran Wellish?"

"No, she hasn't arrived yet. I just don't want you to go to that meeting. It will be bad for...our relationship."

"Are you all right, Nicolas?"

"I have to hang up now. Please don't go."

"Nicolas, I can handle a reporter. It will be very good publicity for Muriel B."

"Lynn, this interview is not about Muriel B."

He sounds very cautious, as if he can't talk freely. Honestly, it feels a bit awkward.

"Don't worry. I know exactly what to say to Chloe."

"Lynn?"

"Yes."

"If you decide to go..."

"Yes."

"Whatever they tell you, and whatever you decide, well, I want you to know that last night was very special for me."

"Are you all right? You're frightening me now."

"I have to hang up."

He does so and leaves me with a feeling of freakiness. He sounded as if this meeting with Chloe was a deadly trap and he'd risked his life to warn me.

It's all so mysterious and...*so* romantic!

The taxi leaves me in front of a lovely little hotel. Oh, you should see me now. I'm the mastermind behind the "Twenty-four-hour Blanchett Complete Makeover."

I have invented sexy-hip-casual wear. You wouldn't believe what I can do with a pair of sandals, jeans, a simple T-shirt, the proper handbag and a fantastic hangover.

And it works. I saw the looks men gave me as I left the hotel. Even the ones with their wives or partners couldn't help themselves. They had to turn and give me the who-is-this-woman-I-wish-I-knew-her-better look.

The concierge opens the door for me and, as I walk to the reception desk to ask for Chloe, I feel the insistent gaze of a man seated in the lobby.

"Lynn?"

He drops his newspaper and stands. It's no one else but Hubert Barclay. You know? The super-sexy-I-would-kill-to-spend-seven-minutes-with-you media mogul. He scans me. He smiles, he is very happy with what he sees.

"How are you? You look...amazing."

Oh boy, he sure looks happy to see me.

"Are you staying here?" I ask.

"No, I came to see a friend. You?"

"I'm looking for Chloe."

"Chloe Destouches. Of course. She's in the restaurant. Is she writing something on you? You deserve it, anyway, for all the good work you're doing for Muriel."

All my good work?

"Where are you staying?" Hubert continues.

"The Four Seasons."

"Le Georges V?"

"Oui."

"Mmm? A bit tacky. You should check in here. It's more your style."

I think to myself that Hubert has no idea what my style is, but I only say, "Maybe next time."

We look at each other. He smiles but says nothing. Obviously he's waiting for me to say something interesting and witty.

"I have to go," I say. Great, Lynn. Real witty.

"Oh. Are you…?"

"What?"

"Would you like to have dinner with me? If you're not too busy, of course."

Dinner with Hubert Barclay?

"Oh! That would be lovely."

"Good. I'll phone you at the Georges V then."

"Sure."

Sure, sure, SURE!

I walk away. Don't turn back. I order you not to turn back, Lynn. Imagine you are Roxanne Green. She would never turn back. Dammit! I turned back and there he was, checking me out with a satisfied smile on his face.

"Was that Hubert Barclay you were talking to, Lynn?" Chloe asks, but of course she already knows the answer. Chloe and Barclay belong to the same world. I'm the odd one out.

"Yes, that was good old Hubert. Isn't it a small world?"

"Do you really know Barclay? I mean, know him well?"

"Hubert has just asked me out on a date, but if you publish anything about us dating, I'll kill you."

She pushes out a chair for me and I sit down beside her.

"You keep surprising me, dear. You're dating the most eligible man on the planet and you don't want everybody to know. What are you? A Buddhist?"

"I just don't want details of my private life published in a glossy magazine."

"But that's why we're here!"

"Well… Except if it can help Muriel."

"I don't think so, Lynn," she says while pouring me some tea. "Nobody cares about Muriel. She is a fake, a spoiled brat, *une sale gosse*. And I won't waste a single drop of ink to help her get out of the shadow she will never leave."

My stomach churns with guilt. I wish Chloe would stop bashing Muriel. Muriel has actual creative talent. *I'm* the fake.

"My real interest is you, Lynn."

"But I'm representing Muriel B."

"Oh, come on! You must have realized what a waste of time they are by now. Muriel's nothing but a rich kid spending her father's money and pretending she is the best thing since denim. She makes me very angry."

Muriel must have stepped on Chloe's stilettos and never apologized for it.

"She makes a lot of people very angry," Chloe whispers.

"I think she has talent," I say.

"Talent! What's that exactly? It takes more than talent to succeed. It takes genius. Your mother has genius. Xu has genius." Chloe goes back to the whispering mode. "You two should meet again and talk. Xu is a very good friend of mine. I could arrange something. *Un rendez-vous.*"

"I don't think so. I'm just starting with Muriel. They trust me. You can't deceive people like that."

"Lynn, you're not a captain. You don't need to go down with the ship. This is not an honorable battlefield. This is fashion."

I reach for the sugar and get a dirty look.

She can't stand *sweet!*

"It so happens that Xavier is staying here, too. I could call him and you two could meet right now."

Call me paranoid, but years of rejections have taught me something. I don't feel naturally desirable. So, when all of a sudden, someone appears very eager to talk to me, I can only imagine that it's to kill me, dry me, salt me and eat me through winter.

"I'm sure that Xavier Urbain doesn't want to be disturbed to talk about corporate treason."

"Not at all, he is actually waiting for us in my room."

The plot thickens. Didn't Nicolas tell me not to come? How did he know that this interview for *Marie Claire* was nothing but a smoke screen?

Chloe stands as if it were a done deal. She promised to deliver my head to Xavier Urbain before lunch, and that's the way it's going to be. She doesn't even turn back to see if I'm following. She is sure that I want to hear what Xavier has to say, and she is absolutely right.

I stand to follow her. I didn't even have a chance to try my tea. And so much for having a feature article about me published in *Marie Claire!*

"No, we're not taking the elevator, dear. My room is on the second floor and my trainer says the stairs are good for my butt."

Chloe nimbly ascends the stairs as I drag behind.

"Have you had sex with him already?"

"Who?" Does Chloe think I know her trainer?

"Barclay!"

Oh, right. "None of your business," I say. No article, no details.

"You know that he has a girlfriend back home. They're talking ring and wedding cake."

"I hope I'll get invited."

"Ooh! That's so continental of you. Very *today*."

"Hubert and I are just friends."

"That's right. You're one of Hubert's special friends. Believe me, I'm so over those kinds of friendships. Five minutes in bed, two days of running mascara."

She smiles and knocks on the door of room 212.

Xavier Urbain opens the door. He didn't bother to dress up. He wears a bathrobe. The little hair he has on the top of his round head is neatly greased and brushed back.

"Ah, Lynn Blanchett! I'm so happy that we meet again. We have so much to talk about."

We enter Chloe's room. Yak! It smells of acrid sweat, strong cologne and soapy humidity. There's very little light and no oxygen at all.

"Please sit," Xavier says, pushing a chair toward me. God, I can't stop thinking that he's the weirdest, most revolting little creature I've ever seen.

"This conversation is well overdue," Xavier says. "You must have realized by now that Muriel is a flake."

"Well, no actually," I tell him. "She is…different, but I see potential in her."

"Wouaf!" Xavier barks. "There's nothing behind Muriel B. Just wind. It takes years to build a serious fashion house like Xu. She thinks that she can come with all her father's money, with all her ridiculous tattoos and all those *things* all over her face and we're all supposed to clap our hands and call her genius."

"I don't understand why she makes you so furious. Chloe and you seem so against her."

"Pretentiousness is infuriating."

"She's not the only pretentious person in the business. Why single her out?"

"Listen. I don't want to talk about her anymore. I want to talk about you. I want to help you."

"I didn't know I needed help."

He eyes Chloe nervously.

"Lynn, would you just listen to what Xavier has to say?" Chloe seems to have lost some of her icy calm.

"We think that you are an exceptional asset. I mean, your name…and your *ideas,* of course!" Xavier says in what he must think is a seductive voice.

"And I would hate to lose you to those buffoons. Understand?"

"No, I don't understand."

"Well, Xavier would like to offer you a position in his organization. A top position. But that would mean that you would need to stop having any contact with Muriel B."

I look at Chloe. I can't believe my ears. I'm the stake in a poker game between Muriel and Xavier Urbain.

"You must be joking," I snap. "You want to double-cross Muriel by using me?" I began to laugh, quietly at first, but soon I was practically in tears.

"What's so funny?" Chloe looked at me and frowned. Or would have frowned if all the Botox in her face hadn't prevented it.

"The situation. And you people. Why do you think I would backstab Muriel?"

"Well, how much is she giving you?" Xavier asks.

"Enough," I lie because we haven't discussed money yet. And actually, she might not be giving me anything at all after she speaks to Fran.

"I was thinking of offering you…enough, too." He writes a number on a little hotel pad and pushes it toward me. I read it. My throat dries instantly.

"It's in euros," he says.

They're waiting for a reaction but I am paralyzed. Are they really proposing to pay me all this money? He takes back his pad and writes another number.

"And this will be your *ipso facto* bonus when you sign a contract with us."

I read the number.

Holly mother of God!

I'm rich! Look at me, Jodie, I made it! I am a freaking European goddess!

"I'm sure that whatever Muriel told you, it will never match those figures," Chloe says.

I thought she was a journalist, but she seems more like Xavier Urbain's dark shadow.

"Well…I have to think about it," I say, trying to stay perfectly neutral.

Think about it? My brain is screaming at me. Are you crazy? Didn't you read the little pad and the huge numbers? Ask them to show you the money and sign the contract immediately. You don't owe anything to Muriel or to Nicolas.

Shit! Nicolas! God, he is going to hate me. I'm a horrible mercenary, only excited by the smell of gold.

"We don't have a lot of time to think, Lynn. Those are the figures," Chloe says. "Now you have to make up your mind."

Sign, sign, SIGN!

"I need time to think about it."

They look at each other.

"You're not going to try to raise the bid, are you?" Xavier asks.

"Lynn knows she is very valuable, Xavier. But I'm sure she realizes that her name is not worth one cent more."

A lovely woman, that Chloe, through and through.

"I just need to think about it," I repeat, managing to sound much calmer than I feel.

They relax. They seem convinced that I will go along with their evil plan and honestly, if it wasn't for Nicolas, I really might.

"Don't take too much time thinking, Lynn," Chloe says. "Opportunities are like trends. They perish fast."

I hate to admit it, but Chloe has a point. What if they change their minds? What if they realize that I'm not worth all that money?

What if I say yes and never see Nicolas again?

Nicolas! Nicolas! You're about to ruin the deal of my life.

With all that money I could just buy fifteen guys fitter than you (not that I have seen you without your shirt on). Guys that would fulfill all my kinkiest fantasies. Guys that would go by the name of Alfredo, or Bernardino. Guys that would not only have sex with me on demand but would also be very good at cleaning the swimming pool or spreading sunscreen on my back with their very, very strong virile hands.

And you, Nicolas? What do you have to offer? A scooter! Just a damn ridiculous scooter and the bizarre feeling that you are the one for me.

Step #10:
You can sleep with Mr. Lovely but you
must marry Mr. Wealthy.

A message left at the reception desk says, "Call me back. Nicolas."

Oh, God!

I imagine Fran Wellish's face when she tried to remember a Lynn, daughter of her ex-boss.

What did you say? Lynn? Hmm… No, no. There was no Lynn around Jodie. She had an ugly little dog called Spark, but I never heard of any daughter called Lynn. Sorry, she must be a fake my dear Nicolas.

Another message says, "Will pick you up at seven-thirty. Kiss. Hub."

Hub?

I can't picture Hubert Barclay as a "Hub."

A Hub can't possibly manage a media empire.

I lie on my bed looking at the two notes.

"The Hub," I say out loud.

Maybe the Hub doesn't give a damn who my mother is.

The Hub might only be interested in the *real* me, the person I am *inside*.

Yeah, right! Based on his reputation, the only inside he's interested in is inside my pants!

Why am I even going out with him? Besides the handsome-rich-powerful thing, I mean. Am I attracted to him? Hub sounds ridiculous as a name. It's like a spaceship is picking me up for dinner.

I read Nicolas's message again. Cold. Straight to the point. Directorial. I'll-see-you-in-my-office-right-now kind of message. A message for someone about to be told she's over.

I sigh and fall onto my bed. I have landed in a crazy world, inhabited by frenzied lunatics, but somehow, I like it here. I have seen the kind of life I could have had. You know, with Nicolas and all the rest, and I want more of it. But instead, I'm about to be cast away, sent back home without fame, without glamour, and probably end up marrying a guy called Rod or Ted out of desperation. I will never show Jodie I can be part of her world.

The phone rings. It's Nicolas. I know it's him. I can feel him even over the phone. There's no point in postponing the kill. I pick up.

"Lynn?"

Yes, it's him.

"Hi, Nicolas."

"Sorry, Lynn. Did you get my message?"

"I was just looking at it. Did you speak with Fran?"

"Fran Wellish? Well, no. She postponed her trip to Paris."

Postponed?

"Postponed?"

"In fact, it's quite weird. She actually wasn't on the flight and now we can't seem to contact her."

Thank you, God! You've vaporized her!

"But what about you? Did you talk to… Where were you today?" he asks rather clumsily.

"I needed time for myself. I spent my day walking." Did that sound as much like a lie to Nicolas as it did to me? He must suspect I went to the meeting.

"Are you angry with me?"

"No… Why should I be angry with you?"

"I don't know. It's the sound of your voice. You okay?"

I'm so far from okay, but obviously I can't say that to Nicolas. Better change the subject. "I walked by L'Escargot. It looks very nice in the daylight."

"That's funny."

I roll on my bed and start to play with the phone cord. "What's funny?"

"I talked to my parents today. They've finally decided to sell the restaurant. They asked me one last time if I wanted to take it over."

"And what did you say?"

"I said no, of course."

"They must have been sad."

"I guess." Nicolas takes a deep breath I can hear over the phone. "Can we see each other tonight?"

"I have a date." Oh shit! I shouldn't have called it a date. "I mean, I just bumped into Hubert Barclay, and he asked me to have dinner. It's a…friends-date."

Nicolas is totally silent. I hear my own words echo in my head.

Definition of friends-date: eat food, drink wine, go home, keep pants on! Everyone knows that, right? Even in France?

"Nicolas, Hubert is just a friend."

It's you that I want, silly.

"I see. I'll see you at work tomorrow, then."

Damn! Why am I screwing this up?

"Lynn?"

"Nicolas?"

We sink into another of our famous embarrassing silences.

"I…" Nicolas starts, then stops.

"Yes?"

"I…"

"Hmm?"

"Well, have a nice evening," he says.

Whatever.

Didn't I tell you that I'd be a princess? I can't stop looking at myself. Front. Back. Three-quarter. Profile. I really did do some walking after my meeting, and I bought a couple of amazing dresses and a pair of shoes to match each one. Then I bought a stunning new trench to complete the outfits. Thank God for the cash Jodie gave me.

The few banknotes left lie on the table beside the Kazo store receipt and look at me with their sad eyes for the loss of all their friends.

Yes, I shopped at Kazo…you know.

But seriously, look at me!

Front. Back. Three-quarter. Profile.

That's what fashion is all about. Transformation and finding one's identity. I have finally found out that I can be cute. Very cute. Super very cute. In fact—dare I say it?—almost beautiful. Wait until the Hub sees me! He is going to drown in his own drool.

I know. I shouldn't go out with Hub. Not with what's going on, uh, or not going on with Nicolas right now. Still, it's going to be fine because, first, it's not a date. It's a friends-date. Second, I feel absolutely nothing toward the Hub and will really be thinking about Nicolas.

And third, I'm just dying to go out in Paris with an all-American legend like the Hub!

I'm the little darling of the jet set! And let's face it. This is probably my one shot at this before it all comes crashing down, so I think I'm entitled to enjoy it.

Har har har!

The phone rings and the concierge tells me that there is a Mr. Barclay waiting for me in the lobby.

It's so incredible!

I would like my entire life to be just like tonight. I mean, how I'm sure tonight will turn out.

I'm so excited I can't remember if I have closed the door to my suite.

I can't remember if I took the card key!

I quickly look in my purse but I've already forgotten what I'm looking for.

How can you do it? How can you stay gracious and have a date (a friends-date) with Hubert Barclay? He is taking me out in Paris. I belong to a long list of celebrities and models that Hubert has taken out, had sex with and then discarded. What a lucky girl I am.

Oops! I mean, of course I'm not going to have sex with the Hub. This is a friends-date. I'm thinking of my angel Nicolas and I feel very guilty for not being with him.

Of course, Nicolas could have asked me out…

I see him. The Hub has his back to me. I walk down the last steps to the reception area. I'm making my Ingrid-Bergman-comes-down-the-stairs impression. He turns to take a good look at me. Ah! There's electricity in the air. I can feel it. I smile my best smile. Bull's-eye! It's working. He likes what he sees. A real girl, finally. Not one of those tall, anorexic spiders. A fleshy girl he could bring to his parents and say, "Yes, Mother, she has curves and large hips, and she will bear my child!"

"Hey, Hubert." Or Hub or the Hub.

"You look…perfect."

He looks "perfect", too.

"I booked a table at La Tour d'Argent. I hope that's not too tacky for you."

"You seem very scared of tacky." I give him my best sexy-but-suitable-for-a-friends-date smile.

"Tacky kills, Lynn."

"Well, I've never been there before," I say. "But I'm starving, so anything will do."

He smiles. He doesn't date a lot of starving women. Or anybody eager to go anywhere. That's the problem with anorexia and self-medication. Low sugar makes you numb. I'm different. I'm all cookies and cream. It gives me the energy to bite into life and plenty of extra fat.

"I haven't had a steak since I arrived in Paris," I say, eagerly renouncing my fake vegetarianism. "Do they have good steak?"

He tries to think about it. "I've never seen a steak at La Tour d'Argent, but I'm sure that if we ask them, they'll send a runner to buy one somewhere."

He's so unfussy. In a way, he acts as if he doesn't give a damn about the world, and at the same time he appears to be very kind and eager to please.

I love this friends-date!

Outside the hotel the night is warm and the sky is pink red. Everything is perfect. Hubert's driver opens the door of a stretch black Mercedes. I sit in the deep leather seat. I could get used to this.

"Should we go for an aperitif first?"

"If that means an alcoholic drink, I'm with you."

"What kind of girl are you? Trendy or classic?"

Er? "Classic?"

"Good. Do you like Bloody Marys?"

"Mr. Barclay? Can you read minds?"

"Dave," he calls to the driver. "Take us to Harry's."

It's something else to be driven in stretch limos. You feel separated from the real world, it's like traveling in fantasyland.

"Lynn, I'm embarrassed to ask you, but where did we meet before?"

"We never met before, Hubert."

He considers that and smiles. I smile back.

"You're something different, Lynn."

"You bet, Hub." I know, it sounds like I'm flirting, but I'm not…. Or maybe just a little bit, in a friendly kind of way.

The driver stops in the middle of a tiny street, blocking the traffic with style. He jumps out of the car and opens the door for me. He gives me his hand and helps me out. Hubert came out by himself and is already waiting for me at the bar's entrance.

"I knew that I couldn't have possibly met you before. I would have remembered."

He opens the door for me. Inside the bar, it's packed, smoky, noisy and dark and I love it. It's exactly the way you would picture nightlife in Paris. It's the way you read about it. The smoke. The noise. The relics of the past hanging from wooden panels. I can only hear English conversations. We're among Americans here, and we are all keeping an eye on the door in case Ernie Hemingway or Scott Fitzgerald come back from the dead to enjoy a last gin and tonic.

"Look who's here! Isn't it a small world?"

Isn't it indeed? Roxanne Green is eyeing us and gives me an inviting smile.

She sits with a handsome, dark-haired boy half her age.

"Lynn! How lovely to see you here. Hubert! Sort us out with some drinks, will you."

"Sure. What's the boy drinking?"

The boy looks up at Hubert.

"Oh. Hubert, Lynn, this is…Guy. Guy is… What is it you're doing again, Guy? *Qu'est-ce que tu fais dans la vie, mon chéri?*"

"*J'ai été dans l'Appart. Mais j'ai perdu.*"

"Oh, yes, Guy was in one of those stupid reality shows they've got here. Now I think he wants to write his biography, but of course, he will have to learn how to read and write first. And he wants to become famous. Bring him a club soda, he already had too much to drink."

Roxanne brushes his cheek.

"*Je me sens pas bien!*"

"So, Lynn," Roxanne says. "I see you've been busy. And you can't say I didn't warn you about Barclay."

"It's just a friends-date," I protest. "Besides, Hubert has a girlfriend back home."

"Tsk, tsk! You're so outdated, darling. Hubert has dumped the poor girl like he dumps any young naive thing that passes through his bedroom. She wanted them to get engaged before fall, so he wanted her out. He came to Paris to give her time and space to move out of his New York apartment. How delicate of him! Aren't you a knight, Hubert?" she says as he returns with our drinks.

"If you say so."

He puts the soda in front of Guy, but the poor thing has fallen asleep on the table.

"I think it's past his bedtime."

"That's the problem when we're dating *so young,* Hubert," she says, sipping her Bloody Mary and stroking Guy's hair.

"Mmm! This is the most delicious Bloody Mary I've ever tasted," I say, trying to shift the conversation.

"You're the luckiest man, Hubert," Roxanne continues as she eases back in the bench. "You're rich. You're successful. And now you're adding Lynn Blanchett to your trophy wall."

"Oh, j'ai dormi!" Guy jerks back to life and looks around.

"It's all right, darling. We didn't miss you."

"I'm sick. I want out," he manages to whine in English.

"You're a big boy. You can go out by yourself."

"It's all right," Hubert says. He helps the boy to his feet and drags him through the crowd.

How decent of him! If this wasn't a friends-date, I would be so charmed.

"Lynn, let me say this—stay away from Hubert."

"Nothing will happen. This is—"

"There's no such thing as a friends-date."

I'm about to protest and explain the terms of a friends-date, but a man falls into Hubert's seat, stares at me and says, "Hey, I know you."

He is an elegant, overweight guy in his midforties. He has curly red hair and the round red face of somebody who enjoys his beer with lots of potato chips.

"I don't think so."

"Everybody knows her," Roxanne tells him. "But nobody knows you. Is that your best pick-up line?"

"Hey, don't be so uptight, lady. The name's Brian. Brian Ferguson from Boston. Are you from Boston?"

He is kind of cute, if you like them chubby and cuddly.

"What do you do for a living, Brian Ferguson from Boston?" Roxanne asks.

He shows his glass of beer.

"I buy and sell wine. That's what I do."

"That's beer."

"I'm unfaithful."

"Lovely job."

"Simply the best. Cheers to that," he toasts, then empties his glass. "Hey, can I buy you ladies a drink?"

Roxanne studies him more carefully. "Married?"

"Divorced."

"Well off?"

"Can't complain."

"Make it two Bloody Marys." She shoos him away. "Doesn't he look like the common Joe for a Brian? I like him."

"I'm not sure Guy is going to like him, too," I say, reminding Roxanne she's here with a date.

"Speak of the devil."

Hubert comes back alone.

"I had to put the boy in a cab," he says.

"Now, Hubert, that's nasty. I had plans for Guy tonight."

"Hey, I was here first, buddy," Brian says and puts our drinks on the table.

"Hubert, meet Brian Ferguson from Boston. Brian sells wine."

"And who are you, buddy?" Brian asks like somebody about to lose his parking place.

"Brian, I have new plans for you tonight. You're going to be my date," Roxanne purrs at Brian.

"Whatever you say, boss."

"Good boy. Sit."

Brian sits with a big smile on his face. Give him beer and women, and he feels complete.

"Can we join you tonight?" Roxanne asks.

"We have a reservation at La Tour d'Argent."

"La Tour d'Argent!" Brian spits his beer back into the glass. "That's for tourists and sitting ducks, buddy."

"Oh behave, Brian."

Brian freezes and gives Roxanne a sleazy look. "Lady, I like it when you talk nasty."

Look at her. She can't stop a *so* un-Roxanne Green smile. He slams the table and says, "I know another *tour,* but this one is Tour de Montlhéry and, ladies and gentlemen, it's the real thing."

I look at Hubert and say, "Why not?" So Hubert smiles courteously and says, "Why not, indeed?"

But we're not ready. We're not ready until we drink enough Bloody Marys to kill a small pony, and when we get out of Harry's Bar, I see nothing wrong with Hubert having his arm around my waist. Because that's exactly what friends do when they go out on friends-dates.

He calls Dave on his cell phone. He looks so much in charge. I feel that for once I can rely on someone else and I'm so touched that I could cry (yes, I'm drunk!).

I turn to Roxanne. I need her moral support.

She's useless.

She laughs and laughs! Roxanne Green laughs a normal, earnest laugh. Not the hyena cry she normally uses to punctuate every sentence. She finds the round Brian hilarious.

"Where's that cab?" he yells, but suddenly, the sight of Hubert's Mercedes shuts him up. But just for a moment.

"Oh, wait a minute, buddy! Are you trying to impress us?"

"No, that's just our ride," Hubert answers, so naturally detached I want to kiss him. But I guess that I shouldn't because first, this is a friends-date and I need to remind myself to feel very guilty from time to time.

Dave offers his hand to help me out when we arrive at the restaurant.

"I told you, it's the real thing," Brian says.

"Lynn, this is going to be by far the worst evening I have ever had in Paris," Roxanne says, but, by God, she's smiling so much she even forgets about the wrinkles it makes on her face.

We enter the small restaurant. Copper pots and various-shaped and -sized salamis are hanging from the ceiling. A woman, apparently the owner, is guarding the entrance. She recognizes Hubert and they shake hands. He speaks in French to her. He makes a joke and she laughs and calls one of the waiters. They start shuffling things around in the tiny restaurant to arrange a table for us.

It seems like there is a special private function going on in there, like a wedding or corporate party, but Brian says, "It's like this every night, a big party with strangers."

It's a gourmets' gang bang!

There are no separated tables. You sit at a long table among perfect strangers. Everybody shares their wine and food.

I don't know if it's all a dream or if this is for real. I feel like a young teenager. Excited and overwhelmed. Hubert doesn't look like an enemy. I don't need to be careful with him. Not tonight. Tonight, he's my partner. He's the one I can rely on. The one who will protect me and see me right.

We've ordered food but I have no idea what I have asked for. The waiter puts a large, deep platter in front of me that contains something that looks like giant dead slime in sauce. I hear Brian laugh out the word *kidney* and I feel instantly sick and claustrophobic.

I need oxygen. I stand up and start to push people out of my way.

I try to smile as I pass by the owner. She sits like an old queen behind the till. She controls who pays and who tips. Money and whiskey on ice are her two things. I smile, so she'll think I'm all right and still a young lady. But you can't fool people like her. She knows that I'm as drunk as a pig and sick as a dog. She tosses me a condescending smile. She has no time for people who can't hold their liquor. I push open the door and reach the street. It's a hot night. I'm disappointed. I expected a fresh cool supply of air and all I get is a warm blanket charged with pollen.

"Do you want to go?" Hubert has followed me outside. He puts one hand on my shoulder and the other on my cheek. I'm trapped. I feel possessed by him and very safe all at the same time.

"Yes," I say, looking back into the restaurant.

"They'll be fine," he says as he pushes buttons on his cell phone.

"Don't call Dave, please. I need to walk a bit."

"Whatever you like," Hub says as he smiles at me. "Lynn, I need to tell you something."

"What?"

"I haven't felt like this in years."

"Sick and drunk?"

"No." He shakes his head and laughs. "I don't know if I have ever felt like this before."

"Oh, come on!" This has to stop right now. Even as drunk as I am I know a line when I hear one.

"Listen! I felt like *this*…tonight. With you."

"Is that the best you can do?" I snap defensively. I'm caught off guard. Men like Hubert Barclay don't speak like this. Not to women like me.

"In fact, you're right. I can do much better." He stops me by grabbing my arm gently. I don't want to see his eyes. I look farther down the street. I look at the passing cars and the traffic lights as they turn to red.

"I want to do much better, Lynn."

I turn back to him. I shouldn't have.

He kisses me. Very fast. On the tip of my lips.

No, no, no! This is not happening. This is not what friends do on friends-dates.

"I don't…" I try to say something to stop Hubert's kiss.

"Shh!"

Oh, don't fool yourself, Lynn. I feel the pressure of his

hand on my back as he comes back for more. I made a mess out of this friends-dating thing. I'm overwhelmed by his charm, by his strength, by his desire. I don't want it to happen but I can't fight it either. I kiss him back.

He breaks our embrace and calls Dave on his cell phone. We both know that the walk is over. We need a ride.

I wake up at dusk. At first it's hard to remember where I am. Then it hits me like a torpedo.

Boom!

I'm lying in bed and the Hub is asleep beside me. This is not a hotel room. It's more like an apartment and as I ease up I see the Seine through the panoramic bedroom windows.

Oh, my God!

I turn to look at him. All I see is his very large shoulders, his face smashed against the pillows.

Alarm bells go off in my head. I've got to get out of here.

I slide out of bed. The last thing I need is for him to wake up and ask me how I feel.

Oh, my God!

Help me!

I find my panties on the floor. My Kazo dress lies like a neglected kitchen towel nearby. My shoes didn't make it farther then the living room. I pick them and tiptoe to the door.

I can't even pretend that I don't remember a thing. I remember all the dirty details.

Him all over me.

His body.

His skin.

How could I have done this? The guy just asked me out

on a date, a little restaurant dinner, and now I'm running out of his apartment after a night of passionate mating and multiple orgasms.

Help me, help me!

It's not what I wanted. I just wanted a medium-rare steak. Maybe some béarnaise sauce.

I try to open the door as discreetly as I can, but I make an awful racket trying to figure out how to operate the lock.

"Lynn!" I hear him calling from the bedroom. "Lynn!"

I slide out onto the staircase and close the door. I run down the steps like a thief. My heart is racing. I imagine him running after me. I imagine that I will never make it to the street. I press all the buttons to get the front door to open and finally there is a *bip* noise and I run out and away barefoot.

I see a taxi and I wave. I finally put on my shoes before I jump in.

"Vous, vous avez fait la fête," the driver says.

"La fête?"

"Party, party…" He winks.

Even the taxi driver knows. And… Talking about a party! We didn't even use condoms!

Well, it was supposed to be a friends-date! You don't take condoms to those.

It didn't stop me.

I'm pa-athetic!

I feel so guilty, but…why? I'm not married to Nicolas. We're not even together-together. I'm a single, young American girl in Paris with boiling hormones in a hot Kazo dress. I'm going out with high-flying American society and having amazing sex with a Hub. Until Nicolas steps up and tells me he wants a relationship, that's allowed. Right?

★ ★ ★

I run up to my room. I look for my card key in my purse but I can't find it. Oh, no. Did I leave it in Hub's apartment? Will he come here later and enter my room? Will he ravage me again and again until I die of ecstasy? Will he—oh! I finally find my card and enter my room.

I lock myself inside and collapse against the door.

He has kissed and he will tell! Everybody is going to know what kind of dirty girl Jodie Blanchett's daughter is. One night, that's all it takes to have me. You don't even need to buy me dessert. Just bring me to a bar, fill me up with drinks, and I'm yours.

I find his business card and go to the phone. It's 5:30 a.m. but I need to call him and set the record straight.

I let the phone ring…and get his answering machine. I hang up and phone again. It's busy. I hang up and phone again. He picks up.

"Nicolas?"

He doesn't answer at first.

I just hear him breathing and I imagine him trying to figure out who in the world would call him at this ungodly hour while he stands completely naked in the middle of his living room with his phone in his hand.

"Nicolas, it's me, Lynn. Wake up, Nicolas!"

"Lynn?"

"It's okay if you hate me."

"Lynn. I… Where are you?"

I'm lying on my bed after a night of frenetic sex with a man I don't really know and I'm talking to another man I don't really know but really want to have sex with. Does that make sense?

"I'm at my hotel. Now, don't interrupt. Just let me talk. You should hate me, Nicolas. I'm a terrible person. I lie. I lied to you. I lie all the time. I'm not the person you think I am. I—"

"Lynn?"

"Yes?"

"Do you want to have breakfast with me?"

He opens his door and there I am. I think I've set a new world record. It took me less then five hours to get from Hubert Barclay's to Nicolas's apartment.

I follow Nicolas, and the sweet smell of freshly brewed coffee, to the kitchen. He wears a baggy white shirt and jeans. I have never seen him look so casual. He asks if I want coffee and I tell him I'd kill for some, with a side of aspirin.

"Did you have a busy night?" he asks while looking for the aspirin.

Busy? Yeah, you bet!

"I had too much to drink, I guess," not mentioning that I hardly slept and that my sense of guilt is squashing my brain to a pulp.

He pours two cups of coffee and takes them to the living room. I follow and ask myself why on earth I came over here?

We sit on his sofa. Nicolas's apartment looks like a student condo. It's tastefully decorated, but it doesn't show the signs of wealth that I witnessed at Muriel's or Hubert's.

"I was worried," he says. "The way you sounded."

I look around and realize how little I know about Nicolas. Maybe even less than I know about Hubert, which is sad since I've seen him nearly every day since I've come to Paris.

I hear a door slam and look up from my coffee cup. Someone else lives in this apartment?

Oh, how naive can I be? I don't even know if he has a girlfriend. I don't know if he is married, or has been married, or has any children. I don't know if he is about to drive his wife to work and bring his two little girls to school.

I'm a mess!

"You sounded in a state of panic," Nicolas starts again. He's clearly waiting for me to explain why I called and where I've been.

"I'm sorry to put you through this. I guess I was a bit freaked out. I had a rough night."

I regret immediately having said that. Better change the subject, fast.

"You have a nice apartment."

"It's small. And too expensive. It's really hard to find something in Paris."

I look around for any signs that will help me to understand who Nicolas is and why I need him so much.

Everything is very orderly. A place for each thing, each thing in its place. There is a huge collection of CDs covering an entire wall, but absolutely no picture of any kind. I can hear a toilet flush and the sound of running water. Somebody is taking a shower. I naively ask, "Do you live alone?"

"I live with Marc."

"Oh."

So what happened to *I'm not gay?* Damn French!

"Marc is my flatmate."

"Ah." What does he mean exactly by flatmate?

"Marc is working at Muriel B," he says as if he was reading my mind. "I think you two met when you came to the office."

"Possibly." I sip my coffee casually and try to remember a Marc.

"He is a very talented designer. He spends most of the day in the workshop."

"I think I remember him," I say, but I have absolutely no memory of a Marc, any Marc.

"You look worried."

"Nah, I'm not worried." I guess my sipping wasn't as casual as I had thought.

"If you're worrying about the position, you should stop. I told you before, Muriel's crazy about you. I'm supposed to prepare a contract for you today."

I want to tell Nicolas I'm not here to discuss the contract, I'm here to understand why I feel so guilty about last night. I'm here to see if I can be that person in the shower one day. I'm here to see if he wants me to be that person in the shower. But instead I say, "What about Fran Wellish?"

He shrugs. "I don't know. She's weird. She refuses to talk to us anymore."

I should be relieved. But in fact, I don't care about Fran Wellish right now. All I care about is the shower and the distinct sound of Marc the Mysterious Flatmate groaning and vocalizing under the spray.

"It's a rather small apartment, I mean, to share," I say.

He shrugs again. "I've been here since I was a student. I like the district."

I don't care about the lodging problem in Paris, either. I want Nicolas to describe fully his relationship with Marc-in-the-Shower, and I want him to tell me that Muriel is wrong and he didn't lie to me the other night just to toy with my feelings. I want him to confirm that I'm not crazy. I want him to say that even though he is an angel, he still looks down at me and sees…and sees… Oh, dammit! I want him to say that there is something going on between us!

But Nicolas doesn't say any of that. He's waiting for me to speak again. "I guess I'll have to start looking for an apartment as well," I say.

"I can help you."

"How's that?"

"We can include a relocation package as part of your contract. I have to discuss it with Muriel, though."

"Ah, bonjour!"

I turn to see a tall, handsome man standing in the doorway, wearing nothing but a pair of boxer shorts on a very athletic body. Now I recognize him immediately. He is one of those very effeminate creatures I've met in the workshop.

"Bonjour," I reply.

"Quelle surprise! C'est gentil de venir nous dire bonjour comme ça." Nicolas smiles at Marc.

Okay, I know Nicolas says he's not gay, but still, I can immediately sense the dynamic in their relationship. Nicolas is the reasonable husband, always reliable and serious, and Marc is the crazy wife, exuberant and unpredictable. They live on the sixth floor and I feel like jumping through the window.

"Lynn needed to talk to me about the job," Nicolas says, switching the conversation to English.

"Oh, I see. Business, all the time business, business, business. Oh, but you must be starving." He has a very strong accent. "Nicolas, the croissants!"

"Are you hungry, Lynn?"

Paris has been very good for my figure. I never eat and I spend my time running in all directions.

"I'm starving."

"Elle a faim, ça se voit!" Marc gestures at me dramatically with his hand.

Nicolas stands up.

"Non, non, I'll go," Marc says. "You two talk…business, and I make breakfast."

He disappears back into the corridor from where he came, like an actor who'd jumped onstage then receded backstage.

"He is a lovely guy," Nicolas says.

I feel so stupid. I should have stayed in bed with Hubert. I should have tried to see if I could love him or even only like him, once the Bloody Mary had worn off.

"Are you still worried about the position?" Nicolas asks again.

"I feel better now," I lie. "It's been a crazy roller-coaster ride since I landed."

"I'm so sorry, Lynn. Everything is so confusing right now. I hope that soon we will see the light at the end of the tunnel."

"Croissants pour tout le monde?" Marc asks. He has thrown a long black coat overtop a pair of sweatpants. He doesn't wait for an answer. He just jumps out of the apartment and closes the door saying, *"A tout de suite, les amoureux."*

"Don't mind him," Nicolas says. "He likes to act bigger than life."

I'm not exactly sure what Marc said. I recognized the word *love* or *lovers.* Maybe he said, *Bye, love.* Or, *I love you, Nicolas, we had really great sex yesterday night, pity the American girl is here, we could have done it all over again before breakfast.*

We have one of our silences and Nicolas breaks it by saying "On the phone, you said that you lied to me."

"I was confused," I mumble.

"When did you lie to me?"

"I was lost, I have…" Oh, what the hell. "I was confused, so I guess I needed to talk to someone. It doesn't matter anymore, I was just…stupid. I thought, because of the night we had together… I guess, I thought… But I didn't know about you and Marc, so you see I was wrong."

"What about me and Marc?"

Oh, I'm so embarrassed. You'd think for a man in fashion it would be no big deal, but he obviously wants to stay in the closet, and I opened it, uninvited.

"No, I mean, I didn't know you were together." I cross two of my fingers to represent their relationship. "I mean together-together."

He looks at me. Silence.

"I thought that you and me might have started something. But…I'm… It's ridiculous, of course, because…"

How could I ever think a guy like him would ever consider a girl like me. Or, apparently, a girl.

Stupid, stupid, STUPID!

"I was wrong. And I shouldn't have come here this morning." I stand and I say, "I should go now."

"Marc and I are not together." He stops me. "Marc is my flatmate," he repeats.

"Nicolas, you don't have to—"

"What part of *I'm not gay* didn't you get? I'm starting to find this very offensive, Lynn!"

What's happening here?

"I also thought that something happened between us that night."

"Really?" For a brief moment I'm thrilled, but then the guilt comes rushing back.

"Lynn, answer my question. When did you lie to me?"

But I can't answer him now. I'm too embarrassed, too confused. "I am so sorry. I need to go."

"Wait! Lynn, what did you want to tell me?"

"No, no. Nothing, absolutely nothing. I had a rough night. I'm better now." I walk to the door. "I'm sorry if I have offended you."

"Lynn, this is crazy. Stay!"

"I'll see you at the office. We have to discuss…the contract and stuff."

When I come out of the elevator, Marc is standing there. "Lynn, *les croissants!*" he says, showing me the paper bag from the bakery.

There will be no more croissants for Lynn.

She has been a bad, bad, bad girl!

Step #11:
Love lasts a year. A penthouse in
Tribeca is for life.

"They've been in the boardroom for the last two hours."
And Nicolas has been waiting for me at the Muriel B reception desk all that time.

"Oh, God, I can't do it," I tell him, cringing at my own whininess.

"You have to do it," Nicolas tells me as he grabs my arms and walks me upstairs.

"Do we have to move so fast?"

"Do you need to wear sunglasses?"

I take them off. The light strikes straight into my brain and I panic I may have just been stricken blind.

The workshop is very quiet. Everybody pretends to be very busy, but under the surface they all seem anxious and excited.

Pierre Boutonnière is in the house and when Pierre Boutonnière is in the house, everybody bows and scrapes. He is the one who gives money for their wages, money for the electricity bill, money for the phone bill, money for the coffee and everything else that makes Muriel B run.

And Pierre came this morning to put an end to the dream before it's even really started.

"On compte sur vous," one of the workers says as I pass by. Did he just say that they're counting on me? I ask Nicolas for a quick translation. Yes, yes, they all think that I'm here to save them. They see me as their last resource. That's why Muriel spent her last dime importing me. To get me inside that boardroom and turn the investors, aka Muriel's brother, into a thankful money fountain.

But I'm late, I look like trash and I'm an emotional mess. I stink, too.

I'm in an awful state to save the ship from sinking.

Nicolas leans in close and whispers in my ear, "Pierre rarely agrees to meet his sister. Especially here, in our office. Mint?"

He shakes a box in my face.

"Thanks," I murmur through closed lips.

"Pierre grew up in France with their father, Muriel in England with their mother. They're like ice and fire."

"Is there some coffee in there?"

He doesn't bother answering. He opens the door to the boardroom and pushes me in.

Two men sit opposite Muriel. Nobody speaks.

"Hello," I say.

"Ah! Lynn! Meet Pierre."

Which one of the two cadavers is Pierre? They both look anemic, wear gray suits and have sickly green complexions.

"How did your…previous meeting go?" Muriel asks.

"Oh… My previous meeting? Yeah! Very well. I couldn't cut it short. Very important. I'm sorry."

I had decided not to sleep at all, but once I sat on my bed in my suite, I don't know what happened. Somehow my brain switched off, and I was awoken hours later by a phone call (Nicolas) and some hysterical banging on the door (Massoud). And darling, I look a mess! They didn't give me a chance to change or shower. I still have the Hub's scent all over me, along with the vague funkiness of cigarettes and sweat, and alcohol breath. Somehow I don't think Nicolas's mint is going to cut it.

"Pierre Boutonnière," one of the cadavers says, and stands to shakes my hand over the table. Surprisingly, the hand's hot. "And this is Georges Duprès, from Finance."

I shake the second hand and it's not only hot but moist. Damn, I need coffee!

"Nicolas, can you arrange more coffee for everybody?" I say.

He can't believe it. He just stands there, looking at me as if I have transformed into a beetle.

"Okay…" he says hesitantly and dials a number on his cell phone. He's making a ten-meters-distance call. I mean, we can hear the phone ringing in his office and the voice of his assistant answering the call. *"Catherine, peux tu nous amener du café dans la salle de réunion?"*

I smile at Pierre. But he doesn't smile back. He doesn't find Nicolas's ego trip funny like I do. But again, he is the one paying the phone bills.

"I hear that you're the best thing that has happened to this company," Pierre says, but the look on his face tells me he doesn't believe it.

"We're lucky to have someone like Lynn," Muriel says.

"This company has to stop relying on luck." Pierre looks at me. "Did they brief you on the financial situation?"

"Lynn is more a creative person than a financial expert," Muriel cuts in again.

She's not herself. She does her best to look calm and fully grown-up, but the way she keeps clenching and unclenching her hands is a dead giveaway.

"Well, Lynn, I hope your financial expertise is good enough to understand that this company has just enough money to survive for the two next weeks, and then it is bankruptcy."

Muriel directs her pen across the table like a cruise missile. Pierre catches it before it falls onto his lap. They've probably been playing this game since they were five years old.

"Do you have to ruin everything all the time?" She's done playing mature. This is not your everyday meeting with your banker. It's family business.

"The situation is slightly different now," Nicolas interrupts. "We're expanding. Valuable people like Lynn are joining us. We're looking into getting some serious investors."

"Investors?"

The word brings back some blood into Pierre's veins.

"Who?"

"We can't talk about it now. We have agreed to total confidentiality, but a major brand is thinking of becoming our financial backer. With your agreement, of course."

"You don't need to hide anything from us. Every single cent you have spent so far came from Crédit de la Cité. We are Muriel B."

"No, Pierre, you're not Muriel B," Muriel explodes. "I'm Muriel B! It's my name on the door. I made this company. I am this company."

Pierre opens his mouth to yell back at his sister, but before he can, Nicolas interrupts. "Kazo."

Everybody looks at him. "Kazo is thinking of investing in Muriel B?"

Georges Duprès has actually moved. His head has tilted an inch to the right. That's how incredible the news is.

"Is this Muriel B internal gossip or something real?" Pierre looks from Nicolas, to me, to Muriel.

"It's real," Muriel says. "We're talking. Kazo wants to invest money in a small independent brand, and he is thinking of us."

"Just thinking?"

"More than thinking. They considered a few companies from the start. Now they've came down to two. It's between Xu and us." Muriel smiles a small but triumphant smile.

Xu? That explains their hatred for Muriel.

"Xu is bigger than you," Pierre says. "I don't hear certainty here."

"Well, one thing's for sure," I say as if I was in the loop. "If we close the company before the show, we'll never know."

They all turn to me. "How much did you invest so far?" Let's see how Pierre likes being in the hot seat.

"Too much," he answers.

"Imagine it. When Kazo comes in, all your expenses will be refunded and you get to control the finances of a branch of Kazo's empire." I draw a little square on my notepad. "But if we close now, you lose everything." I tick the square. It really appears as if I know what I'm talking about.

I turn to Muriel. I detect a smile on her face. Pierre is done listening to her. Or to Nicolas. But he will listen to a new girl from the U.S. with a guaranteed Blanchett pedigree.

"I was talking to Hubert Barclay this morning," I continue.

"You had a meeting with Hubert Barclay regarding Muriel B?" Pierre says.

Oh, boy! Did I ever.

"Well, yes. Barclay is an old friend. We talked about Muriel B. And he said…"

I can't repeat what he really said, not without an X-rated warning.

"Well, he was interested in doing a TV show on the birth of a fashion company. You know, reality-TV style."

I turn to Muriel. "All this is new to you, but that's what we discussed last…this morning."

I search for Nicolas's eyes. I look at his notepad. He writes Hubert Barclay on it and then adds three question marks.

The coffee comes in and Nicolas's assistant refills all our cups. Pierre sips some. He is thinking. He turns to Georges Duprès. They don't say a word. They communicate by telepathy like aliens…or twins.

"But if we're closing in two weeks, well, all that's over," I repeat after sipping some of my coffee.

Pierre opens and shuts his mouth a few times like a confused guppy before finding his voice. "Do you have a figure in mind?"

We won!

"Nicolas needs to work it out with you," Muriel says. "We're the creative people, you do the boring stuff."

Oops. Wrong timing, Muriel. That takes Pierre twenty years back, when she broke his bike and went to tell their father that he pulled her hair. "Muriel, we're going to open another transfusion line for you. But that's the last one. It will be minimal and will help you to survive until the show. After the show, if nothing major happens, like Kazo backing you up, it's over. And Dad will agree with me."

"That's why he put you in charge of the family's finances. Because you're such a good daddy's boy."

"That's great, Pierre." I jump in and turn to Muriel, giving her a stern don't-fuck-this-up look. "That's all we needed to hear."

My head is about to explode.

"Which one should we waste?" Muriel asks again.

The entire staff is standing around the boardroom table. All the sketches are spread in front of us. Françoise Neuton, all the designers, the assistants, even the receptionists, everybody is in here. It's a moment of pure democracy. We don't have enough money to produce all the dresses for the show. We need to dump a few. I stay with Muriel who helplessly contemplates the drawings, I really want to go back to the hotel, take a shower and go to bed.

"Let's think the other way around," Nicolas proposes. "Which one don't you want to waste?"

"Please, Nicolas, things are already hard enough without you trying to confuse me! Lynn, help me!"

I look at the drawings once more.

"I don't know, Muriel. The red ones give me a headache."

"The red ones are my favorites!"

I cup my head in my hands. "Do you really need me for this? I mean, you know better than anybody which ones to trash."

She sighs. She has had enough of me. "Nicolas, take her somewhere else, she annoys me so much right now."

"But… Don't you need me to…make the selection?" Nicolas sounds truly hurt by Muriel's dismissal.

"Since when do I need you to make creative decisions? Go. Take her away."

I don't give him a choice anyway. I stand up and wait for him to show me the way out.

"Lynn, tomorrow, we are going to make this—" she moves her finger in between me and her "—official. Nicolas will see to it."

"Sure."

Great. That leaves me twenty-four hours to decide once and for all, Xu or Muriel B.

Life is all about choices.

"Do you want to go back to your hotel?" Nicolas asks. "You look exhausted. I'll call Massoud."

We're back in the street. Busy. Chaotic as usual. "Listen. I'm sorry for this morning. Being late for the meeting. It was untactful."

"It was…a bit unsettling."

"Will you forgive me?"

"It depends."

"Depends on what?"

"On you. On this afternoon."

"Are you blackmailing me, Nicolas?"

He smiles. Boy, when he smiles, you would give him the moon and ask no change.

"Are you hungry?"

"I could eat a horse, with you sitting on it." Suddenly that shower and nap are forgotten. All I want is Nicolas.

"I know just the place. It's the best restaurant in Paris."

"I hope it's the best and the closest, or else I might not make it alive."

"It's the best and the most fun. You actually pre-buy your food and cook it yourself."

"Can't we just grab a bite anywhere?" Only the French would think it's fun to make you work for your own lunch.

"And we'll pick up some wine."

"Oh, no, no alcohol."

"Wine is not alcohol."

"No, it just so happens to make people drunk."

He stops. He looks at me and smiles.

"Why did you think that I was gay?"

Oho!

"Um…I didn't." Maybe I can play dumb.

He doesn't buy it. "You've asked me if I was gay almost each time we've met."

Well, when all else fails, there's honesty. "You're all sensitive, and nice."

"Does that make me gay?"

"You're…cute."

"I'm cute?" He likes the sound of that. "Well, does that make me gay?"

"You… Well, you don't look at me in that way."

"That way?"

"You keep your distance. Like you're…not interested."

"So…if somebody is not interested in you, he is gay?"

"No!" God, I didn't mean for it to come out that way. I'm so not conceited like that. I mean, guys like Nicolas are never interested in girls like me.

"And if I was looking at you *that way,* I wouldn't be gay?"

"No…I mean. Why? Are you?"

"What?"

"Interested?"

"You're a funny girl."

"Is that interesting? For you?"

"I guess it is."

He didn't just bring me to any restaurant. He brought me to L'Escargot, his parents' restaurant. It's just been through a complete cleanup and I can still smell a mixture of bleach and wet wood.

"They've asked me to get it ready for sale. Lots of people have already asked to see it."

He unlocks the front door to let us in. It's a funny thing to enter a restaurant like that, when it's completely empty. At least this explains why we had to buy our own groceries.

"Can you cook?" I ask.

"Yes, I'm very good at cooking."

Well, isn't he perfect?

He seats me at a table. Puts two glasses in front of me and opens the bottle of wine we picked up on the way over.

He toasts: "To success."

"I'll drink to that. What's on the menu?" I paid little attention to what he'd bought at the market.

"My specialty: Beans à la Nicolas."

"Great!" I hope that sounded as enthusiastic as I intended it to.

"I'll take you somewhere else. I just wanted to show you the place."

Uh-oh, I guess not. "No. I like it here. Beans will be fine. Beans and wine."

I follow Nicolas to the kitchen. The equipment is still well organized, ready for guests.

"It's a second home for me, this place." Nicolas pulls more food from the grocery bags. "Beans and… What do you call these in English?" He passes me a can.

"Artichokes"

"I can make a salad with these."

"That would be lovely."

"Look, I found a real treasure!" Nicolas smiles broadly as he pulls a lone jar off a shelf.

"What the hell is that?" I ask, inspecting the glass jar. It looks like a brown-red stew full of white beans and gore.

"It's cassoulet. It's my father's specialty. This one must be a vintage one. I bet you it's still edible."

He opens the jar. He sniffs it and proclaims the sludge inside "one of the best dishes in the world."

I take a whiff. Not so bad.

"You just need to warm it up. But it's meat."

"I'll have meat. For once…"

"Really!"

"I'm *so* over being a vegetarian."

So that's what he prepares instead of beans and artichokes. Cassoulet. And we go back to the table with a bowl each of steamy goo.

I try a small bite.

God, it's awful!

Revolting!

Yaaaaaak!

I tell Nicolas *"very hot"* but I wish I could spit it back into my bowl. Thank God I still have my wine.

"You don't like it, do you?"

Dammit. I have offended him. Again! But honestly, I'm not surprised his parents had to close down the restaurant if that's the kind of food they served.

"They're really famous for their cassoulet. People would travel hundreds of kilometers to have my parents' cassoulet at L'Escargot."

"It's very good, Nicolas," I say and force another forkful of the stuff in my mouth. It's fatty, stinky and revolting. But I swallow and smile. God, we're not in any sort of real relationship yet and I already have to fake a culinary orgasm.

"Do you want to see upstairs?"

"Upstairs?" What's upstairs?

"There is a studio upstairs."

I don't feel very comfortable about going to a studio upstairs. But it's going upstairs or eating the freaking cassoulet.

"Sure."

We go through the kitchen and into the courtyard. I follow him up a very old and narrow staircase. It's extremely dirty, dark and moldy and makes me feel even more uncomfortable.

He unlocks a tiny red door on the first floor.

"I used to sleep in here, waiting for my parents to close the restaurant and take me home."

He opens the door. It's a very tiny room with a very small window. It's very dark inside.

"Come in."

I step cautiously inside.

"Oh! It's..." It's disgustingly dirty and old. "It has a lot of character."

"Yeah. It's special for me. I feel safe in here. I feel protected." He points at the bed.

"The bed," he says.

There is a bed.

I mean that's all there really is in this room—a bed.

I look at him.

We have a moment.

This place is not only a refuge. There is something erotic about it. It's isolated. Calm. Nicolas's love for it is practically palpable. And there's nothing but a big bed looking at us.

I need to say something. Do something. "It certainly needs a good cleaning." Oh great, that's all I can come up with? Something that sounds like another insult.

"Yeah, sure."

I'm so close to him. So close. Even closer! I'm so happy! I… I—

His cell phone rings.

"It's for you," he says and passes me the phone.

"For me?"

"Hey, Lynn. Hubert here!"

No! Not now!

"How did you…?"

"I phoned your office, darling. You can't escape me."

"This isn't a good time."

"It never is, darling. I have something arranged for tonight. Dave will pick you up at eight."

"Wait! No!"

"Got to go."

Hubert hangs up on me.

It's gone. The moment between Nicolas and me is gone. Hubert is in the room with us. He lies on the bed looking at us. He sits beside the window and winks at me. He stands by the door, eating my bowl of cassoulet, and asks, "Did you really eat this shit?"

Step #12:
There will be plenty of Mr. Lovelys,
very few Mr. Wealthys.

I'm sitting on my bed. It looks like I'm anxiously waiting for my anti-Prince Charming to pick me up, but oh, no, that's not what I'm doing. I'm rehearsing. I've been rehearsing since I've come out of the shower and slid into another lovely Kazo garment.

Yes, I know. I'm all dressed up and sexy again.

But it doesn't matter how sexy I am. It's not how I look but what I will say. Want to hear my speech? Listen: Hubert, I don't want to see you again. I love someone else. Yes, *love!* Leave me alone with your incredible magnetism, your fame and fortune. Just fuck off, will you!

And I'm going to deliver the message in my lovely Kazo outfit.

Knock knock.

I jump to my feet and mentally run through my speech

again, because I already feel a bit terrified and empty minded at the idea of seeing the Hub.

It's Dave, the driver. Hub sent him to bring me to his master and he says, "You look lovely, Miss Blanchett," and smiles warmly at me.

The Mercedes is parked in front of the hotel. Dave opens the door for me. I can feel the looks of the passersby. They try to guess the identity of this amazing lady in Mr. Barclay's car. Yeah, that's right, I'm a goddamn princess.

Hubert, will you just fuck off. I repeat it in my head. Get lost. Beat it. Shoo! Shoo!

Dave drives us toward the Eiffel Tower. I need to make some time to climb up there. That's what tourists do after all.

"Are we going to the tower?"

"No, much better than the tower."

Better then the Eiffel Tower?

We make a right and the Mercedes slides along the Seine. Dave slows down.

"I wish I could bring my lady here. Mr. Barclay has very good taste," Dave says.

We stop in front of the *Mississippi*. Hubert is already on board this reproduction of a genuine American steamboat.

I can't believe it!

A steward in a white uniform waits for me by the boardwalk, carrying a silver tray with a glass of sparkling champagne. It's all rehearsed and perfect. I grab the champagne and walk on board.

"Chin chin," Hubert says and lets his flute touch mine. Only, he leaves the two glasses together and looks at me. You get it? The two glasses are like the two of us. The condensation on them is like the sweat on our skin. Oh, God, this *fuck off* business is *so-o* hard.

"Shouldn't we drink now? I think it's bad luck to toast without drinking."

"Lynn, luck can't touch us."

"What should we toast to?"

"To us."

"To Paris, and to the crazy things we did in Paris," I propose.

"Did?"

We drink the champagne.

He looks at me and lets the silence do the hard work. A guy dressed in a tuxedo breaks in. "Are you ready to leave now, Mr. Barclay?"

"Yes, we can go."

"Go where?" I ask.

"Who cares where we're going?" Hub says as the boat leaves the bank and starts its journey.

"Would you care for a top-up," the steward asks and refills our glasses with Veuve Clicquot. Then he disappears behind the bar and all of a sudden romantic piano music begins to play.

I'm trapped.

"Would you like to dance?"

"No."

"So let's go upstairs," Hub purrs in my ear.

The second deck is a lovely dining room with a panoramic view of Paris. A table is set beautifully for dinner. We're just above the waterwheel and beside a lovely champagne bar. The Seine is everywhere around us as we glide past the Eiffel Tower. The sky is orange, and the champagne is going straight to my head. Hub tries to kiss me, but I turn away and look at the seagulls following the boat. I pretend to be a keen ornithologist.

"You…" I need another hit of champagne before I can spit out my speech to Hubert. I grab the bottle on the bar and refill my glass. The steward's horrified. He was supposed to anticipate my every desire.

"Hubert, you're—"

You're a nice guy but I don't want to sleep with you again. I'll swim back to shore.

"I was sad when I didn't see you this morning," Hub interrupts. "Last night was very special. We connected."

Am I everyone's special night?

"Yeah, we connected big-time," I say.

Like really big-big time! Okay, I have to focus and tell Hub this isn't going anywhere.

"I'm not the kind of girl that ends up in somebody's bed on the first date. I find it…depressing." Depressing? God, I sound so lame.

"I'm not judging you, Lynn. Yesterday was magic and it ended up…magically."

Magic, that's right. Hocus-pocus and shazam! Multiple orgasms!

The steward doesn't even wait for us to finish our drinks. More champagne flows in.

Is that Bowie playing on the lower deck? Bowie can be so romantic.

"Did you know that Bowie is my favorite artist?"

"Bowie is a friend," Barclay says.

Bowie?

Does he actually know Bowie, the real Bowie? My Bowie?

I stay very silent and sip more champagne. Remember, Lynn, you're on a date with a legend.

"I like his music, too. I think it can be very romantic. Are you hungry?"

"I could eat a horse, with you sitting on it."

Oops.

I said the same thing to Nicolas earlier, didn't I? And I got my mouth full of greasy gore for it.

Hubert turns to the tuxedo man and nods. He was hiding there, by the dining table, invisible, but as soon as Hubert nods he lights the candles and slides to the lower deck, gliding like a hovercraft.

"Let's take a seat."

The boat makes its way under a bridge, and when we come out the other side, we're in the middle of Paris.

My, oh, my!

"You look astonishing in this light," Hub says, and as he says it, another boat overtakes ours. It's one of those tourist boats, with very strong spotlights. We're blinded for a second. We disappear in the white light. We're dead and in paradise. Hubert vanishes. The boat passes by and his face reappears a few inches from mine. It's perfect. Everything is perfect. I wish it was a dream, because if it was a dream, I could indulge in a kiss and not feel guilty about it.

Come on, blame it on the champagne…and Bowie. I lean over and kiss him. It's a gentle kiss. He traps my lips. I feel his hand on my shoulder again. Is this one of the tricks he uses? He knows the right spot to press on my back and I'll be his. I'm melting. I ease back in my chair. The steward and the tuxedo man gently lay our starters in front of us. They must have been waiting for the kiss to be over. Those people are extremely well trained for romance dining.

In the middle of our plates is a little golden coffee cup with a tiny portion of orange soup. The smell couldn't be more delicious.

"This is your *amuse-bouche,* consommé of pumpkin. It's just an appetizer from our chef."

"Do you know that *amuse-bouche* means mouth foreplay?" Hubert says.

"Oh, that's very appropriate," I say and feel blood rushing to my cheeks.

What was I supposed to tell him, again? Something about going our separate ways because I have another love interest that I haven't slept with yet? I think about it and decide to…to eat my consommé.

"I'm invited to the Sony Music party tomorrow. Would you like to be my date?"

Tomorrow? No, I promised Nicolas I'd go to his place for a dinner party. "I have to work tomorrow night," I say. "Sorry."

"What about the Louis Vuitton party on Friday?"

Friday?

"Are you invited to parties every single night?"

"Yes, but I'm only going to the most dazzling ones."

Ah!

"I own Sony Music stock. And…well, I'm a good client of Louis Vuitton. Lots of handbags."

"Lots of breakup gifts?"

He frowns at the "B" word.

"Generally, I give away cars for breakups. Interested?"

Well, actually… But then, how many days of relationship

do you need before you can count it as a real breakup? I mean, a car-compensated breakup?

"Cars or apartments," Hub says with a smile.

You even get a choice of breakup packages when you let go of the Hub. That's very different where I come from. The only breakup gifts I ever had were a long-lasting sense of desperation and worthlessness, coupled with unpaid phone bills.

"That's very generous of you. Especially knowing the number of breakups you must have gone through."

"Oh, is that what you heard?"

"Isn't it, like, what everybody hears?"

"The less people know about me, the more they pretend they do."

"Meaning?"

"I have fought to avoid every single breakup I've ever had, and all of them have been devastating but unavoidable."

If I had to give away a car or an apartment each time, I would go by the same principle.

But I don't tell him that.

I don't even make a joke about it because Hubert is staring straight at me. He leaves a deep meaningful silence to explain it all. I know. It's a technique men like him use. They let you know how much they have suffered in the past. It gives them depth and emotional reliability.

And for a second there, I even wanted to believe him.

I'm running out of excuses to explain why I keep ending up in bed with the Hub.

I wake up in my suite. The bed is empty beside me, but the shower is not. It's full of a singing Hub.

But make no mistake. Members of the jury, this woman is guilty as charged. She was sexed so much and so well, her vocal cords hurt. She won't sing today. She won't sing any day soon. Unlike the man who is taking a shower in her bathroom right now.

I'm so confused. I messed up again. I achieved exactly the opposite of what I wanted. It's this city. This charming guy. This romantic feeling. His voice. His kisses. His touch.

I'm so weak. That's exactly why I have messed up my life so far. Look at Jodie. That's a strong woman! Unlike me, she says no when she has to and she has been perfectly happy for the last forty years.

I'm a tramp!

And unless this room has soundproof walls, everybody in the hotel will know that by now. Soon all Paris will know. And soon Nicolas will know.

Why did you force me to eat your goddamn disgusting cassoulet instead of being the one to bring me on board a boat, supply me with unreasonable amounts of champagne and declare your love to me?

I ease up on my elbow to look at Hubert as he comes out of the bathroom. He has wrapped a towel around his waist, and is drying his hair with another towel. He looks like the man in the shower-gel ads.

"I'm sorry I woke you up."

He sits beside me on the bed and kisses me on the forehead. "I have to be in London for the day. Come with me?"

I shake my head. "I have a job, too."

He kisses me on the forehead again. "Tonight, then?"

"I told you, I have to work."

Who took the jam out of my doughnut?

He shrugs and goes back in the bathroom. "Can I use your toothbrush?"

"No!"

There is something amazing about being in a bad mood. You can see yourself being a bitch and you hate it, but there's nothing you can do to stop it. "It's not hygienic," I say and immediately hit my own forehead. Lynn, you schmuck! Not hygienic, really? After last night?

Thankfully he is gentlemanly enough not to protest.

"You have to promise to come with me to the Louis Vuitton party."

"Maybe."

"Maybe is better than no." He comes out of the bathroom with his black shirt on. He smiles at me. "You should go back to sleep. You sound very tired."

Give me a knife! I want to jump on him and stab him in the face. Tired? Sleep more? What part of "I have a job, too" didn't he understand?

He tries to kiss me before being on his way, but I turn away.

"Okay…" he says, not really complaining. He has a you're-just-in-one-of-those-moods look on his face. "I'll phone you when I'm back from London."

That's it! Get out of my room! Get out of my life!

I hate you!

I hate Nicolas!

I hate myself.

I hate myself the most!

Nicolas asks me to come to his office.

"We need to arrange some office space for you. We can share my office in the meantime."

I look at him and it hurts so much I could cry. How could I do this to him when I know that he is the One? How could I do it *twice?* I'm so…

"It's…not very practical, is it?" I snap.

That's the way it is going to be. I make all the mistakes in our relationship and Nicolas will pay for them.

"Just for the time being and—"

"I cannot work in a shared office. I need to…" What do I need exactly? "I…need privacy."

He nods. "I'll arrange something."

And stop being so nice. It drives me nuts.

He gives me a white cardboard box. I open it. It's a cell phone.

"The company will pick up the bills," he says encouragingly. "But don't go too wild with the calls. We're not that rich yet. The number is on the box."

"Thank you," I hiss, drop the phone in my purse and throw the box in the bin.

"We need to be able to contact you all the time. And—" he picks up the box "—the number is on the box."

"Yes, you said that already." I snatch the box from him.

I sit in front of his desk.

"I tried to phone you yesterday but you weren't in your room," he says gently.

I stare at the wall because there is no way I can look at Nicolas.

"I left a few messages for you."

God, don't I know. The concierge passed them on to me but I just trashed them and then felt more ashamed and enraged.

"So it was you phoning again and again," I bark. "When

I don't pick up the phone, Nicolas, it means that I don't *want* to be disturbed."

I would jump through the window if we weren't on the first floor and therefore perfectly useless. How maddening!

I look at him again.

You're all I ever wanted, and I'm losing you for a fling with Mr. Wealthy.

I'm so sorry!

"I'm sorry, Nicolas. I'm...so tired...again."

That's the thing with men. They know that they should forgive everything when we are...well, tired. They know they shouldn't investigate more.

"I don't want our morning to be like this," Nicolas says.

"What?"

He smiles. "Let's start again. Good morning, Lynn. How are you?"

He caught me by surprise: I smile back. I can't believe it, he made me smile. "I'm good, Nicolas, and what about you?"

"Well, I couldn't be better. Would you care to have breakfast with me?"

"No, Nicolas. I had breakfast already. But a cup of coffee would be nice."

"A coffee would be nice indeed, Lynn."

We look at each other. The first one to laugh loses. I crack up first. I have never been good at holding back emotions.

He laughs with me. "That's much better."

His assistant brings us coffee and passes him a document she has printed for us. Nicolas wants to go through it with me.

It's Muriel B's road map. I look at him. I listen to his voice. He sounds like my English teacher. He explains what's to happen every single day all the way to the show. I'm not too focused. His voice sounds like music. I forget last night. I forget this morning. There is a ray of light that breaks through his office window. I look up from the document and nod. It's just an excuse to stare at him. I wish he would close the folder and say, "Look, let's take my scooter and drive around all day." Instead, he points at a figure and says, "That's our estimated budget."

"Yes, yes!"

"Do you want me to go through it with you?"

"Well, listen…"

"I know. It's probably way under what you expected. But that's all we have."

"It's not what I wanted to talk about, Nicolas. What I wanted to say is… Do you want to take your scooter and go for a ride? We can consider it as apartment scouting, you know, for my relocation to Paris. Does that sound crazy?"

"Oh… No, it doesn't sound crazy, but—"

There is a but.

"We should be meeting Muriel at Fjord—" he looks his watch '—about now."

"Well, another time maybe."

"Yes, another time."

Instead of a scooter ride, we got Massoud to drive us to the Fjord Agency to select models for the show.

"Prague is everything America isn't. Americans love it," one of the girls says. I nod and take a bite of my blueberry muffin. The girl tries to be overfriendly with me because I'm part of the selection process.

"You must go to Prague," she insists. "Promise me that you will go to Prague!"

She sounds like a travel agency.

"I must visit you when I come to New York. I often go to New York." She laughs. Is she drunk? She swallows her tea nervously. "New York is great."

She doesn't know what to do with her long, slim arms. Her body language is very disturbing. She is trying to be sexy and intriguing but her lack of confidence is slipping through. How can she lack confidence? She's gorgeous. Next to her, I look like an ugly dwarf. So does Muriel. Not to mention Louise, our booker at Fjord.

Louise is one of the ugliest women I have ever seen. And her job is to manage some of the most beautiful girls in the world.

"Allez les filles! Numéro quinze. Jolanta." Louise calls. *"Allez, ma puce! On n'a pas la journée, merde!"*

"Oh, that's me. It's my turn," the girl from Prague says and runs to the casting room. I follow.

Muriel and Nicolas are already in the room when I enter. I sit beside the video camera operated by Louise. The girl from Prague stands against the white wall.

"How old are you?" Muriel asks.

"Sixteen."

Sixteen? Shouldn't she be in school or something? She brushes away her long hair. She strikes a pose. She is looking at Nicolas.

Just like the other fourteen previous gorgeous creatures that came to sell themselves in the casting room. They couldn't stop looking at him.

Don't you dare think about him!

He is *my* angel!

Grrr!

"Would you turn around?" Muriel asks.

The girl turns around.

"What are your hobbies?"

"I love traveling. And fashion. And going out." She laughs.

There it is again!

She just smiled at him. What kind of smile was that? Does she wonder what it would be like to kiss him? She's sixteen!

"What do you think?" Nicolas asks me.

"I think exactly the same as you." Because I'm better suited to you than these teenagers, I finish mentally.

"Can she walk?" Muriel asks Louise.

"She's done a few catwalks already. She's good. Do you want her to walk for you?"

"Please."

Louise gestures and the girl starts to walk back and forth. Twist. Turn. Pose.

Why not ask her to show her teeth while she's at it?

"She's good," Nicolas proclaims.

The girl stops walking. She is balancing her long, thin arm in the air, looking at us, the ugly, small potato-women group and the angel, waiting for our decision.

Only we will decide later.

She walks lazily out of the room, as if dragging it out a few extra seconds will increase her chances of getting selected. She stops and turns back to us. "Can I take a muffin home?"

"Of course, darling," Louise says. "You can take as many muffins as you like. And send in number sixteen. Kristy."

A tall, athletic girl comes in. She wears a very short skirt, a very tight T-shirt and high leather boots. She looks amazingly beautiful and sexy. And there it is again! She's grinning at Nicolas.

Dirty bitch.

"Hi, I'm Kristy. I'm nineteen and I've been with Fjord for three years," the girl says with a British accent. She smiles and smiles and smiles at him and he falls for it.

He smiles back!

"Can you walk?" I ask, annoyed.

Everybody turns to me.

"You're very pretty," Muriel says.

I can't believe she said that. Can you tell a model that she is very pretty? Isn't that…unprofessional or something?

"You're very feminine, I like that," she goes on. What Muriel means by feminine is that even though the girl is so skinny, she still has a pair of gigantic breasts.

"Very feminine, that's right," Nicolas confirms.

Look at them!

They are *so* unprofessional.

Especially Nicolas!

Shame on him!

And, by God, I need another muffin.

My mind is still browsing through the different Kristys, Jolantas and other Ulrikas when the elevator door opens to Nicolas's floor. It was a long day and I'm ready for the dinner he promised me.

I can't compete with models. I'm a frog and no matter how long you kiss me (ask Hubert) I will not transform into anything else.

I knock on the door. Nicolas opens.

God, you're so damn beautiful.

I'll never get use to it.

If only I could be more like…like them. I wouldn't feel so challenged by you and I could start to see you the way you really are.

I enter the apartment and it smells of…of…

Of saffron. Which reminds me of home.

"I cooked vegetarian," he says.

I follow him into the kitchen. There are chopped vegetables all over the place. Dirty pots and pans. It's all happening in there.

He grabs a bottle of wine and two glasses. "It's a bottle I've been saving for a long time. And tonight is the night."

He pours a little splash in each glass and passes me mine. He sniffs it. Shakes it. Makes a big fuss about it.

"Should we make a toast?"

"Yeah, sure."

What would be an appropriate toast? "To the future and to Muriel B," I propose.

"No, to you."

"To me?"

"Yes, to you and to our luck to have you here in Paris."

"Okay." I'm about to toast but he stops me.

"Actually, it's the wrong toast. To my luck to have you here in Paris."

Oh!

We toast and we sip a bit of wine. God, is this how a good red wine is supposed to taste? It really tastes like fungus.

He looks at me with big wide-open eyes. So I swallow this disgusting liquid and say, "Mmm! Very delicious!"

He spits his back in the glass.

"Oh, no! It's so corked," he says. "I'm so sorry."

I laugh. "Good, I was scared you would force me to drink the whole bottle. Yuck!"

He takes my glass away. "It's funny. I have been waiting to open this bottle for years. I have waited and desired it and when it finally happens, it's crap. I'm so disappointed."

"That's the story of my life."

"How do you mean?"

"Do you believe in destiny?"

"I believe that you make your own destiny. You make your own choices."

You know, angels can be so naive.

"I believe destiny is free will at work. I'm an existential-ist. You know…Sartre?"

"But what about luck?" I ask.

"What about it?"

"Don't you believe in luck?"

"I'm not a superstitious person, no. But I believe in chances, and in taking chances."

"So this corked wine is not bad luck?"

"Definitely not, it's bad cork, bad storage or bad wine."

"What about us? Isn't it luck bringing perfect strangers together?"

"Luck has nothing to do with it. People meet and break up all the time. You came to Paris. I was in Paris. It's what you decide to do about it that's important."

Does he mean that I should blame myself for sleeping with Hubert twice instead of blaming some invisible and de-structive superpower? That is so…scary!

He empties the red wine into the sink. All these years of

expectation ruined and discarded. Bad luck! I can't stop thinking this way.

The world is run by luck.

You either have bad luck or good luck. Thinking otherwise will only attract bad luck. Considering a world without luck feels like a sin. I touch wood discreetly. I would spit three times on the floor if I didn't think it would get me kicked out of the apartment.

"I think you're wrong," I say. "We follow the road that has been set for us. Look at me in Paris. It would be impossible if it wasn't a trick set up by destiny."

He laughs. "Somehow, I believe your being in Paris has a lot to do with who your mother is."

Touché!

"Sorry," he immediately says when he sees all the blood leaving my face. "I didn't mean it that way."

"It's all right, Nicolas, I get it all the time."

He touches my face gently. That's what I get as compensation for being humiliated. It's better than nothing.

"What I meant is, if I had followed the road set for me, I'd be running a restaurant by now. I made choices, and I worked my own way up."

"Look at us," I say because I like to bring back my favorite subject. "Don't you think that somehow destiny has something to do with us being here, drinking corked wine together?"

He opens another bottle and says, "This should sort out the cork problem. As for us…I think…" He sips some. "Mmm! This one is simple but very nice."

I try the new wine. It's very good. It's sweet and fruity. I like simple.

"Very fruity, don't you think?" he asks.

Beware! Frenchmen avoid real conversation by talking about red wine. Someone should put that in a guidebook.

"You don't think that destiny brings two people together?"

He goes back to his pots and pans. Frenchmen avoid any real conversation by cooking and talking about food, too.

"I told you. I don't believe in destiny."

Before I can respond, Marc enters with his date.

"Lynn, this is Eddie. *Eddie est banquier.* Moneyman. Ha ha ha! Eddie, this is Lynn. Lynn is a star. Ha ha ha. Cocktails?"

"J'ai ouvert une bouteille de vin," Nicolas says.

"Oh, he's so boring with his wine. Anybody wants a cosmo or a mojito?" He turns to Eddie, the moneyman. "Oops! Do you speak English, darling?"

"I studied management in England," Eddie says to me. "A long, long time ago."

Look at Eddie. He looks like the perfect boring gray accountant. But once he leaves his office, the gray man becomes crazy Marc's partner. What, if not destiny, brings two people so different together.

"I could trade my wine for a Bloody Mary," I say.

"But of course! Nicolas, you are so old-fashioned." He turns to me. "Nicolas is so cute but at the same time so French. Eddie used to be very French, too. But I changed him." He laughs heartily.

Marc mixes the drinks for us. He and Eddie have set their minds on whiskey sour, with the iced cherry and all. Nicolas sticks to wine. He is *so* French!

"Before I came into his life, Eddie had a girlfriend. A girlfriend! Poor thing. I changed that, too…." He bursts out laughing again.

Before me, Nicolas didn't believe in destiny. Can I change that? If you can change somebody's sexual orientation, can you also change their beliefs?

"Wine is an art. Vodka is just alcohol," Nicolas snaps.

"*Alors,* look who's upset now!"

"I think that Nicolas is very sexy," I say boldly. "Old-fashioned is sexy. It's classic. It's beyond fashion and trend. I like that about him."

"Oho!" Marc and Eddie sing together.

"Thank you, Lynn. I knew that finally there would be something sexy about being ancient," Nicolas says jokingly.

"An old man trapped in this gorgeous Apollo's body. Mmm! Darling!" Marc is playing suggestively with his iced cherry. "Lynn's right, that's hot."

"I didn't say hot, I said sexy."

"Girls say sexy when they mean hot and hot when they only mean sexy. Ha ha ha!"

"I'm hot," Nicolas says proudly.

And we drink to that.

"Lynn, you look like a fun girl." Marc points at me. "Let's go out tonight!"

I'm about to tell him that I'm exhausted and that I need some rest tonight, but my handbag starts to vibrate.

I swear. It didn't vibrate when I bought it in Kazo's shop. It's like a weird paranormal phenomenon.

"Your bag…" Marc says and passes it to me.

Not only does it vibrate, it plays a famous dance tune. I open the bag and take my new cell phone.

"I'm so sorry." I should turn the phone off, but my curiosity takes over. Who could be phoning me?

"Hey, you," Hubert says. "I'm back."

"How did you get this number?"

"I phoned Muriel. I told you, I'm a very good friend of her dad's."

"You phoned my boss to get this number?"

"Actually, she had to phone somebody and she called me back with your number."

"You're using my boss as your personal assistant?"

"Come on. I've watched the girl grow up. Muriel's father and I, we go way back."

"Give me a second."

I stand and walk away from Nicolas. I walk all the way to the entrance and leave the apartment. But that's not enough. I run down the stairs and only start to talk again once I've reached the courtyard.

"I told you that I'm working tonight," I say.

"I'm happy to hear the sound of your voice, too."

"Hubert!"

"What's with you? Each time we're separated for more then twelve hours, we have to start all over again."

And each time I see you, I fall for it again.

"Actually," he says, "I like it. I feel challenged. Not played but challenged."

I'm his own private rhino, and he is thinking of adding my head to his collection.

"Hubert, I can not talk to you right now."

"I need to see you tonight."

"It's not a good idea."

"Where are you?"

"I'm with someone."

I look up. From here, I can see Nicolas's silhouette in his living-room window.

"I'll find you, Lynn."

It's entirely my fault. I should have stopped this thing with the Hub from the start, so I say it, "We need to talk, Hubert."

"Who is this *someone?*"

"Does it matter?"

"I have been in this situation before. It's nothing that cannot be fixed."

"Well, *I* haven't been in this situation before and I sure don't like it."

I hear some footsteps. The courtyard light comes on. Nicolas stands there, behind me. "Are you all right?"

"Is that him?" Hubert asks.

"Listen, I'll call you later."

"What's the problem?" Nicolas asks.

I'm frantically looking for a way to turn off the phone. "Don't hang up on me, Lynn!" I can hear Hubert say.

Off, off, OFF!

"Who was that?"

"It was Hubert Barclay."

"Oh?"

"We needed to talk…and we talked."

"Okay."

"What do you mean by…*okay?*"

"You sound weird again, Lynn."

He comes closer to me.

I feel so confused! "I'm sorry, Nicolas, but I need to go, I'm so…tired."

"What about dinner?"

"I can't do it, Nicolas. Not tonight. Will you say goodbye to Marc and Eddie for me?"

"You're going to see Barclay, aren't you?"

I don't feel obliged to answer. Instead, I give him a reassuring kiss on the lips. A quick one.

"Stay, please."

"Nicolas, trust me."

He comes back at me and kisses me again, the same way. The quick way. He needed two kisses to feel in the safe zone.

Once I'm in back in the street, I finally manage to get basic brain functions going again.

I've kissed him.

For real!

Not a stolen kiss, or the double-cheek trick. The real thing, where he kisses me back and asks for more!

Step #13:
Once you have convinced yourself,
convince the others.

"Are we there already?" Muriel asks with unusual sweet-ness. She's been sleeping in the car, but wakes when Mas-soud slows down to pull into a gas station.

"*On vient de passer Lyon,*" Massoud answers.

"Halfway," Nicolas explains for me.

Yes, we're on our way south to Saint-freaking-Tropez. Oh, we're not going on holidays, no, no! Muriel decided that we needed the isolation of the Boutonnière villa to gather forces and prepare the show in serenity. She calls it a work seminar.

We get out of the car while Massoud starts to pump the gas.

"Nicolas, would you buy me a diet something?" Muriel asks, yawning. She puts on her shades even though the sky is dark gray. "Actually, make it a bottle of rosé."

To tell you the truth, we don't really look like three young professionals on our way to a seminar. We look like three spoiled kids with money to spend, a deep craving for rosé and a chauffeured car.

"Have you ever been to the Boutonnière villa?" I ask him as we stand in front of a huge wine selection in the gas station.

I know. The French need easy access to wine even on the highway.

"She never did me the honor," he says and picks up a bottle.

"It's funny all you do for her. You run the company. You deal with her staff. You're even her sommelier, by the looks of it. You must be by far the most versatile human resources manager ever."

"Yeah, you're right. It's funny."

We both turn to Muriel. She's standing in front of a row of coffee-vending machines. She looks as if she can't understand how to handle them without involving her PA. She slides her shades down to get a better look at the instructions.

Nicolas and I exchange a quick glance and laugh.

"I'm telling you, she's lucky to have you," I say.

Muriel turns to us. "What?"

"Do you need help?" Nicolas proposes.

Vending machine conquered, we sit at a table with three horrible plastic-cupped cappuccinos.

"We always stop here," Muriel says moodily. "I must have stopped here about a million times."

"Is your father living on the Riviera then?" I dare ask, because mentioning her father always fuels some fire in her.

"Nobody lives at the villa," she says. "It's there for fun."

And work seminars, of course.

Nicolas lifts his left eyebrow at me while sipping his coffee.

He's impressed I had the guts to mention the *F* word.

"Is he not living in France, then?" I insist.

"Dad lives in his jet," Muriel breathes. "He doesn't do anything like normal people." You can almost see the rage slowly building inside her. "I don't really care where he is as long as it's not in my way. Can we talk about something else now?"

I've ruined her bad-cappuccino moment.

"Fuck it *anyway!*" she snaps. She takes her cup and empties it in the trash bin. "I need to take a piss!"

I know, you're not supposed to empty liquids into trash bins. That's why it looked so cool.

She really is the creative one.

"Nicolas," she calls.

She didn't make it to the toilet. Something more interesting caught her eye on the way. She stands fascinated in front of a gift display.

"We need this. It'll be good for concentration." She grabs a small plastic hedgehog and hands it to him. "Look. It's really ugly."

"It's some sort of local mascot," Nicolas explains.

"I *hate* it," she laughs. "Buy it, and ask them to open the bottle, will you?"

I can't believe my eyes. The place is amazing.

Massoud drives along the coast. The skies are not gray anymore. It's dusk and the sun shines with all kinds of orange above the quiet sea.

It's so…Mediterranean!

On one side of the road, a rocky coastline dives straight into the sea, on the other, pine trees and amazing villas stand proudly.

We've crossed a lovely little village called Saint Raphael, so Muriel says, "We're almost there."

"Presque," Massoud confirms and yawns, too. "Here!" he says as he takes a right.

All I can see is a row of secluded villa gates, security cameras, angry-dog warnings and other invitations to shoo. But I can already hear the frenetic sound of what seems to be billions of grasshoppers.

And the smell!

It smells of pine trees, hot ground and the sea. If you could bottle that smell, you'd call it Holiday and make millions selling it.

Massoud stops and takes a remote from the glove compartment. He presses the single button and a massive wooden gate opens in front of us.

I turn to Nicolas.

He's smiling just like me.

What a place!

Can we relocate here?

Forever?

We come to a final stop in front of what appears to be the mad dream of an architect escaped from a *Star Trek* convention. The Boutonnière Villa.

"Shit," Muriel whispers as soon as she exits the car. "That's my fucking luck!"

"What?" I say, trying to see what could be wrong, now that we made it to paradise.

"Don't you see it?"

What?!

"The lights!"

"Beautiful," I say, because I thought she was speaking of the sun finding its way to the villa through the pine trees.

"The lights!" she repeats then kicks one of the spots illuminating the villa.

Oh! Muriel is mad because Francis—that's her absent father, Francis—is already in the villa.

But when we make it to the swimming pool, it's my turn to be shocked and furious.

"That's impossible," I say, not because Muriel was right, but because Jodie's there, dressed in a summer-white ensemble, smiling at me and drinking what looks like a glass of chilled white wine. And that alone kicks me in the gut, because I can't remember Jodie drinking alcohol ever.

I ignore the James Coburn look-alike standing beside her, drop my bags and spit "What are you doing here?" in a defensive-teenager tone I've never used with her before.

"Oh, Francis…" She turns to the James Coburn carbon copy and with her detached Jodiesque voice, says, "This is Lynn, my protégée."

I look as if I'm unpacking my Adidas bag into the lovely wooden cabinet, but what I'm really doing is trying to look away from Jodie, who, for some reason beyond my comprehension, has followed me into my bedroom and now observes me, calmly sitting on the bed.

"It's funny to see you here," she says as she plays with her wooden necklace. She looks much younger than I ever remembered her. Maybe it's the brand-new suntan on her face.

"I mean, Francis and I used to come here centuries ago. I don't believe you were even a plan then."

I've already lost my bite. I'm back to my normal Jodie-is-here submissive self.

"It's a lovely place," I say.

"It wasn't lovely at all then. It was wild. Your generation would never know. You're so…"

I'm finished unpacking. I want to find something else to do to escape her, so I walk to the sliding doors and pretend I need to air the place.

If only I had a mop, I'd clean!

Oh, look at that. My room has direct access to a washed-wood terrace falling straight into the swimming pool.

Everything is wood and white.

Even Jodie.

"Are you here on business?" I ask, to try to understand what she is doing here, in my room.

"I came to see you," she says, and I have to take a good look at her.

See *me?* Come on!

"There is also this little retrospective of my designs in Saint Paul de Vence. But that's secondary."

Ah! That sounds more like it.

"But I'm here, aren't I?" she says. "Isn't that what's important?"

I try to figure out what's behind Jodie's sudden interest in me. Hypothesis 1: She's dying of cancer and is experiencing remorse for being such an absent mother. Hypothesis 2: This is not Jodie and this is just a look-alike convention. Hypothesis 3: I'm dreaming and will wake up screaming and drenched in sweat.

"We could go together to Saint Paul," she suggests, and my whole body straightens as she stands up from the bed and walks to the closet. She looks through the clothes I've just unpacked. She lifts the Jodie Blanchett dress with one finger, like a scientist looking at some interesting scum. "Oh! That's an old model. I don't remember giving you this one. It must have been ages—"

"You didn't, I bought it."

"You bought one of my dresses? Lynn, that's so absurd! We're trashing them by the ton."

Why did I even mention it?

"It was on sale, anyway."

She frowns. She obviously doesn't like the idea of being on sale.

"I met a friend of yours. Roxanne Green," I say, to change the subject.

Jodie drops the dress and tries really hard not to look annoyed.

"Why on earth do you have to meet people like Roxanne?"

What?

"I met her on the plane by accident. She mentioned your name."

"Of course she mentioned my name," Jodie says as she checks her tan in the mirror. "What is the old tramp up to nowadays?"

"She writes books."

"Books? Roxanne? What about? How to live a normal life with gonorrhea?"

"Self-help books. Quite good ones, actually."

"Trust me, you don't want someone like Roxanne to give

you any sort of advice. And don't accept any drugs from her."

"No, Roxanne is a respectable lady."

"She's too old to bed society, darling. That doesn't make her respectable."

I decide right then to keep the copy of *20 Steps to Success* for myself. It would be wasted on Jodie.

"She says she hasn't seen you in a long while. It's like you disappeared," I strike back at her.

But I'm way too green to play the wit game with a master like Jodie. "I don't feel the urge to see people like Roxanne anymore. My fascination with prostitutes is behind me."

Oh, God!

"You know what we used to call Roxanne when she used to come down here. The hose. Do you know why?"

"No, actually, I don't want to know why," I snap.

"Anyway, ask Francis. The hose!"

I wish I was more like Muriel. Bold, courageous and fast. I would be able to keep up a conversation with Jodie without feeling the need to go hide somewhere. I try to think of something to say next, but Jodie beats me to it.

"Come with me tomorrow," she says. "It'll be fun."

Now my doubts dissolve. Hypothesis 1: Cancer! Incurable!

"We have to work. We don't have much time before the show," I say.

She shrugs it off. "Francis is flying us back tomorrow night. We'll soon be out of your hair."

The work seminar is collapsing by the minute.

Instead of laying down big ideas and brainstorming our

way to success in today's fashion scene, we hide in the kitchen, get drunk on rosé and lend a hand to the caterers.

Nicolas is helping unload their equipment and Muriel and I are making room in one of the three gigantic refrigerators. Next we'll peel potatoes and do the dishes.

Muriel would actually make us do anything to avoid being in the monumental living room where Francis and Jodie are having a jolly good time remembering how Roxanne got rebaptized the hose all those years ago.

Nicolas comes back to the kitchen carrying what looks like a hundred-pound crate full of pots and pans, but he does it in style, as he is dressed in a lovely Gucci summer ensemble.

"Is it just us and…them?" he asks, pointing at the living room, "The staff has enough equipment to cook for an army."

"How the fuck would I know?" Muriel barks back. "He wasn't supposed to be *here* to start with."

"Let's just make the best of it. I'm sure Jodie can add her five cents' worth to our show plans. Why don't we go speak with them," Nicolas suggests, brushing off his Gucci shirt.

"That sounds good," I say, because strangely, I'm in the mood to see more of this new Jodie.

Muriel grabs her wineglass and jerks it toward the stairs. "Be my guest," she says and sits down on a stool, apparently determined never to leave the kitchen again.

When we arrive upstairs, it sounds unexpectedly quiet. The living room is empty.

"They're gone," I say.

Maybe I dreamed the whole thing. The friendly Jodie was just a mirage.

Clap, clap, clap! Jodie's stilettos beat the wooden floor. She's back!

"Where's Muriel?" she asks as she enters the room. She wears a light coat and her hat, and looks as if she's on her way somewhere.

"You're not staying?" I hear myself ask.

"Francis is taking me to Cannes. We don't want to be in your way."

"Are you ready to party?" Francis reappears in a white summer suit. "Ah! Lynn. Tell Muriel we'll be out for the night."

Dammit!

"It would have been great to get your input on our collection," Nicolas says to Jodie.

"My input," Jodie repeats, amused by the word.

She's so keen on him. Jodie loves beautiful people, no matter what. "Another time."

"It was great meeting you," he says sadly.

She smiles at him. "You take care of my…girl."

"You're not coming back?" I'm surprised at the surprise in my own voice. I should be used to being abandoned by Jodie by now.

"We'll stay at the Martinez for the night, and then…" She shrugs.

I feel like telling her, *Oh fuck this work seminar, I want to stay with you and come to Saint Paul Something,* but she doesn't leave me the opportunity.

"The show on the street," she says vaguely.

Oh, yes, the proof that I have a spark of her own flair in me.

"Be careful," she tells me. "It's been done before. You need to do more thinking."

* * *

"Is he gone? Really gone? Gone *gone?*"

"They'll be sleeping at the Martinez," Nicolas confirms.

Her face opens up. She breaks into an earnest smile. "So let's move, then."

Muriel's not disappointed to lose them to Cannes. *Au contraire.* It's like someone put the batteries back into her. She's done hiding in the kitchen. She wants to show us around so we get a good feel of our working environment before getting down to business.

We leave the caterers to their cooking and head toward the beach, following a lovely little path in the woods.

Night is setting in slowly, but I can still hear children running, screaming, calling each other names. Female voices are hurrying them to stop drowning their little sisters, or leave the dog's ears alone, or stop playing with the sprinklers because it's dinnertime. Things that mothers normally say to their kids, instead of *Sit here and by God don't touch anything and be quiet while I finish working on this piece.*

"Do you know any of the people who live around here?" I ask Muriel.

"Oh, this one," she says, pointing to a villa, "it used to belong to President Mitterrand, before he died, of course. Galliano lives nearby. Everybody that's somebody has a villa here."

We don't make it to the beach. Muriel is ready for another drink and she knows exactly the place. We turn into what looks like the entrance to a villa, but it's not. It's a campground packed with tents and people coming back from the beach or playing cards. There are little kids chewing on chicken drumsticks from dinner picnics and rinsing sand off their feet. A sign reads, Camping de la Pinède.

She keeps surprising me, this girl. When she said, "Let's get a drink," I pictured us in a trendy bar in the middle of Saint-Tropez, looking the part. But, no, we're making our way to the Buvette de la Plage, the epicenter of the campers, surrounded by a crowd of young people very happy to see three new faces and wondering to which tent we belong.

"Qu'est-ce que vous buvez?" the barman asks, though he doesn't look like a barman, but like the janitor, corraled into pouring drinks for the night.

"Un Bloody Mary," I try.

No luck. No tomato juice. Orange juice and vodka, he proposes. I say why not, but I'm out of luck again, he's out of orange juice until tomorrow morning, when he'll find five minutes to go to the supermarket. Oh, to hell with it. I do exactly as Muriel and Nicolas and order a glass of chilled rosé.

The Buvette de la Plage is just a wooden shed with a few tables and a dance floor. It's illuminated by hundreds of colorful lightbulbs. Red, green, yellow.

It's packed.

Noisy.

I turn to Muriel. "This doesn't strike me as your kind of place or your kind of crowd."

"See that guy, there?" She points at a twenty-something blond guy engaged in a flirtatious conversation with two laughing blondes. "That's Vincent de la Pinotière, son of Marcellus de la Pinotière. One of the richest families in the country. Real estate. Movies."

"Telecommunications," Nicolas adds.

"Their villa is just next door to ours. And there—" now she points at a group of teenagers drinking and smoking at one of the tables "—those are the Pouik kids…and friends."

"The Pouiks are famous industrialists," Nicolas explains. "They're filthy rich. *Nouveau riche. Très m'as-tu vu.*"

"And who's that?" I ask, pointing at a middle-aged man drinking beer and balancing one of his flip-flops on the tip of his toes. "Prince Albert of Monaco?"

"Nah. The rest of them are...you know...*campers.*"

We move to a table.

"You like it here?" she asks Nicolas.

He shrugs. "It doesn't have that exotic charm it has for you."

"What do you mean?" I ask.

"This is exactly the type of place I used to go to every year with my parents. As campers, of course. Only, we preferred Bretagne over the Riviera."

"Bretagne is so..." Muriel just hisses, not finding the proper word to defame Bretagne.

"It's less pretentious than down here," Nicolas tells me.

"Boring!" she finally decides.

"It depends what you're after."

"I'm after more of this," she says, tilting her still-full glass of rosé. "Go buy a whole bottle, Bretagne Boy."

"You shouldn't be so mean to him," I say while Nicolas is away talking to the barman, probably about the rest of tomorrow's shopping list.

"What?"

"Treating him like some sort of servant."

"You really say whatever pops into your mind, don't you? Sometimes it's cute, sometimes it's just plain dull."

"Nicolas is the best thing you have going for you. Be careful with him. That's all I'm saying."

"Listen to you. The best *thing*. The best thing I have

going for me is *me*. Oh, quit playing the offended *mistress* and get into the mood."

Mistress?

"What? Do you think I don't see what's going on between you two? And who doesn't, really!"

Oh, look, the room turned bright red again—must be one of those lousy bulbs.

"Who's...*who?*"

"That's the only thing the boys are talking about in the workshop. You broke their hearts, you know. Nicolas was something of an item for them." She laughs. "What did you call him again? Ah yes, yes, *hot! Fizzza,* like a blaze! Ha ha ha!"

Marc, damned Marc!

"Nothing's happening between us."

"Lynn, what the two of you do in the privacy of his office is your business. Close the door, that's all we ask. Actually, the boys would love the door to be slightly open to catch a glimpse." She laughs again. "His poor Catherine. She used to be madly in love with him, you know, like PAs usually are. Ha ha ha!"

I want to grab her by the shoulders and shake her until she understands that there is *nothing, nichts, niente* going on in Nicolas's office or anywhere else. But a thin young man pops out of a group of other thin young men and is delicately caressing his suntanned six-pack under a light, open shirt as he says, "You are lovely. Are you English?" with a tasty Italian accent.

"She's American," Nicolas says as he sits down with a bottle of rosé.

"I'm English," Muriel says with an inviting smile. That's

all he needs to sit with us, introduce himself as Giorgio and ask in which section we've planted our tent and if we want to go for a swim with him and his friends later tonight.

"I *lo-ove* your piercing," he tells Muriel. "I have piercing, too." He pulls his tongue out and there, smack in the middle, there's a gigantic stud. "It's very, very nice. For se-ex." He laughs.

"I have tattoos like you, too," he continues. This time, he needs to stand, and pulls down his shorts and there, just above his crotch two little teddy bears, a blue one and a pink one, are hugging each other.

"Very cute," Muriel says. "I bet you show it to all the girls."

"No, not to all the girls. Only to the be-eautiful ones, like you."

"Do you have a tattoo?" I ask Nicolas, hoping and smiling.

"Never got the time to arrange one," he says and looks tense because the rest of Giorgio's gang is slowly invading our table, about seven or eight lively young boys, all of them ready to display their secret tattoos to the two new girls. The rest of the girls at the Buvette de la Plage, the German, the Dutch and the Swedish ones, have already seen all their teddy bears and other brandings many times around.

"I want to bring you to a very special pla-ace," one of the boys says to me. "It's very be-eautiful, like you."

"Hey, don't mind me," Nicolas tells him.

"Okay," he agrees. If it's so kindly proposed, he will just ignore Nicolas. "You like Italy?"

"I don't know, I've never been." I laugh.

"I could take you to Italy, after."

After what?

"That's nice but…hey, listen, I'm with him," I say and put my hand on Nicolas's knee.

"I'm not jealous."

"I am," Nicolas says, and now that I have my hand on his knee, he takes this Italian invasion more lightly and smiles earnestly.

After all, if the entire workshop at Muriel B is commenting on our sexual *prouesse,* we might as well get to it.

I look around.

I know why all the rich kids are coming down here even if the toilets never work.

They get the kind of spice that has been cleansed from their existence since birth.

The dirty spice.

The one of life.

"Can you dance?" I ask Nicolas.

"Like a brick."

"Oh, who cares? Come on!" We go and dance like two happy bricks.

We found Muriel, finally.

She's lying on the beach with Giorgio. He smiles bitterly at us. The poor thing looks exhausted.

He must have been trying all his tricks for the last two hours, but what works on eurocamper girls doesn't necessarily work on Muriel. No matter how many times he tells her how beautiful she is, she keeps her own tricks for the ladies.

"I'll see you tomorrow," he says suddenly. She has badly dented his self-confidence.

"Yeah, and then, you'll take me to Italy, right? *Ciao, bello,*"

Muriel calls to him as she gets up and walks away with us, laughing.

"What we need now… Oops." She trips, Nicolas catches her. She looks up at him. "Yeah, we're getting naked and—" she mimes an expert diver with her hand "—we jump in the swimming pool."

She's perfectly toasted.

"Naked!" she repeats.

Naked! I don't think so.

I don't do naked.

Ask the Hub.

Lights out.

"Nicolas," she continues, "I've always wondered how you look in the nude. I'd like to see that. On Monday, the boys will kill me to get all the details."

"Sure," he says. His flat tone tells me he is not amused by Muriel's antics.

"Oho! Nico! I hope I didn't hurt your feelings again. You sensitive thing. Lynn asked me to be oh *so* careful with your feelings, poor darling. Don't hurt his feelings. He is the best fucking man in the entire world."

"I didn't say that," I protest. "I said…oh, who cares what I said. And I'm not getting naked."

"What?"

"I have a lovely swimsuit and I intend to wear it."

She shrugs. Whatever perversion rocks my boat.

Step #14:
Remember to always look like you're listening. People will love you for that.

We all have the same question when we get home: who's giggling in the living room?

"Ah, Muriel," Francis calls when he sees us. "I met your friend Jolanta in Cannes. I brought her back for a snack."

"She's not my friend," Muriel snaps.

That's right—Jolanta. I recognize her from the casting. The girl from Prague.

"Oh, no, we're not exactly friends," Jolanta says. "We're going to work together. For her show."

Somehow, by the look on Muriel's face, I don't think so.

"That's right," Francis confirms. "You're a model, aren't you, Jolanta."

"She's sixteen," Muriel says coldly.

"Actually, I'm nineteen," Jolanta snaps. "My agent tells me

to *say* sixteen. It's good for my career. I want to be an actress, you know."

"Please, sit down with us. Come on, Nicolas. Did you have any dinner? You cannot think properly on an empty stomach," Francis continues, ignoring the age controversy.

Nicolas was right.

The caterer has cooked for an army and set three beautiful buffets in the living room.

"Jodie decided to stay at the Martinez," Francis says for my benefit. "One of the maître d's, a certain Henri, used to be an old flame of hers. He was working as a beach steward back then. A real Apollo. Oh, God, that is such a long time ago!" He laughs.

Nicolas and I sit down with Francis and Jolanta. Muriel sits last. I'm thinking of removing the knives from the table for Jolanta's well-being.

"Have you been to Prague?" Jolanta asks me again.

It's an obsession of hers.

"It's definitely on my to-do list."

She turns to Muriel. "My agent hasn't contacted me yet for your show. I'm doing Dior, though."

Muriel gives her a dirty look. "Is she for real?" she asks Francis.

"We know each other from Prague," Francis says, ignoring Muriel's question. "Wine?"

"I have a feeling for you," Jolanta says to Muriel. "I really hope I'll do your show."

"You're so beautiful." Francis touches her hand. "Of course you will."

"We haven't decided yet," Nicolas tells her.

"Oh, good! I love to do young new designers. It's so

much fun," she says and spoons a bit of melon. Her eyes are locked on Francis and she seems not to have heard Nicolas at all.

"How did it happen?" Muriel breaks in.

"What?" Francis asks, amused.

"How did you turn into this fucking joke," she says calmly, as if we've all disappeared and there's only her and her father left in the room.

"A joke? Well, darling, I'm happy to keep you amused, then."

"Do you hear anyone laughing?"

Silence. Jolanta is all smiles—she's not sure if it's some sort of family joke she's just not getting.

"Maybe we should eat something," I propose.

"That's a good idea," Nicolas backs me up.

Francis pushes his plate away and wipes his gray beard elegantly. Muriel has ruined his selection of desserts. "Well, it's getting very late. Jolanta, have you finished? We should let them work."

"I wanted more of the chocolate mousse," she complains and laughs like it was the funniest thing she has ever said. "But…I'm eating too much! I'm a pig."

She springs out of her chair and cuddles up against Francis. Look at her. She's just gorgeous…very, very young, but gorgeous.

"We're off," Francis says.

"Good night," Jolanta adds innocently. She probably thinks Muriel and her are just like sisters now.

Muriel gazes silently at the two empty seats left by Francis and Jolanta. Francis has shut the mirror doors to his wing of the villa. Sleep tight, hope the bedbugs won't bite—oh,

God, I just pictured him helping her into her pajamas and reading her bedtime stories.

Stop, Lynn! Think of something else. "Did you try the ham?" I ask. "It's delicious."

Muriel shakes her head and empties another glass of rosé.

"What are we going to do with all this food?" I try again.

Muriel shrugs.

What's wrong with me? Her father is bedding a girl even younger than herself and all I can think about is food.

I turn to Nicolas for help but get only an empty smile.

"I think I upset him," Muriel mumbles. "It's a first."

She grabs the bottle and empties it into her glass. She shakes it to get the very last drop. "Nicolas!" she moans.

He stands.

Tonight, *Nicolas!* means *get me another bottle presto.*

"Nothing upsets him. But tonight, I upset him. Why? Who cares!"

She drinks the whole glass.

"Ah!" She remembers something. "What was her name again?"

"Jolanta," I say as Nicolas leaves me alone with her. I did it again. I looked up at the closed mirror doors. "Hey, Muriel. Maybe we should call it a night. Tomorrow is another day."

"It's just fucking starting," she mumbles and slams the empty bottle on the table. "Jolanta? Yes, Jolanta. She's a funny girl. Very fashionable, isn't she? She has the debutante touch, the little bitch. What did I read recently? Celebutante. You know, celebrity plus debutante. Celebutante."

"I got it the first time," I say carefully.

"Celebutante. Debutante. He'd fuck anything. Sometimes

I wonder why he didn't fuck you, too. Do you wonder that too sometimes?"

Oho! I don't want to hear any of this.

"I'll make us some coffee," I say and run away to the kitchen.

Oh, God, oh, God! Nicolas! Help!

"Hey? Where the fuck is everybody?" I can hear Muriel yell behind me.

Nicolas is sitting on a stool, holding a bottle of rosé and looking at his reflection on the glass wall. He looks so sad and tired.

"Coffee?" I ask as a greeting.

He shakes his head.

I pour myself a cup from the thermos the caterers left.

He uncorks the bottle.

"I think she's had enough," I say.

"She never has enough, Lynn. She needs to go all the way, like with everything else she does."

He glances up toward the living room. There. He does it again. Dreamy, silent and introspective. Only, I can tell he has had enough of being pushed around and crushed simply because *she's something special*.

I sit beside him and stare at our reflections.

"You really look like your mother," he says to my mirror image.

"Oh, no, no! Jodie and I are very different. In every way. She's elegant, beautiful."

"You're charming, too."

Hey, look at my reflection. It's smiling.

"I bet you say that to all the girls."

He puts his hand on mine and kisses me softly.

I needed this so much. His kiss. I can't stand it here anymore. I just want it to be him and me. Everything else, Muriel, Francis, Jolanta and Jodie—yes, especially Jodie—could disappear.

He's such a good—

Kaboom!

We stop to turn toward the living room. Some ugly breakage and lots of Muriel's filthy swearing are coming from there.

We nod at each other. Better go back to rescue her. But before we can stand, we hear more swearing and the splash of something falling into the pool. "Oh, shit," Nicolas mutters.

We're on our feet and running through the terrace to try to fish Muriel out before it's too late. It's completely black out there.

"Muriel!" I call, then turn to Nicolas. "Do you see her?"

"I can't see a thing."

I run back to the kitchen and think, oh please God, don't let her drown. I hear another *splash!*

I press every single light switch there is and the terrace and pool finally come to life.

When I come back, Nicolas is floating in the middle of the bright blue water looking around for Muriel's body.

"Where is she?" he asks anxiously.

Only, there's no Muriel in the swimming pool. Instead, there's a sofa floating in there.

"She's not in there," I say and help him out.

"Dégage!" Muriel yells at her demons in the darkest part of the park.

It's easy to find her. She leaves a trail of destruction.

She unpots trees and plants.

She kicks African art.

She fights with the fences surrounding the Boutonnière villa.

And she swears like a sailor.

When she finally stops we're not on the Boutonnière property anymore. We're on a construction site next door.

"There used to be nothing here," she complains when she realizes Nicolas and I are standing beside her.

I look at her in the moonlight.

I'm not scared of her anymore.

I feel sorry for her.

I imagine her coming here alone as a kid and crying, and now it's all fucked up because they're building another villa and there's nowhere to cry anymore.

"Let's go back, I don't think we're supposed to be here," Nicolas tries.

Useless.

Muriel is already making her way toward the foundation walls.

"Maybe she just needs some time alone," I say, thinking privacy might help Muriel make peace with herself.

But some more glass breakage proves me wrong.

She's not making any sort of peace.

Instead, she has decided to demolish the building, and to turn this place back into the quiet haven she used to come to.

We run inside the building and there she is, armed with a crowbar, breaking every window that happens to stand in her way.

"Muriel! Enough!" Nicolas tries to stop her but she turns and almost whacks his hand off.

I can't believe it!

"Who do you thing you are?" she yells at him. "Don't do this! Don't do that! Fuck you!" She takes a step toward him, raises the bar as if she wanted to break his head open. "I do exactly what I want!"

Nicolas just stands there in front of her, ready to take it, so I shout, "Muriel!" trying to wake her up.

"Oh, fuck it!" She drops the crowbar. "You don't belong here!" she spits in his face. "Leave me alone."

Slowly, slowly, I approach her and take her gently in my arms.

Oh, she resists a bit, of course. Tries to fight me off with some more cursing and battling, but, by now, I've got a good grip and she's not likely to escape.

"Leave me alone," she mumbles.

Too late. The tears have started.

I sit her down on the concrete, and rest her head on my chest. I hold her forehead. Hush, hush, little Muriel. I rock her slowly as I listen to her crying.

Hush, sweetie.

I look up. Nicolas stands beside us. I know he feels so awkward he would like to run away and jump back into the swimming pool.

One, because Muriel just tried to kill him and could still change her mind. And two, because this is girl stuff, stuff he doesn't want to be a part of.

I reach for him and pull him down beside me.

That's exactly what you do during work seminars.

You bond and break windows.

Step #15:
Don't be who you are, be who you want to be.

We slept on the concrete, right there in the middle of the construction site.

I know! A multimillion-dollar property with fresh beds and proper bathrooms was just a few yards away.

It was cold, so I'm spooning Muriel, my arm still over her shoulders, and Nicolas is spooning me.

I wake up first, feeling somehow in charge, and take a good look around. What a mess. It's all broken glass and general mayhem. I turn and murmur Nicolas's name to wake him up. I want us out of here before the construction workers arrive and start asking questions.

Muriel brushes her sleepy eyes, yawns, stands up and makes her way back toward the villa.

"Muriel," I call. I want to ask if she's all right, but she

doesn't give me the opportunity. She just walks away without a word.

I stand.

Shit! I'm in pain! There's not a muscle in my body that doesn't cramp.

"Did you sleep well?" I ask Nicolas and wink in the sunlight.

Muriel turns back and holds some barbwire for us. "Come on then!" she orders, avoiding any eye contact. She rushes past the pool and darts into the kitchen as if there was nothing to see here. But, in fact, there's plenty to ponder.

"The gardeners will fish out the sofa," Francis says. "Quite a night you had there."

"Yeah…er…yeah…" I can't really concentrate on what to say. He stands by the edge of the pool, a cup of coffee in his hand, completely nude, his…his *thing* hanging in the blue light. He squats and checks the water temperature. Mmm… Not bad!

"The sofa! It's so funny," Jolanta cries out as her head emerges from the water. She's an optimist, that girl. She swims to the edge of the pool and drags herself out. She's also completely naked. "Did you have breakfast yet?" she asks Nicolas.

Nicolas, darling, close your eyes!

"The coffee's still hot," Francis says, smiling at me.

"I drink tea. Coffee is bad for your skin," Jolanta points out and makes a moue. On second glance I see I'm wrong. She's not completely naked. She wears plain underwear gone utterly see-through in the water.

"I already had breakfast, but with all the swimming, I'm still hungry."

"How's the water?" Nicolas asks matter-of-factly.

"Funny! With the sofa! Oh, Francis, can we leave the sofa in?"

Francis sips more coffee. "We'll see." He smiles at his crazy young *belle*. "Another beautiful day on the Riviera," Francis comments, turning to the Pinède, flashing me his aging butt. "I want to retire here."

The caterers haven't been back to pick up the leftovers from the three buffets, so we resume breakfast where we left dinner.

"We should do some work, really," Nicolas insists, eating some chocolate mousse.

"We need to go to Saint-Tropez," Muriel counterattacks, eyeing the empty bottles of rosé. "I need to do some shopping."

She looks in a very poor state. She holds her head with both hands trying to keep it from exploding. Work holds no appeal for her today. All she wants is more and more coffee and to go shopping in Saint-Tropez, or boating, or fishing or anything that will get us away from the villa, really.

I'm concerned about the damage she did in the construction site. I wonder if we should contact the owners and offer some sort of compensation, so I ask, "Should we talk about last night?"

"Oh, come on," Muriel explodes. "We were drunk! We were stupid and it's not like we are connected now or something!"

"I meant about the windows. Shouldn't we pay something for the windows?"

"Oh, that… They're probably rich. They won't mind."

"I can go and talk to them," Nicolas suggests. "But it's not like we have a lot of company money to pay for the damage."

"Forget about the fucking windows," Muriel insists. "It will be their fee for ruining…the scenery."

There's no point carrying Muriel from shop to shop and holding her in front of fashion displays pretending she's getting some sort of inspiration. She's complaining she's going blind. Her eyes are going to pop out of her head. Actually, the whole head is going to fall off her body. Bring me to a bar, she begs. Lynn! Nicolas! A bar! Le Sénéquier. Please make it stop! Make it stop! I need a perroquet! perroquet! perroquet!

She practically jumps at the waiter's throat as we find a table on the busy terrace. She wants two drinks straightaway. She wants them fast, now, go!

The waiter hisses insolently and walks away.

This place, this terrace in the port, is a proper institution. It is part of a monument to Saint-Tropez's past glamour. The waiter doesn't hurry for anyone, not even Bardot. So, sit, be quiet, wait for your drink like everyone else, and look the part.

"Nicolas, can you ask everyone to stop smoking? Oh, my head! No! Get me a cigarette, instead. Please!"

If you ever go out with Muriel, let me warn you—she's a handful.

The waiter's back after what seems like an eternity. He wants us to pay right now. He has identified us as potential troublemakers. Nicolas passes him the company credit card while Muriel is downing her first drink.

"Ts! Une carte de crédit! Un dimanche!" the waiter complains. *"On aura tout vu!"*

The mention of the credit card brought Nicolas back to planet Earth. "Work," he says enigmatically.

"Don't worry." Muriel is now sipping her second drink. "While you two lovebirds are walking around smelling flowers, I'm developing tons of new ideas."

"Like?"

"It's all up here," she says, taping her head. "But now it's locked and painful. Later. Later."

When the waiter is back with the bill, Muriel orders a new set of drinks.

He hisses again.

"Leave him a good tip. I like his attitude," Muriel jokes.

"What kind of ideas, Muriel?" Nicolas insists.

"I thought about the wedding dress. I had a revelation. It's going to be a masterpiece." She taps her head again. All up here. No worries—we didn't waste our time at all.

"Ah! And I want a new tattoo," she says as if this alone justifies our presence in Saint-Tropez. "Georgio gave me the idea."

"Bears?" I ask.

She laughs. "Don't make that face, Nicolas. Seriously, I think we should use tattoos as a part of the collection. We could draw them on the models. Imagine."

He nods. There's something to it.

"Haute couture tattoos of course. Designed by me."

"We could make it a trademark. You buy a Muriel B piece, you get a personal designed tattoo motif signed by you," I add. "It would give the fashion editors something to chew on."

"What else?" Nicolas is waving for service. He wants a pad and pen. He wants to note everything down. What would we do without him?

"Wait, we'll continue this later. We're going," Muriel suddenly says, standing clumsily.

We turn to see what she's looking at.

Jolanta and Francis are sitting at the other side of the terrace. The young model waves at us. Smiles. Laughs. It's her five minutes in Saint-Tropez with the famous Francis Boutonnière.

"Don't be silly." Nicolas holds her wrist and she sits back down. "What else?" Nicolas repeats, eager to turn our adventures into superproductive bliss.

She sighs. The creative process is locked down again. Francis is like kryptonite.

It's a very noisy terrace. Still, we can hear Jolanta laughing with our waiter. She's either telling him about the sofa in the pool or the chocolate mousse she didn't eat.

"Embarrassing," Muriel mumbles.

The waiter slaloms back to our table. He even breaks into a smile. He tells us that Monsieur Boutonnière and his special friend invite us to their table. He starts to collect our drinks to help us relocate, but Muriel snaps her drink back. *"On est très bien ici. Allez vous-en! Allez!"*

I shrug for Jolanta's benefit. Sorry, can't come, we're glued to our seats and they're bolted to the floor.

She shrugs back at me and turns away to look at Francis.

Le Sénéquier: infected.
Saint-Tropez: infected.
The villa: infected.

The swimming pool: infected because Jolanta's undies were drying there, even though now they are where Muriel threw them, in the undergrowth.

I've retreated to my room for a hot shower. I'm so sore from last night.

I walk to the terrace. The sofa is drying under the evening sun. Jolanta's going to be so sad. For losing her underwear, of course, but for the sofa, too. She really liked it submerged. It was like wreck-diving.

I take a quick look at the large bed in my room.

The crisp bedcover hasn't even been…uncrisped. It looks so comfortable, to sleep and to hold Nicolas in perfect privacy.

Knock, knock.

"May I come in?"

Speak of the devil.

"Sure," I say, and feel surprisingly uncomfortable, just like the day he showed me the little room above L'Escargot.

Only now, we've spooned.

He closes the door and smiles clumsily.

Oho! I make a mental note: Must sleep with Nicolas NOW!

And before I have time to share my decision, he is pressed against me and we're kissing. He gently lifts me and we finally uncrisp the bed.

He pauses to just look at me. His hand is playing with my bathrobe belt.

My whole body stiffens.

Noticing I've suddenly become a brickwoman, he looks at my face quizzically.

I'm actually staring at the little terrace behind us, and

when Nicolas turns to see what's captivating my attention, he realizes that Muriel is standing on the terrace, a few feet from us, watching in shock.

"I'm…I wanted a word with Lynn," she says awkwardly.

"We'll be there in a minute," Nicolas says with surprising self-control.

"Okay," she says and walks away.

I make a sliding movement to get out from under him and prudishly close my bathrobe again. We sit up side by side on the bed and he takes my hand.

"I'm sorry," he says.

Oh, don't be, Nicolas! I'm not sorry. Not sorry at all.

So I kiss him on the neck and caress his cheek.

Work seminars are the best!

When I arrive in the living room, ready to take the whole incident lightly and joke about it with Muriel, she looks all packed up inside winter clothes and Massoud is already carrying her luggage to the limo.

"I'm calling this thing off," she says immediately. "We're going back to Paris."

"Now? But what about—"

"Yeah, what about it!" she snaps.

"We…you know…should work. That's why we're here."

"Are you fucking kidding me? We're done, we're gone!"

"Because of Nicolas and me? Muriel, it has nothing to do with you."

"This place is bad for us. Don't you feel it? The vibes?"

All I feel is an urge to return to my room and wait for the night to let Nicolas in.

"It's late. Can't we just leave tomorrow morning?"

"Lynn! You heard me. We're done!"

Dammit!

In under an hour we're back on the highway headed north, and as soon as we leave the shore the sky starts to pack gray clouds.

I turn to look at Muriel.

She stares moodily at the landscape, and when we pass by the gas station, the one she always goes to on her way to the Boutonnière villa, I can see her twisting her neck to look at it just a bit longer.

When I wake up, we're back in Paris, locked in a traffic jam.

I see the Eiffel Tower in the distance and it immediately hits me: Paris equals Barclay.

"You snore," is the first thing Muriel says. But at least she smiles about it. So I guess she feels less sore about everything.

"You actually do," Nicolas confirms.

Humiliating, humiliating, HUMILIATING!

"Do you feel it?"

"What?"

"Better vibes. We're adults, we're going to fix this."

"There's nothing to fix," I say.

"Oh, yes there is! What happened in the villa…" She shakes her head. "Let's not part straightaway, it would be awkward. Nicolas?"

"Sure," he says and turns to me.

"Let's go to my apartment," Muriel suggests.

I shrug. All I can think about is the Hub. It's like a huge shadow swallowing me, and I'm sure about several things. There will be no more partying, no more Nicolas, no more anything before I end everything with the Hub. So I say, "I can't go out tonight, I have…plans."

Before Muriel has time to protest, I lean forward and ask Massoud to drive me to the Georges V. A little while later, as the porter opens the door, Muriel leans forward and grabs my hand.

"You keep this one," she says and gives me the hedgehog. "Friends?"

"Friends," I say and before I know it, she gives me a quick kiss on the mouth.

"I like you," is the last thing I hear before Massoud drives away, leaving me in front of my hotel, with my Adidas bag and a little plastic hedgehog, staring back at Nicolas's worried face in the back window of the limo.

I'm not going to my suite though.

Oh, no!

I grab my cell phone and switch it back on. I manage to find the call-back function in the French menu.

"I need to see you now," I say before Barclay has any time to take control of the conversation.

"I'll send Dave," he says.

"No, you're not going to lure me into one of your ultra-romantic traps again."

"What?"

"I'm coming to your apartment right now. And please, don't make any plans."

"Okay, you—"

"I nothing! Give me the address!"

I hang up on him. Be strong, Lynn. You can manage a breakup with the Hub.

Step #16:
Don't get too attached to Mr. Lovely.

The taxi stops in front of Hubert's building. I pay the driver and stand across the street from the apartment. A very light rain starts falling on me.

I walk across the street and press the H.B. button on the interphone. There is a little camera looking straight at me.

"Come on in," Hubert says.

"What floor?"

I make a little mental lottery. Odd numbers, all will be fine. Even numbers, it will all turn to shit.

"Second."

"That's what I thought."

I climb the two floors slowly. The door to the apartment is open. I hear Hubert's voice. He's not alone. He is talking to a woman and even though I can't hear what they're saying, her voice seems awfully familiar.

"Here you are," Hubert welcomes me with a killer smile.

"Marion has just arrived in town. I hope you don't mind her joining us."

"Who's Marion?" I ask.

I step in the living room and I see who the fuck it is. I need to sit. I know her voice because we all know her voice. I mean *us* as in *us the entire planet*. What I didn't know is that in private people call her Marion.

"Do you know each other?" Hubert asks. "Probably you do. Marion, you must have met Lynn."

"You're Jodie's daughter, aren't you?" she asks.

She actually knows me! But I'm goddamn sure we never met before, and I'm also sure that Jodie would never have mentioned me to her.

"Oh, y-yes," I stutter.

She offers her hand. I discreetly wipe mine on my dress and shake it.

Please, Lynn, don't say anything stupid. Like *I'm one of your biggest fans* or *I love your music* or *Is yoga really the answer?*

"We must have been to some of the same parties," I lie because Jodie never takes me to any functions and prefers to lock me in her amazing loft apartment whenever she's in the mood to see me.

"I'm a big fan of Jodie's. She designed some of my favorite pieces."

I nod as if that was a compliment for me.

Hubert proposes a drink. Marion asks for a refill of sparkling water and I say, "Sparkling water, oh that sounds lovely," and regret that no one mentioned vodka or something stronger.

Marion excuses herself and goes to… She is going to the toilet. She doesn't even ask where to find it. They are such good friends. Mmm…

Hubert passes me my sparkling water. "I know that we were supposed to talk. But Marion is going through something and she needed a friend."

"Of course, of course!"

"She needs to go out, you know…."

"Yes, yes…I understand."

"We thought we could go to Mean Ray. Just the three of us. It will be good for her."

Poor Marion, confused and lost with her own emotional troubles.

"The media has been on her back, since…the scandal…."

He frowns suggestively. I have no idea what he's referring to but I nod all the same.

"You don't mind, do you?"

"Oh, no, if…"

Wait a minute! I'm not here to cheer up poor Marion. I'm here to get the hell out of Hubert's life.

"Actually, that's not okay…." My breakup mood is back, but Marion has returned to the living room.

"Mean Ray?" she asks. She looks at me. "I don't want to be a drag."

Hubert smiles at me. If I smile back it means yes, let's forget about breaking up and have fun and then sex. If I start to convulse and white froth comes out of my mouth, it would mean no, leave me alone.

I smile hesitantly.

"Should we go, then?"

What, now? We haven't finished our mineral water.

Marion dials her cell phone and says, "We're going now," very coldly, as if she were speaking to a computer. She hangs up. "Paul will be here in a minute."

Paul? Paul McCartney? Paul Weller? Which Paul, for Chrissake!

"My driver," she says specifically at me.

Oh, *that* Paul!

There is no queue for us, no wait, no effort at all. We fly through people like three ghosts. We're untouchable and everybody would kill to be with us. That's how important we are.

We don't need to speak either. We sit in the VIP corner and a waiter brings mineral water and three glasses. They can read our minds.

Hubert orders drinks for us—Marion sticks to the water—two Bloody Marys and a conversation about London real estate later, Marion wants me to accompany her to the toilets.

I'm her toilet partner!

"Sure," I say, standing. Hubert pats my butt and I really can't tell him to fuck off because I have to stay all hunky-dory not to hurt Marion's feelings.

We make our way to the toilets, and everybody—I mean everybody!—looks at us. I feel the collective envy crawling all over me.

"I'm sorry," Marion tells me.

"About what?"

"About invading your night like that."

"Yeah, but look, I get to go to the toilet with one of the most famous women in the world!"

Oops!

"You're funny," she says.

In all the hottest clubs in Paris, there's a much greater party going on in the toilets. That's where things really happen.

It's not only about doing the business, it's a space where one regains composure with oneself.

"He's a great man. I envy you," Marion tells me from her cubicle.

"You must be envying a lot of girls. His entire address book, actually."

"I never met any of those girls. You must be someone special to him."

We get out of the cubicles and a young model type spots Marion in the mirror, moves away gracefully and leaves us her precious mirror space. She gets rewarded by a smile from the Queen of Pop.

I mean, what wouldn't you do for that?

"Hubert doesn't mix his friends and his…girls." She takes a prescription bottle from her bag and drops a pill. She rinses her face under some cold water. She looks at her reflection. "So, I envy you."

"Can I tell you how much I love your music? And you," a young girl with a French accent says.

"Thank you," Marion replies kindly.

"Oh, thank *you*, you're so graceful," the girl says and walks away all grateful. Marion gets thanked for accepting compliments. You have to see it to believe it.

"Hubert is a lucky man, too. I don't know you, but you seem to be a genuinely nice person. Hubert sees you that way, too, I can tell."

Marion, that's what I used to be before I jumped on that plane to Paris. I have killed that honest and true person.

I lie! I deceive! I hurt! I'm out of control. I'm a monster.

"Are you all right?" she asks as she watches me collapse inside myself.

"I…hope you're right."

"Lynn, you're an honest and nice girl. It radiates from you."

Hubert is no longer alone at the table when we return. Muriel has joined him and I'm suddenly covered in goose bumps.

"I thought you had plans, Lynn!" Muriel laughs like a camel and turns to Hubert. "Oh! *He's* your plans! You're a busy girl."

This is not happening!

I try to look calm and sit down.

"Is Nicolas here?" I ask matter-of-factly, but she doesn't answer. Instead, she eases up in the sofa, tries to embrace me, stumbles, misses and lands on the table, knocking down our drinks. I help her up. "Hi, Marion!" she yells when she realizes who's sitting with us.

"Hi, dear, how's your dad?"

"My dad?"

"How is he?"

"Good."

Muriel's not smiling anymore. It sobers her up to be reminded that she's Francis's daughter.

"I've got to…" She stands and walks away. *Dad* is the secret word that turns her into a zombie.

"You'll send him my regards, won't you?" Marion says, but Muriel is already gone.

I'm about to follow her, but Hubert stops me.

"Muriel will be all right," he says authoritatively.

I look more carefully into the crowd. The dance floor is clear. The bar appears clear. Oh, God! I want to hide under the table, just in case.

A handsome young man detaches himself from the crowd. He's wearing glasses. It makes him look smart rather than nerdy. He sits down next to Marion, as if it is the obvious thing to do.

"They told me you were here," the man says. "I didn't believe them. I told them you're not going out anymore. I told them you're locked up in your fucking castle in London." He turns to us. "Hey, Hub."

"Joe, this is…" Hubert tries to introduce me.

"Yeah, one of your girls, who cares." He turns back to Marion. "We've missed you."

"I missed you too," Marion says and embraces him.

Wait a second. This is not your common Joe. This is Joe Tip, the actor.

"He owns the club," Hubert explains.

"Marion, Marion, a picture, please?"

We look up. A woman, a professional photographer, already has her camera glued to her face.

"I know her. She's all right."

Joe and Marion turn to her and they freeze in a pose. They look straight into the camera. I'd swear they sucked their cheeks in. They look perfect. I can imagine how the picture will look. The photographer takes a few more pictures and turns to us. She asks again, "Hubert, do you mind?"

He takes my hand. He nods and she takes a few pictures of us together. Flash, flash, flash. Hubert Barclay with his special friend. Oh, dammit! I didn't suck my cheeks in.

"Hey!" somebody shouts from the crowd. *"Qu'est-ce que tu fais là, princesse?"*

Moi? Princesse?

I look up. God, no, it's Marc and he is completely drunk! Or high. Or both.

I turn to Hubert. "It's all right, Marc is a friend from work," I say, but my heart is about to explode. I already feel exposed and I look around for a possible escape route.

"You know this guy?" Joe Tip asks.

"Ah!" Marc shrieks suddenly. He's realized that Marion's sitting with us. "You are my GODDESS!" he yells at her.

She looks away. She's not enjoying herself anymore.

"Marc, I think you should go," I say, immediately regretting being so rude.

"Oh!"

Before I can apologize, two bouncers grab him and drag him away.

Hubert puts his arm around my shoulder. "It's all right. They're just going to put him in a cab."

"Hey, buddy!" Joe snaps. "Don't you know that it is impolite to stare? Fuck! Who let those people in?"

What? Who's staring? Where?

Oh, God. Nicolas!

He is there, by our table. Staring at me. Me with Hubert's arm around my shoulders.

Joe waves for service. He's going to have Nicolas kicked out, too.

"No, it's okay. He's one of Muriel's employees," I say.

"Muriel who?"

"Muriel B."

"The drunk girl, Boutonnière's daughter," Marion explains. She's getting very annoyed with all this mess.

A waiter has arrived at our table.

"So…you know this man?" Joe asks again. "Do you know all the freaks that make it into my establishment?"

Nicolas steps toward me. He looks completely confused.

"We work together. He is all right," I say.

Joe scratches his chin. Mmm? He turns to the waiter. "Offer the man a drink." He turns to Nicolas. "Sorry, I thought you were a creep."

"He's not a creep," Marion says. "He is far too beautiful for that."

I can feel Hubert's body tensing beside me.

"Come on, then! Have a drink. It's on me," Joe repeats.

It's all so awkward.

"What would you like?" the waiter asks.

"What?"

"What drink would you like?"

Nicolas shakes his head. "I don't get you," he says to me and walks away.

"Wow!" Joe laughs. "Who's in trouble now?"

"So, that's the *someone?*" Hubert asks.

I don't have time to answer Hubert. I abandon them and go after Nicolas. I hear Marion say, "It radiates from her." And her voice disappears in the club noise.

When I reach the street, everybody is gone.

I shout. "Nicolas!"

I wait.

I shout again because, well, it radiates from me.

"Nicolas!"

"*Ça suffit!*" one of the bouncers yells at me. "*Il est parti, votre Nicolas.*"

"*Il est parti?*" I repeat word for word.

"*Parti.* Gone. Zouf!"

"Zouf?"

My love has zoufed away.

Nothing has gone as planned. Not with Hubert. Not with Nicolas. Might as well try the last person on my list. I ring the doorbell.

"What do you want?" Carolina spits. She's still sore for not making it to the Riviera with us.

"Hi," I say, as if it was normal for me to come to their apartment at daybreak. "I need to see Muriel."

"She sleeps." She closes the door with no further ceremony.

I ring again and again and again.

She reopens. *"Mais t'es folle, toi!"*

"I need to see Muriel. Er…*besoin* Muriel."

"You want to wake up Muriel? Okay!" She lets me in. *"Elle va te tuer.* Ha ha ha!"

She's actually eager to see what Muriel's going to do to me once I've dragged her out of bed.

Muriel lies on top of the bed still wearing the clothes she had on in Mean Ray, cuddling the bedcover around her. I approach. Oops, I stepped on something crisp and noisy. There are a few sheets of paper spread on the floor. I pick one up. It's…sketches. A woman with a huge spider over her head. She must have drawn it just before crashing.

Carolina drops her silk kimono, and, completely nude, slips back into bed.

"Muriel?" I try.

Muriel mumbles, turns and dives deeper into the bed-cover. Not available. Sorry.

"Muriel? It's me, Lynn." I approach, give her a tap on the shoulder and step back carefully. "Muriel? Come on!"

"She's going to kill you," Carolina murmurs like she's been there before.

I take my cell phone and speed-dial Muriel.

Her cell phone rings. She has it on her. She's not really awake but she looks for her phone instinctively. She finds it and still with her eyes tightly shut yells "What!"

"Muriel, it's me, Lynn," I say in the phone.

"What?"

"Muriel, I'm standing just beside you. Wake up, please."

"What?"

"Open your eyes, for Crissake!"

She does. I'm there. With my cell phone making a two-meters-distance call.

She doesn't need any more information. She throws her cell phone at me. "What the fuck are you doing here?" she yells.

"I told her," Carolina clears herself.

"Xavier Urbain offered me a job."

"What?"

"He offered me more money than you could ever afford. But I'm going to reject his offer."

I'm not sure she understood anything I just said. She fights with the bedcover and grabs her alarm clock. "Do you know what time it is?"

"Muriel, I have decided not to work for you, either."

She slams the alarm clock back on her bedside table.

"I lied to you, Muriel."

"What?"

"I lied to everyone. I'm not the person you think I am."

She looks around. She's trying to get a better feel for where she is. She turns to Carolina. "Did you let her in?"

Carolina just shoves the duvet over her head.

"Did you hear what I just said?"

"Lynn, are you on drugs?"

"Listen to me…I can't do the job! I'm not like Jodie! I'm nothing like her. I'm nobody. I lie! I lie all the time! I have no idea what I'm doing here. I'm NOBODY!"

Silence.

"You did coke, didn't you?"

"Listen to me! I didn't do any drugs! I'm just not the kind of person you expected."

"Can we discuss this later, when you calm down and I've had some fucking sleep?"

"Muriel, I can't do this job. I'm going back to New York."

She breathes deeply. "Leaving?"

"Yes."

"Leaving me?"

I want to say something self-deprecating so she won't regret losing me, but I'm far too busy fighting back tears.

"Leaving me, huh? Okay, then!" Muriel pulls the duvet away from Carolina and kicks her butt quite rudely. "You, out! Now!"

"But… It's not my fault! I told her not to wake you up!"

"Out! Out! Out!"

Carolina mumbles something about me being such a troublemaker, picks up her kimono and flashes me her butt on her way out.

"And close the door!"

"I'm going to sleep with Irena and Jacky!" Carolina threatens and slams the door.

"You, in!" Muriel orders, opening the duvet for me.

"I don't think—"

"In, I said."

I hesitantly sit down on the edge of the bed. She pushes me down until I lie beside her.

She throws the duvet over us. It's completely dark under there. I almost jump out when her voice breaks the silence.

"Lynn?"

I can't find my voice to respond.

"Are you crying?"

"No, I'm not crying," I lie.

"I don't care who you are and who you think you're not," she whispers. Her voice is so low, it's like little raindrops on wood. "Yesterday."

"Yesterday?"

"You know, *there*." Muriel is referring to the villa. I can't believe it really was only yesterday we were there.

"I would give everything to be back there, in your arms," Muriel continues. "Only it won't be the same. Because it was…*there*. You understand?"

Silence. I don't know what to say.

"Why did you do it?"

"You were breaking all the freaking windows!" I sniff and wipe my eyes. "You were sad."

"No one ever bothered before."

"I didn't want you to be sad," is all I can reply.

"Lynn, you can't leave now. I need you, Lynn."

"Oh, stop, please! I just want to go home!"

"Lynn?"

"What?"

"It's about Nicolas, isn't it?"

"My God, Muriel! What have I done?"

"We'll fix it, love." Her hand has found mine. "Don't worry about Nicolas. He'll forgive you."

Step #17:
What people think of you doesn't matter,
as long as they don't work for *Vanity Fair.*

Good God, great creator of *things,* evaporate me and let me flee through the ventilation system!

Here we are, in his office.

I'm so ashamed. Muriel dragged me in and wants me to tell Nicolas about my meeting with Urbain. And that's what I'm trying to do with a throat so tight words hurt. What I really want to do is jump at his feet and beg for forgiveness.

I gather enough guts to look at him. He doesn't appear to be listening. He is analyzing the sky, the white colors of the walls, the smoothness of the desk. Anything to avoid looking at me.

"First, there's the Fran Wellish situation, and now this," Muriel comments.

"The Fran Wellish situation?" I ask.

"We invited the bitch to Paris, paid for everything, and

yesterday she went to Xavier Urbain! That's why she disappeared. Don't you see it? It's a war! And the fat bastard is winning it! Nicolas, for Chrissake!"

Her tattoos are turning from black to red.

"I've met with Xavier Urbain, too," Nicolas says coldly. "He offered me a position."

This is just too much for Muriel. She sits silently on the floor and waits for him to say more.

"The condition was that I would resign from Muriel B on the spot," he continues. "I was also supposed to stop any sort of further contact with you."

"Why didn't you say anything?" She's still trying to sound tough, but she's lost her steam.

"I was actually considering their offer."

"You bastard!" Okay, some of the steam is back.

"I had decided to stay with you anyway," he says and turns to me. "I liked our team. I believed in us. I trusted...*us*. But now..."

"I'm so sorry, Nicolas," I mutter.

Muriel claps his hands and brings us away from last night's mayhem, back into her office. "You listen to me, you two. I don't care who's screwing who. This is a business not a dating service!" She turns to Nicolas. "We started this together, Nicolas, and we're going to finish it together. You got that?"

Nicolas just shrugs, eases back and resumes staring at the gray sky like a keen meteorologist.

"I need to talk with him, alone," Muriel tells me. She looks as if she's going to say something nice, but instead adds, "And Lynn, if you try to get on a plane and leave me, I will find you. And I will kill you."

★ ★ ★

Out in the workshop I see Marc and I walk up to him. "Marc, I'm so sorry about last night."

"Sorry for what?"

"Don't you remember? In Mean Ray?"

"Did I go to Mean Ray? *Oh la la,* I don't remember a thing."

I fill him in on how he met Marion.

He screams.

"Did I behave?"

"You were very…enthusiastic."

"A-ah! Keen-o! I'll never drink again! I'm going to join a convent and become a nun."

Nun? Marc?

He points at Muriel's office. "It's very electric this morning. What's going on?"

"They're discussing my future with the company."

"Oh, I see. Money talks." He put his finger across his mouth and invites us not to talk about it. "Dirty talk."

I nod and look at the fabric he is working on. It's some sort of a metallic web with trapped silver pearls.

"What are you doing?"

He grabs a few drawings lying at the side of his table.

"It came in this morning. It's the wedding dress. See, it's like a spiderweb."

I recognize them. They are the sketches that were lying around Muriel's bed.

"Muriel, she is different. She doesn't work with a simple drawing. She makes different sketches. She lets you visualize the dress from different angles. So you don't just see it. You feel it."

He turns the pages and the dress comes alive in my mind. He's right. Muriel has drawn the different sketches to give you a full mental picture of the piece.

"Isn't the design a bit morbid for a wedding?"

He stops and looks at me as if steam were coming out my ears.

"It's symbolic, don't you get it? The bride has caught herself a husband. And he's going to bring her money. See the silver pearls? That's the money. It's symbolic. It's simply genius."

"I see it now. It's very cynical."

"You want cynical, look at the hat."

The hat is a huge black spider holding the web that has captured the bride with its legs.

"So the bride is not the spider," I say. "The spider is the institution of marriage and the victim is the bride, who has been seduced by the pearls."

The dress is like a Polaroid of Muriel's mind. It's clever and truly beautiful, in a dark sort of way.

"Hmm, I guess you're right." Marc looks up.

There're some roar and commotion coming from Nicolas's office. I guess the forgiveness business isn't going down that well after all.

It's five o'clock. This has been the longest day in my life. I had absolutely nothing to do all day but make sure that the clock was progressing one minute at a time and wait for Nicolas or Muriel to call me back into his office.

They've been locked in there all day just yelling and yelling at each other.

Catherine was running in and out, bringing food, water,

coffee and documents. I wish she was wearing a helmet, for safety measures.

The door opens at last. Muriel steps out and looks at me. She appears exhausted. Disheveled. I stand. I take a few steps toward her. "Oh, Lynn, not now!" she breathes and walks away.

But...

Nicolas comes to the door and waves for me. You! In my office! Now!

He closes the door behind us.

"Nicolas, I'm sorry for all the trouble I brought on you," I start.

"Yes, you said that already. Please sit down."

I'm back at school sitting in the principal's office after skipping class.

"Muriel wants to offer you the position of public relations executive assistant."

"Assistant?" What happened to consultant?

He pushes a little folder in front of me. I lift it from his desk. It's strangely light.

"You can return it to Catherine or Muriel," he says, "once you have read it and signed each page. It's in English."

I open the folder and look through the shortest contract in the history of employment. It's written on four single pages.

"You'll be on a trial period for the next three months. During that period Muriel can choose to terminate the contract without notice."

"Nicolas, it doesn't need to be like this."

He had prepared a notepad with each point and ticks them as he goes. "She wants to propose a salary of thirty thousand euros per year."

"Are you just going to talk to your notepad or talk to me?"

"We will help you find an apartment. We will help you to obtain a work permit and we can help you open a bank account."

He ticks "apartment," "work permit" and "bank account" on the pad. I reach over the desk and push the pad away from him.

"Will you listen to me?" I'm trying hard not to scream.

He looks up at me. I can sense how much he hates me now.

"I made a mistake, Nicolas."

"You sure did. Any questions? About the contract, I mean."

"Do you really hate me?"

He finally closes his pad. He doesn't need any time to think about it. The answer is there ready in his heart, and he says it. "I don't care about you anymore."

"It can't be like this, Nicolas, not if we're going to work together."

"We're not going to work together. I don't want to see you. I don't want to hear about you. I don't want to have anything to do with you."

Did you hear that? It was the sound of my breaking heart.

"I've quit," he says. "And Muriel has accepted my resignation."

I'm just going to walk until I find the Seine then throw myself into it.

What happened to *"He will forgive you—I'll fix it"*?

I'm starving. If you want to lose ten pounds, don't start

any crazy low-carb diet. Like I said before. Just come to work in France. It's slimming.

I find a falafel stand and take my order to a nearby table. I open the contract folder. I read the first lines and then slam it shut again.

What's the point of going back to the office, anyway?

Nicolas is gone.

He hates me!

I've finished my falafel and it sits in my stomach like a lump. Things are really hard to digest today.

Call me paranoid, but I'm hesitating before asking for the card key to my room. You don't put assistants in these kinds of hotels. I picture Nicolas phoning the desk clerk and asking him to cancel my suite and throw me and my things onto the street. Assistants should deal with their own accommodation.

"You have a message, Miss Blanchett."

The desk clerk hands me my card key and a little envelope. I open it and the note says, "Hi. Hubert."

"Anything else," I ask, hoping that there would be something more comforting then just "Hi."

"No, that's it, Mademoiselle Blanchett."

I drag myself to the elevator. I'm worn out. I categorically refuse to think. It's a survival thing. I know that the minute I start to think, I will crumble and collapse. I just take one step at a time, and keep breathing in and out.

I open the door to my room and I have to clap a hand over my mouth not to scream. First, I thought that somebody was standing in the middle of the room. But it's not human, it's flowers. Right there, beside my bed. It's beautiful. It's one of those designer compositions. Like a beautiful tall white tree. I can't believe it.

"You must think that I am the tackiest person in the world."

Oh, it's the man that was scared of tacky.

I turn to see Hubert standing in the corridor right behind me. "How did you…"

"You're not happy to see me?"

I'm not sure yet, so I say, "I'm not sure yet."

"I tried to contact you today, but…apparently you were busy."

I recall my day watching the clock at Muriel B and counting the seconds. "I had a weird day today."

"Because of last night?"

"Because of me. Because of Muriel. Because of everything."

He points at his flower tree. "I didn't know how to do that. I'm not used to the running-after-the-girl game."

"Nobody asked you to run after me," I say and hear how unkind my voice sounds.

"There's something real happening between us. You can't lie about it forever."

You know what I really need now? I really need to fall into his arms. I could cry on his shoulder and feel secure again. I could forget everything about Muriel B and Nicolas and just accept being one of Hubert's girls and getting a choice of cars or apartments later.

Argh!

"We had too many Bloody Marys and too much champagne, Hubert."

"Give me a chance, Lynn."

"Hubert, you're a nice man. I really mean that. But…" I look at the contract. "I need to think about it."

"About what?"

"About us."

"What is there to think about?"

"That's exactly my point."

He puts his hand deep in his pockets and walks back into the corridor. "I don't want this to sound shallow, but I've never been dumped before."

"I'm not dumping you," I say like a coward, because that's exactly what I should be doing. "I just need some time for myself."

"Well, when you're done thinking about us…"

"I'll phone you."

"Yeah, I know."

I just came out of the shower. I'm not in anybody's arms but I have slid into a thick fresh bathrobe. That's as good as it will get tonight.

I sit in the middle of my king-size bed and look at the contract folder before me.

I pick up the phone.

I dial and listen to the very familiar ring tone.

"Bill Blanchett."

"Hi, Dad, it's Lynn."

"Oh, Lynn, finally! I was beginning to worry. When are you coming back?"

"I was actually calling to talk to you about that, Dad."

"Of course. By the way, Jodie phoned me. She said she met you in France and she was worried about you, too."

Jodie? Worrying about me?

"Are you all right, pumpkin?"

No, Dad, pumpkin is slowly dying out here. Pumpkin is breaking everybody's heart, including hers. Pumpkin is a monster.

"Maybe you should come back if you're homesick. You have nothing to prove, pumpkin."

"I'm all right, Dad, but I'm calling because I won't be coming back anytime soon."

Silence.

"I've been offered the job I've been dreaming about all my life. I'm in the middle of a fairy tale," I say, forgetting to mention that the fairy tale looks more like a nightmare right now. "And I've decided to stay in it."

"I'm happy for you, sweetie."

"Thank you, Dad."

"And, Lynn..."

"Yes, Dad?"

"I love you, pumpkin."

Don't cry, no, don't!

Ah shit!

"I have to go," I say and hang up before he starts to ask why I'm crying.

"Well, Muriel, it's just you and me, then," I say out loud as I open the contract folder.

I reach for the pen and sign each of the four pages.

> # Step #18:
> ## You can have talent but no success, but you can't have success without talent.

Today is great.

First of all, it's 6:00 a.m., and I wake up in my own apartment. My own apartment in Paris! Of course it's not much of an apartment, but for me it's just as good as paradise on a second floor.

It took three weeks to get to this. And don't go thinking that I could have stayed at the Georges V.

Yeah, that's right. I had to give up my suite.

In the last three weeks, Muriel has moved me in and out of three different apartments including hers. I have flatted with all kinds of crazy young Americans, broke artists and rich kids playing bohemian before going to Yale and then joining Dad at the practice.

She even put me in a flat for models! Imagine me living with four Russian, Polish and Estonian models. I felt like the ugly dwarf crawling around the apartment leaving slime traces behind.

But today, this morning, I'm the happiest person in the world. I have found an apartment in Rue des Martyrs and I just moved in.

It's expensive. It's incredibly small. It's old.

But it's the hottest, hippest district in the city right now and it's so fashionable. It's young and bohemian and happening and it's *so* lively. Even now at six in the morning, you can hear the market people setting up their stands and shouting at each other joyfully.

And know why else today is great? Our show is scheduled for tonight.

My first apartment in Paris and my first fashion show! I am so proud of it! Because, I might be an (executive) assistant, but I pulled this thing up from the ground all by myself.

During the last three weeks, I've had to jump over so many obstacles, I thought I was an athlete.

Since Nicolas is gone, Muriel expects me to fix absolutely everything. And fixing things is everything in France, because it's the land of the *no!*

No, Lynn, we can't make the show in the street because we don't have the authorization.

No, we don't have the light equipment.

No, we don't have the marquis for the models.

No, we don't even have the models, to be honest.

No, we can't have the traffic stopped.

No, the press won't come.

And when they come, no, we don't have enough money to build a press stand.

We can't do this!

We can't do that!

No, no, no!

It's enough to make a girl go mad, but fortunately I have set clear goals:

1. I will have this show take place in the street.
2. I will keep Muriel focused and away from any work-site or activities involving crowbars or windows.
3. I will forget Nicolas since he hates me, and move on.

So far, I've been good at keeping the first two resolutions.

I'll be in Rue Saint Denis all day supervising the preparations. Let me tell you something, I'm the most respected assistant in this business, mostly because we don't tell anyone that's my title. Muriel presents me as her *collaboratrice*. I thought she might give me Nicolas's title since I inherited all of his duties. But since he left, Nicolas has become complete taboo within the Muriel B corporate world. Especially since everyone knows he works for the enemy now.

Yes, that's right, Nicolas works for Xu. We found out when Carolina came back from her modeling agency with an invitation to the opening of the new Xu store, and it was signed *Nicolas Bouchez—PR Manager*.

PR!

He even stole my turf!

And there was a phone number to confirm attendance. So one day when I was alone in my office, trying to forget all about Nicolas, well, I called the number.

I asked for Nicolas and said it was Lynn Blanchett from

Muriel B, and it was very, very important. I waited for his assistant to tell me that he doesn't want to talk to me, since he hates me, but instead, I heard his voice say, "Lynn?"

"Ah, Nicolas!"

"So, what's so important?"

Er…

"Well, I found an apartment," I said joyfully.

Silence.

"Rue des Martyrs."

"Lynn, I'm quite busy right now."

"Oh, yes, yes. So, how is it at Xu?"

"Very busy," he repeated.

I needed to think of something to say before he hung up on me. I blurted out the first thing that popped into my head: "I'm in trouble, Nicolas."

"Lynn, it's not really my problem anymore."

"I know, but…I would really like to see you. Really really!"

I waited, and he finally said, "Where?"

"Why don't you come to my apartment? I can cook dinner."

I heard him breathe. "I don't think so."

"Could we at least talk about it on the phone?" I said, trying to prolong our conversation a bit longer.

I know. Pa-thetic!

"Lynn, I agreed to have no more contact with you or anyone at Muriel B when I joined Xavier's team."

"Oh! But it's not related to Muriel B."

"Are you phoning for *personal* reasons?"

"Er…yes."

"Bye, Lynn," he said and hung up on me.

I looked around my office, which used to be his office actually, to be sure nobody had heard me. I was shaking.

My whole body was shaking.

I arrive at the office. You couldn't tell that it's our big day, except that the dresses are ready, covered in plastic and suspended on racks to be transported out of the workshop.

I sit behind my desk and look at the guest list. I have printed little question marks in front of all the names of the people who haven't confirmed attendance yet.

There are question marks in front of all the biggest celebrities and all the editors from the most prestigious newspapers.

There are fundamental differences between a major fashion show, like, say, the latest winter collection of Jodie Blanchett, and a fashion show by a young new designer. When Jodie presents her pieces, I know people who would actually kill to be there. Fashion editors would drink their own ink for a word or two with her.

A show by a wannabe like Muriel is a different game. Nobody wants to come and see it, especially the people who should be the most concerned with fashion and new trends.

Nobody cares.

The editors are not interested in going to another semi-to-not-known designer's show. You need to phone them every day and every day they cancel. So you have to convince them all over again and they have another chance to cancel the following day.

Muriel, who? Muriel B? Oh, does the young thing still exist? Sorry, we are too busy. We're going to a brunch with Kazo or another celebrity designer who's not coming to your show, either. Har har har!

Your guest list is just melting in front of your eyes.

And, please, forget about talent.

Forget about beautiful garments.

You see, in fashion, fashion is not enough. Editors are not interested in fashion. They are interested in celebrities. You need celebrities on the catwalk, in the audience, at the after party.

Bring celebrities to your show and the press will come like flies, attracted by…oh well, you know what.

And it's sort of a twisted relationship, because in return, celebrities need the press to come and watch them, so it's my job to bring all these people together.

But you don't find celebrities grassing in paddocks.

I pick up my phone and dial the number to Martin Villiers, one of the most respected publicists and agents in Paris.

I know how hard it is to get him on the phone. That's why I came to the office so early. I phone him on his private phone number and get him before he has a chance to put his PA between us.

"Oui?"

"Hi, Martin. It's Lynn Blanchett, you remember me?"

"Er…Blanchett? Where…"

"We met at the film premiere the other night. The funny American woman? Me? Jodie Blanchett's daughter? Do you remember?"

"Ah…oui, I remember. You were with Kazo."

Oh, that's right. I should take you back a bit.

About two weeks ago, I was invited to join Muriel for the premiere of some artsy film by Paris's hottest young director.

I was still flatting with models and let me tell you, those

girls would have killed to be at this premiere instead of going out clubbing with some rich but anonymous serial model-dater. Secretly they all want to be actresses.

The phone rang. It was Muriel. She was calling from her cell phone and asked me to look down on the street below. When I did, she was standing by a white stretch limo waving at me.

I flew down the stairs, wondering if I looked good enough in my Kazo dress, and just before getting in the car, I looked up at the window. There they were, my four flatmates, staring at the ugly little Lynn getting the star treatment.

Yes!

I could imagine them cursing me in Eastern-European accents and applying extra foundation.

Muriel wasn't alone in the limo. An old Asian man, soberly dressed as a priest, was staring at me. I sat in front of him and began wondering if he was some kind of butler.

"Hi there," I said.

He nodded elegantly and Muriel said, "Lynn, this is Akiro Kazo. I don't believe you've met before."

"I'm so pleased to meet you. I love your work," I said. I couldn't help wondering if it was okay to wear a Kazo dress while traveling with the man himself in a limo. There might be some kind of etiquette for that, too.

"You've probably noticed, but I'm wearing one of your dresses."

The old Kazo looked at me while Muriel was trying to uncork a bottle of champagne.

"Prêt-à-porter model, yes," he said.

"Lynn has a thing for casual clothing," Muriel explained as the cork popped. "Champagne?"

"No alcohol, yes. *De l'eau.*"

Muriel poured him a long drink of mineral water. "Sorry, Akiro, but we are two alcoholic ladies," she said and handed me a flute. "Cheers."

Kazo didn't toast with us. It seemed as if he was living inside his own protective eggshell, almost unaware of the world surrounding him.

"Are you looking forward to the movie?" I asked him. It might not have been the most brilliant conversation starter, but at least I was trying.

"I don't like movies, yes. *C'est très vulgaire.*"

No champagne and no movies in Kazo's life.

"What do you do when you're not working?" Muriel asked.

"I buy houses."

"Is it fun?" She refilled her flute. You had to give her that. She was not intimidated by him.

He didn't answer. He probably didn't know the meaning of the word *fun*.

"You must be working most of the time anyway," I said, coming to his rescue. "Creating magnificent dresses."

"I don't work anymore. People work for me. I buy houses. I travel. I see vulgar movies with alcoholic ladies."

He smiled, enjoying his own joke.

We arrived at the Champs-Elysées, and I could see a large crowd packed around the theater entrance. I could hear them scream and see the flashing lights.

I was going to get the red-carpet treatment! Our car stopped and a security man opened the door and helped me out. I was out first. Kazo followed. He didn't pause for the press. He just walked straight into the cinema.

It was insane!

You couldn't see or hear a thing. Your instincts told you to smile and look happy, but walking those hundred feet to the theater was like crossing a battlefield.

A hand grabbed my dress and stopped me. I turned toward the press stand.

"Who are you? Who are you?" somebody shouted. A few microphones and tape recorders were shoved straight in my face.

"Lynn Blanchett. I work at Muriel B."

The hand let go of me and even pushed me forward. The microphones disappeared just as fast. Not important enough. Not important at all. I looked around for Muriel. I couldn't see her. I was disoriented. Where was the entrance? A young woman with an earpiece and a clipboard walked to me.

"Vous avez votre invitation?"

I didn't have any invitation. All I had was Muriel picking me up in a limousine.

"Do you have an invitation?"

"I'm with Kazo."

"Your name is?"

First she looked through a pink list and didn't find me there. She lost her smile. She looked through a green list. I wasn't there, either. I was going down and down on the color-coded social hierarchy.

She found me on a plain white list, the last one on her stack of documents. She passed me a credit card-size badge.

"Use this to get in." She pointed in the direction of the entrance. "And please move on. You're stopping the real VIPs from getting into the theater."

She was very annoyed with me. I was stealing precious

press exposure. I walked on and I could see Muriel and Kazo entering the theater in front of me. They didn't seem to care that they had lost me.

I had to flash my white pass about a dozen times to different security staff. I was pushed and kicked and yelled at before finally being forced into the first row and seated all the way to the left. Great! From where I was, I could only see the top right corner of the screen.

"Ah, Salut," I heard, and turned to see the young Frenchman Roxanne was dating sitting in the next row up. I had forgotten his name. All I remembered about him was that he was in one of those French-TV reality shows.

"Oh! How are you doing?"

"Tu es avec Roxanne, toi aussi?"

"Roxanne? No, I'm with Muriel B."

I turned to show him who Muriel was. Dammit! Roxanne. She was actually sitting next to Kazo and Muriel, and among the other celebrities. They had great seats, right in the center of the theatre. While Mr. Reality Show and I were seated in the servants and gigolos section.

"C'est Roxanne qui m'a invité," he went on.

I was looking at Roxanne, trying to attract her attention, and suddenly I realized the incredible truth. Brian—winedealer Brian—was making his way along her row to sit beside her. Roxanne had invited the two of them, her young gigolo and the funny wine dealer. Only she had seated one in the outcasts section, beside me, and had put the other one at her side.

"Tu travailles dans la mode, non?"

"I don't speak French that well."

"You work fashion?"

"Yes."

"Can you help me work fashion?"

"What's your name again?"

"Guy, I was in *L'Appart*. You know, the French *Big Brother*."

"Guy, I'm not interested."

"Okay," he said and eased back in his seat, clearly forgetting all about me. It didn't disturb him to be rejected. He was very much like a prostitute trying to turn tricks. Sometimes he got lucky, sometimes he didn't.

After a bit, the film director came out and made a short speech. I gave Roxanne a last look before the lights went out. She didn't see me.

I would love to tell you that I was like a Buddhist monk, in touch with my inner self, but thinking of wine dealer Brian up there with Kazo and the gang, and me down here with the Guy type, I couldn't stop feeling jealous and humiliated.

"Enjoy the movie!"

Yeah, right.

I met Martin Villiers at the after party. I was lucky enough to have regrouped with Muriel and Kazo and I had shaken off Guy. As for Roxanne, she disappeared with Brian before I had a chance to talk to her.

Kazo presented me to Martin. He didn't know what to say about me exactly so he said, "My friend Jodie Blanchett's daughter."

"His friend Lynn," I said.

"My very good friend Lynn," Kazo corrected.

"It's fantastic to meet you," Martin said, looking around

for a possible escape route from a complete nobody like my-self. "I…your mother…you know!"

"Sure."

"It was lovely talking to you," he said as if we'd been at it for hours. "I have to leave you now, I have to see one of my clients." He pointed in a random direction. "You know how these parties are. Work, work, work! Right?"

"Yeah, right."

He smiled and walked away.

"You see," Kazo said. "I prefer to buy houses and go to bed early. Vulgar movies very tiring, yes."

I stayed with Kazo for most of the evening. We found a sofa to sit on and we watched people without saying much. I just made sure that his glass of mineral water was kept full, and I think that he appreciated me for that.

"Your mother. Great genius," he finally said.

"Thanks."

"I see it in you. You can be great genius, too. It's in waves around you." He moved his hand around me, de-scribing the invisible waves of geniusness surrounding me. "I like you. I like silent-type woman," he concluded, and offered me a ride back to my models flat in the white limo.

"Yes, Martin, I was with the Kazo group," I say. "I hope that I'm not waking you up."

"No, but…did I ask you to call me?"

"Yes, don't you remember?" I lie. "We were supposed to go through the list of your clients coming to Muriel's show tonight."

"Ah."

"Do you remember?"

"Yes," he lies in turn. "Refresh my memory. Who was supposed to come?"

I give him five of the top names I'm after.

"Mmm?"

Mmm sounds bad.

"Is there a problem?"

"Muriel B is too small to get these people."

"Maybe they will just enjoy being there."

"No, they don't enjoy being anywhere. There must be something in it for them. Did I give you the names myself? Surely I didn't."

"There will be a lot of press coverage."

"I can send Samantha Cock. She is attracting lots of publicity and I'm sure she would love to go."

"Samantha *who?*"

"She's getting big in the adult industry. Trust me, they are the new stars."

"A porn star? You must be joking!"

"It would be perfect—a porn star coming to a fashion show on Rue Saint Denis." He laughs like someone possessed.

I repeat the five names. "Those are the ones I need. Help me out here."

Curse! Never use the word *help.* They hate it.

"You can't have them. I'll send you Fernando Galton."

"Who's he?"

"A writer. He likes catwalks. He's really interested in meeting models."

"A writer and a porn star, that's all you can do for me?"

"It's a perfect match." He sounds deeply annoyed by now.

"Listen, I don't remember promising you anything, especially not anyone you mentioned, so—"

"Kazo will attend," I lie.

"Kazo… What is Kazo doing at a show by an unknown designer?"

"He likes us. Muriel B could become big, you know. She will remember every bit of help she got along the way."

Shit! I said "help" again!

"Give me your phone number and I'll call you back."

Getting a call back is never a good option. They never call back. I give him my phone number and he hangs up.

I close my eyes and recompose myself.

I dial a new phone number.

"Résidence Kazo."

"Hi, Jean-André, this is Lynn Blanchett from Muriel B."

"What do you people want now?"

Now?

"I need to talk to Mr. Kazo."

"He is busy."

"He's expecting my call."

"What is the purpose of your call?"

"It's about Mr. Kazo's attendance at Muriel B's show."

"What about it?"

"Well, will Mr. Kazo attend?"

"We've already had this conversation. Mr. Kazo will attend."

Already?

"Mr. Kazo and I start to be annoyed by the constant harassment from you people at Muriel B."

I haven't talked to Kazo since the vulgar movie. I mailed him an invitation, but that's it. Jean-André hangs up on me before I can discuss his definition of *harassment*.

I look at what I have: Kazo, a list of question marks, a writer and a porn star.

How can the journalists resist coming?

I look at my watch: 9:00 a.m.

I pick up the phone and dial the cell-phone number of Marie Matisse. She's probably the most important fashion editor in town. I call her every day. One day, she says that she will be at the show with her team, the next day she says that she is tied up with something else.

"Lynn Blanchett? Isn't that a funny coincidence? Guess who I am having breakfast with? Come on, guess! We were almost talking about you."

Almost? "Well…"

"Hubert!" Marie says impatiently. "I'm having breakfast with Hubert Barclay. You bad girl! Do you want to talk with him?"

The Hub.

I guess I need to take you back a few weeks again.

The Hub and I are not seeing each other anymore, but somehow we keep bumping into each other all the time. Paris is a very small city for two highflyers like us.

Anything that has to do with Hubert confuses me enormously.

Well, he is a lovely guy.

Very attractive, too.

Intelligent.

Rich and successful.

He says he's crazy about me and nobody—I mean no-body!—has ever been crazy about me before.

Yet, I know that our relationship was wrong, that we

shouldn't push it any further, but I like him. Actually I like him very much.

About a week ago, Hubert left a note for me at Muriel B. It said:

> You should have told me you moved out of the George
> V. Do you want to come with me to the Riviera?
> Hub.

It was written on a Post-it and waiting for me on my computer screen. It was the last of many unanswered messages he sent me.

So I decided to meet him.

So we could put a full stop to our story.

But it's hard to let go of the Hub.

I told him we should meet for tea. I didn't want it to be too private, so I chose a public park. We met at Le Jardin du Luxembourg. He wanted to see me at the Lovers' Fountain. I suggested the tennis courts as it's more neutral ground.

He was already waiting for me when I got there. He was looking at a couple of young tennis players yelling at each other.

"I think he's right," Hubert said. "The ball was out. But she won't let go. And now she's telling him how unfair he always is. They're going to break up over it. How are you, anyway?"

"They were probably ready to break up before the match started. They just waited for the right moment."

"Are you coming to the Cap d'Antibes with me?"

He knew I hadn't come to discuss the details of our trip south. He was like the doctor advising you to take your pills and rest, knowing you wouldn't make it through the night anyway.

I sat beside him. The guy on the tennis court gave up and granted his partner the point.

"That's the same old story. We give up before you do."

"Women have more endurance and a higher pain threshold. We give birth, you know."

"I have another theory," Hubert said. "Women need to put their partners on trial. But the trial never ends. The jury will never reach a verdict. The trial will go on forever and ever. While we want to reach a settlement fast."

"I'm not putting you on trial, if that's what you mean."

"This week has been one of the worst in my entire life." He looked at me with this sad-sad-sad look and it was hard not to fall for it.

"I can't think. I can't sleep, and I don't want to go down that road. I have seen other men crawling like this before and I want to believe I'm better than them. But then I think, what the fuck! I don't care what anyone else thinks. I don't care if I'm tacky or stupid or vulgar, or even ridiculous. I want to be with her, I want to be with Lynn. That's all I can think about. But you don't even return my calls."

"I needed to think," I said, and it sounded so shallow. I had thought that breaking up would be much easier. I had pictured him distant and blasé saying, *Well then, goodbye, dear. I have a rendezvous with a young model of about your age after this. She's Asian and I've been told she does things to die for with her tongue!* I hadn't expected it to be these heartbreaking emotional gymnastics.

"I thought we were not playing a game."

"It wasn't a game, Hubert. But it didn't work. I mean, it

didn't work in my head." I didn't make any sense, did I? "Oh, Hubert, why skirt the issue. I don't love you. I like you. But I don't love you. I can't do this."

"Love wears off. We can have everything else but love."

"It doesn't work like that."

"Give it a chance."

We both looked at the young couple on the tennis court. They had stopped playing and they had stopped fighting. She was crying and he was holding her tight in his arms. They hadn't come on the court to play tennis. They'd come to sort out their problems and it looked as if they had succeeded.

I stood up. I knew that we would go nowhere this way. "We shouldn't see each other for a while."

I'm so bad at breaking up with him. I just can't let go completely.

"You can't keep me away from you."

"Please, Hubert. You know that we're not going anywhere."

"I have never been dumped before," he said again. He was right. It didn't sound obnoxious at all. It sounded desperate and sad.

"I'll see you around," I whispered like a coward and walked away. That was the last time we saw each other.

"No, I don't want to talk to Hubert right now," I say to Marie. "I'd rather talk to you."

"You young thing! You're driving our Hubert crazy. I've never seen him this way."

"Yes, well. That's the way it is. But I'm calling regarding tonight's show."

"What show?"

There you go.

"Muriel B's."

"Oh, when is it?"

I'd told her about fifteen times already.

"Tonight, at five. It must be written on your invitation."

"Tonight? Oh, God, no! I'm busy tonight. I'm going to the Dior party. Bad luck!"

Is there any point in telling her that yesterday she confirmed that she would come? Rather, I say, "Well, Kazo will be there and…" And I tell her the names that Martin wouldn't give me.

"Is that right?" she says, sounding impressed.

No, actually it's not right, so I choose not to answer at all.

"I might arrange some time to see the show then. Really, we wouldn't like to neglect Muriel B, would we? I'll see what I can do. Do you want to talk to Hubert now?"

"Marie, if you'd ask Hubert, he'd tell you that he doesn't want to talk to me."

"You are so wrong about that!"

"See you tonight, then," I say and hang up. I hate fashion people.

I look up to see Catherine coming into my office with a beautiful bouquet—small but delightful. "For you," she says briefly. She'll never forgive me for pushing *her* Nicolas out. The day she realized I was to move into *his* office and she was to work for me, she developed a permanent speech impediment—inability to address me with sentences longer then three words—and called in sick for the rest of the week.

I look at the card, it reads:

Good luck. Can't make it this time. Very sorry. Jodie.

I ponder the message. *This time!*

If it wasn't so tragic it would be kind of funny.

She probably means she was there for my birth, so I can't complain if she can't make it to the rest of the events that add up to *my life*.

It's not like it's a surprise.

I met up with Jodie a few days ago. Well, *met*—more like crashed into her trajectory. She was on her way to a some-thing-something in Moscow connected to her new perfume. She called me from Charles de Gaulle Airport. She was connecting in Paris and thought it would be *nice* to catch up while she was waiting in the terminal.

"It's a real headache. It will be hours before I can board my next flight. I'm going to kill Nathalie (her PA) over this one." Please note that she's been killing Nathalie for many, many years over absolutely everything. "Anyway—be fast."

I was running through the terminal when I caught sight of her. She was sitting on the other side of a glass wall, all alone in her bubble, staring obsessively at a TV screen list-ing the next departing flights.

I knocked on the wall. She turned. She tapped her watch. Not a lot of time left. She stood and came to the wall. She looked tired and upset.

She said something but she was all moving lips and no sound, so I shook my head and pointed at my ears. She looked around and waved over a security officer like she was calling a waiter in a busy restaurant.

Once they identified who and in what awful mood she was, they arranged a private room for us—one of those tiny cells they normally use to strip-search suspects.

"I received your invitation," Jodie said. "For Muriel's show. It's very unfortunate."

"Unfortunate?"

"The date's all wrong. I can't make it. We're launching JB2 that week."

A satellite?

"My new perfume. I'm all tied up. Anyway, how are you for money?" she asked as she took one of her it'll-fix-it-all envelopes from her purse.

"Wait a minute. How can you not make it?"

She looked awkward, frozen in midmovement, holding an envelope I wouldn't touch.

"Are you going to take it?"

"No."

She put the envelope back in her purse. "You make it personal, Lynn. It's ridiculous. It's business. I'm launching a product. I'm busy. Point."

"Oh, that's funny."

"How's that?"

"I didn't receive *your* invite."

"What invite?"

"The one for the launch of the perfume."

"I never… What are you talking about? You never liked being dragged to those things."

"I'm not eight years old anymore and it's not like you have to bring me to a nightclub and abandon me in a corner because you couldn't find a baby-sitter."

"Why are we talking about that now? I'll ask Nathalie to send you an invitation, if it's what you want."

Her phone rang.

"Look. It's probably her," she said. "I'll tell her."

"Please, don't pick it up."

"Why?"

"We're not finished here."

Oh la la!

"Do you realize I'm too tired to do this right now?"

"Oh, Jodie, trust me, I'm *very, very tired,* too."

She looked at her cell-phone screen. "Nathalie," she confirmed, sounding annoyed. "I thought it would be nice to see you, I didn't know you'd make it such a *pain.*"

"It's important for me to have you there, at the show."

"Even if I wasn't so tied up, I generally never go to other designers' shows."

"The problem, Jodie, is that it's not just another designer's show. Another graduation ceremony. Another birthday party. The problem is that it's *me.*"

Her phone rang again.

"I'll think about it," she said, to put an end to the conversation, and took the call.

"Don't think about it, please, just come."

"Ah! Nathalie!" She stood up. "I am going to kill you this time," she said on the phone. "Do you have any idea what I'm going through?"

She was about to leave me in this white, sterile cube, when she looked at me over her shoulder and said, "You're becoming very confrontational. Very French! Muriel is having a very bad influence on you."

* * *

I'm very French!

Very confrontational.

Ask Jodie!

That's why I stand on the Champs-Elysées right in front of Martin Villiers's agency about to press the intercom even though the plate reads: *CCA—Sur rendez-vous uniquement.* By appointment only.

Obviously I don't have an appointment. He wouldn't even return my call.

I ring.

"Oui?" the intercom says.

"Delivery for Mr. Martin Villiers," I say, looking away from the camera lens.

The door buzzes and opens. I take the elevator and walk into the CCA reception area. Oh, but I'm not in yet. The real treasure is behind two monumental wooden doors tightly locked behind the reception desk.

The receptionist, one of those long thin snake all-skin-no-muscles types, looks up from her computer and seems puzzled not to see a courier.

"I have an appointment with Mr. Villiers," I lie before she has time to press her get-this-woman-out-of-here-right-now button.

"And…you are?"

"Tell Mr. Villiers…"

Tell him what? That I have a gun, his address and a picture of his children in my purse?

"Tell him it's very important."

She shakes her head as if it was as impossible for her as

sprinting up and down the Himalayas. "Mr. Villiers is out of the office," she says.

Like hell he is! "Can you tell me where I can find him then?"

"I can't give you that information."

I'm feeling frustrated. "You might get fired over this," I threaten her.

"No, but I will certainly get fired if I tell you his whereabouts."

Smart-ass! I'm about to change strategy and start to cry and beg, when the gigantic doors open and the breath is knocked out of my body.

Nicolas!

Even more gorgeous than I remembered.

And not alone.

He is all smiley and touchy-touchy with a tall blond girl, walking out of Villiers's office as if it's a natural thing to do for beautiful, successful people like them. While the toad-kind like me stays at the reception desk begging for an interview with the god of agents!

I want to kill them both.

So that's what he's doing with his days since he resigned from Muriel B, huh? Dating a blond goddess when I spend my life crying at the memories of us.

"What are you doing here?" he asks when he finally notices me.

Well, dying of humiliation, obviously!

I just shrug because I can't manage to get my voice back.

"You remember Clarice," he says clumsily, pointing at the blond bombshell.

Wait a minute!

I recognize her.

She's not a movie star. She's the beautiful blonde that was flirting with me in Kazo's garden.

"You really should have come to the Gucci Party," she says with a moue. "It was, like, completely mad."

"I should have, shouldn't I?"

"We're going down to the Dior breakfast right now. Do you want to come with us?" she asks.

Yeah, that would be great, so I can refill your coffee while you French-kiss Nicolas.

"I don't think it's a good idea," Nicolas says.

"Oh, but why?" She pouts seductively at him.

"Sorry. Can't, anyway," I say, trying not to yell.

"We've just signed a deal with Clarice," Nicolas explains. "She will be the new face of Xu."

Ah! Does it mean that she has to have sex with you, too?

"So tonight is the big night?" he asks.

"Yeah, I sent you an invitation."

"I know."

"Are you coming?"

"I don't think so."

"Too bad!"

The elevator doors open and Nicolas jumps in dragging Clarice along, happy to have an escape route.

"Wait!" I scream.

"What?" Nicolas holds the elevator door open and stares at me.

"Did you see Villiers in there?" I ask, pointing back at the magic doors.

"Martin? No, he is at the Dior breakfast like abso-*fucking*-lutely everybody!" Clarice says before Nicolas has a chance to pinch her.

★ ★ ★

Clarice manages to get me inside Le Troyen. This girl should get my job. She's everyone's little darling. She even kisses the security hunks.

"This place is very special," Nicolas says annoyingly.

Since she wanted to invite me and insisted that he come along, he has no choice but to take this ride with me.

It's a sunny day. Le Troyen is like a little white castle slash greenhouse slash wedding cake in the middle of a flowery part of the Champs-Elysées. It's lovely, with blooming roses and hummingbirds.

"It's been open since the French Revolution," he says. "I think that it's one of the rare restaurants in the world to have three Michelin stars."

Oh, God almighty! I've stopped caring about the beautiful restaurant setting, and the history of French gastronomy. I'm onto something much bigger. Past the entrance of the white castle slash wedding cake, there is a perfect concentration of international celebrities.

"What is this," I ask Nicolas, "the annual who's who convention?"

Hey, I got a smile out of him!

Clarice turns to me. "Ha ha ha!" She overheard me and finds me very funny. She is so perfectly gracious and at ease among the stars, like a little celebrity fairy.

"So how long have you been together?" I ask Nicolas.

"We just signed her an hour ago."

"No, I mean together," and I make my famous finger together-sign.

"Oh, *that* together," he breathes. "Sorry to disappoint you but we're not…" He does my finger trick.

"Oh, it doesn't bother me if you date models," I say, and mentally jump for joy that they aren't together.

"She's not a model! God, don't you know her?"

Apparently, I am the only person in the world not to know Clarice.

"Come on! She's the heiress of Kleron. You know. The hotels."

Ah! That explains the name! It's not just a funny coincidence.

"And now she's Mademoiselle Xu!"

Clarice turns to him, laughs, winks and runs into Miller Yourt's arms. Yes, Yourt the rock star, who happens to be standing by the champagne bar. He calls her babe. She calls him sugar, and she forgets all about us.

Nicolas leads us into the ballroom. A small catwalk is surrounded by large tables set for a lovely continental breakfast.

Champagne, coffee in real silver pots and mini-croissants!

"Isn't Dior's show supposed to be this afternoon at the Carrousel?"

"This is not the show. This is the preshow breakfast," Nicolas explains.

A preshow?

"It's a sneak preview for VVIPs."

Here's the thing. To get into the top show, you need to be a VIP or well connected to one. But these days there are too many VIPs so they have invented VVIP, and special exclusive breakfast fashion shows to accommodate. Weird!

"Here he is." Nicolas spots Villiers sitting at one of the front tables eating a croissant all by himself.

I cruise like a torpedo toward Villiers.

"Oh! Vous!" he says when he sees me.

"Do you mind if I sit with you for a minute?"

"Well. Yes, I'm waiting for my real guests."

I sit down anyway.

"Is it about Muriel B again?"

No, it's about saving the whales of Australia!

"You said you would call back."

"Are you kidding me?" He looks up at Nicolas who stands right behind me. "Did you explain to her how this game is played?"

"I have nothing to do with her," Nicolas says, lifting his hands. "I'm not even working for those people anymore."

Villiers sighs. "Well, that's not the way we play the game, here."

"We need to talk," I start.

"*Elle est incroyable celle là!* I don't care what you need. Look around. Nobody cares what you need. The day Muriel B will be like Galliano, I will call you darling and love you for real. In the meantime, I want you to leave me alone. Bye now."

"I don't want to give up," I reply.

Maybe Villiers is like some Jedi Master testing my willpower, and if I hold on long enough, he will break into a smile and teach me how to control the force.

"Trust me, I *will* make you give up!"

And then comes a real surprise.

It comes from my shoulder.

It's Nicolas's hand on my shoulder. It's both an encouragement to give up and a comforting touch.

Come on, Lynn, he seems to say, you're disturbing all these good people. Give up. Get out. Leave my life! Because I hate you, you know.

I turn to look at him.

He doesn't look like he hates me. He just looks plain sad for me.

He has been there, you know. Working for Muriel and trying to get people's attention. Now he is hanging out with celebrities and getting the real thing at Xu.

"To be continued," I say to Destouches.

"Au revoir et à jamais, mademoiselle!"

That means goodbye forever. I didn't need a translation.

I stand and look at the catwalk. The models have started to glide around, clothed in the latest Dior collection. It's not like a real show. They are more like fish in an aquarium in a Chinese restaurant.

"Oh, Lynn! Nice to meet you again."

I turn to see my favorite toilet pal, Marion. "I'm awfully alone. Can I join you?" she asks.

I look down at Martin. His mouth hangs half-open. "Is it all right with you if Marion joins us?" I ask him.

"Sure! Sure! Great!"

I sit back down, and push out a chair for her. "Martin, you must have met Marion," I say.

Marion looks at him. "No, I'm sorry, I don't think we have."

Even for Superagent Martin Villiers, Marion is big news. "Oh! Yes we did, Marion. We met numerous times." I swear there are large sweat drops forming right under his wig.

"I'm sorry, I…don't remember."

I put my hand over Marion's as if we grew up together in the Brooklyn Covent School for Girls and ask, "Marion, are you coming to Muriel's show tonight?"

"Oh. Well…"

"You know, it's the street show. It's going to be quite something."

"Well…"

I press her hand real tight. "Tell me you are. It would mean *the world* to her."

"I guess…well, yes, sure."

I turn to Villiers. I know he heard her but he pretends to be looking at the dresses on the catwalk now. He is actually the only person in the whole ballroom looking at the poor models.

"How's everything, anyway?" Marion asks while glancing quickly at Nicolas.

"Things are…well…you know…" I shrug and turn to Villiers. I know exactly what he is computing in his rotten brain. If Marion goes to Muriel B's show, why shouldn't my clients?

"Martin! Darling!" Miller Yourt has set Clarice free and she decided to join our group. "Hi, Marion! What's up?" she asks casually.

"You know, Dior in the morning, Muriel B in the afternoon."

"Ma-artin?" Clarice whines. "Are you going to Muriel B's show, too? Because I think I want to go now!" She sucks her thumb thoughtfully.

We turn to him.

He stares at me, so I grab the pastry basket and offer him one. He finally chooses the one with raisins, smiles and says, "Oh, well, how couldn't I?"

"Well," Marion says. "I haven't seen Muriel's father for ages. It will be a kick to see him again. I wouldn't miss it for the world."

Thank God Muriel's not here!

As others at the table chat with Marion I let her hand go.

I have more important business. I slide my hand under the table and grab Nicolas's.

I squeeze it.

But instead of squeezing back he takes it away and gives me a dirty look.

I try to keep smiling at him.

I try so hard, my face hurts.

Nicolas says, "We need to talk," with a serious face, so we leave Villiers, Marion and Clarice Kleron to their breakfast.

We go backstage, out of everyone's sight.

He shakes his head and sits down on a carry box. "What was that all about?"

"It was nothing. Just a friendly handshake, for old time's sake."

I sit beside him and draw my biggest card in this game. "Hubert Barclay is out of my life, if that makes any difference to you."

"It's too late, Lynn. Why don't you understand?"

Because I don't want to!

"Please, Nicolas. Barclay was…"

"Was what?"

What was Barclay, indeed? Why didn't I just prepare a neat speech, huh, full of emotional picks and heartbreaking gimmicks?

"Barclay was a dream. Barclay was…like this job."

"What job?"

I point at the part of the catwalk we can see from under the seat stand. The models are still turning absently.

"This job! What we do. I dreamt of something like this all my life, you know. I looked up to Jodie and thought, I want glamour. I want the glitz, the spotlights. I want to be a part of it. And now that I'm here, I realize that there's no glamour. There is no glitz. It was just a stupid dream."

"Barclay was just a stupid dream?"

He wants me to say it.

"It was a charming dream," I tell him the truth. "But yes, it was just a dream."

Can we kiss now?

"You know what? You're right, Lynn, this is all a dream."

God!

"And I want to wake up and realize that you never existed, that you never came into my life and made a complete mess of it."

When I feel this way, there's only one thing—rather one person—who can save the day—Muriel.

I've located her. She gave me an address on the flashy outskirts of Paris, near Le Bois de Boulogne.

The taxi leaves me in front of some threatening-looking gates. I go through the scrutiny of yet another security camera and make my way toward a tall, dark mansion covered in moss and surrounded by a spooky English garden. Muriel is just inside, waving at me from behind one of the French doors.

"What is this place? The Parisian residence of Count Dracula?"

"Almost. It's my father's house."

It couldn't be more different from the villa in the Riviera. It's dark and clotted with intimidating antics. The walls are covered with old paintings. Dead people posing for the artist.

"It's very intimidating, like a museum."

"Typical *grande bourgeoisie française,* very attached to the things of the past," Muriel says. "So what is this great news then?"

"We have Marion and a couple of big cheeses from Villiers coming to see what a genius you really are."

"Good," she says moodily and drops her tush onto a throne.

"What's wrong?"

"This." She hands me a sheet of paper. It's a printed e-mail. It reads:

Muriel. I won't be able to be at your show. Pierre will represent me. I know it will be a great success. All wishes of luck. For F.B.—Lilian Meredith, personal assistant to M. Boutonnière.

"Did you get flowers?" I ask, ready to compare our fortune.

"Flowers?" She smiles. "No, fruits and chocolates. Best quality! Hediart. Oh, and a box of champagne to celebrate."

I look really useless with my damn bouquet. "You're spoiled."

"I came here to make him eat his e-mail, or his assistant's e-mail, to be fair, but…he's already gone."

Francis is back in his jet—flying all alone above some unknown ocean looking for his own immortality.

"You know, Lynn, we're messed up, but at the end, we'll be fine."

Oho! Not quite.

Someone is fiddling with the lock in the foyer. I give her back the e-mail. "Well…*bon appétit.*"

We stand and tiptoe to the foyer to give Francis a proper welcome, but we don't get Francis, we get Jolanta.

"Oh…hello," she says, more disappointed than surprised. She steps in and closes the door behind her.

She looks up to Muriel with those poor kitten eyes. The light is gone. The honeymoon's over.

"He dumped you, didn't he?" Muriel asks calmly.

She shrugs. *Oh well…don't they all!* and gives Muriel her keys. "I… He asked me to just leave them anywhere." She looks upstairs. "I have a few personal things to…you know."

"Feel free."

"He didn't tell me you'd be here. He said I could stay for the weekend as long as I would be gone on Sunday evening."

"The place is yours." Muriel gives her back the keys. "We were actually about to leave."

We watch her climb the monumental stairs.

"I envy her so much," Muriel says enigmatically.

I know: she's so freaking slim!

"She can just give back her keys, pick up her things and, on Sunday, it's over. No more Francis Boutonnière in her life."

I'm so shallow.

Shallow, shallow, SHALLOW!

Step #19:
Every success story has its climax.

Damn!

Nothing's working. Nothing's ready. Nobody's here. They can't stop the traffic. Cars are slipping through our roadblocks. None of the models have turned up. There are no journalists. No photographers. I mean, where is everybody? I'm like the pathetic birthday girl without any guests for the party. Where is Muriel? It's going to be a disaster! Where did I leave my handbag? I need my cell phone! I need to phone everybody! Help! Help! Help!

When I locate Muriel, she seems strangely calm. That's a bad sign with her, let me tell you. It means that she is very close to exploding and having a full-scale mental breakdown.

"Where are the models?" she asks because, indeed, where are they? There's only one hour left before the show starts and the technicians have just finished setting up the backstage marquis. One hour! What are we going to do? All the

Muriel B staff is here, under the marquis, sitting beside the racks of clothes, waiting for something to happen. And they all look at me.

I just smile. "The models are on their way. Not a problem at all."

"We're not going to be ready on time, darling," one of the hairdressers complains.

"It'll be all right," I repeat and phone Louise at Fjord Agency. I get her voice mail again. I walk away from the marquis to leave her another angry message.

"Louise, call me back. Where are the models? This is an emergency."

I look at my watch. Fifty-five minutes to the scheduled start. Oh, no! I wish something would happen. I wish a flood would destroy Paris and take me with it!

I walk to the catwalk. They're still working on it. "How long will it take to finish the catwalk?" I ask one of the carpenters.

"Don't know. About an hour. Maybe."

I look at the stand for the photographers and television crews. It's empty. Completely empty. Not a single tripod to be seen.

Dear Lord, make me invisible.

A woman walks up to me. I recognize her immediately. Yeah, that's right, she frowns. She can't remember where she's seen me before. But I do. She was the security girl at the entrance of the movie premiere. She carries the same clipboard, but today she works for us.

"Vous êtes Lynn Blanchett?" she asks.

"No English. I mean…no French. Just English." I try to look composed, but I realize how stressed out and incoherent I sound.

"Lynn Blanchett," she says, grabbing my wrist, trying to calm me down.

"Yes, yes, that's me," I manage to say, but really, I'm about to cry.

"I'm in charge of check-in and security. I work with SecuryShow. We have a problem."

Oh, really, we have a problem?

"We've finally managed to stop the traffic, but we can't guarantee security during the show."

"What security?"

"This place is too open. Passersby will be able to come in and out. It's impossible for my people to stop gate-crashers. You understand?"

"Oh!" Will that really be a problem knowing that no one will come? "That's the spirit. We want it to be a street event. It's fringe, you know what *I* mean?"

"No, I don't know what you mean. Whoever had this idea didn't think it through," she says and walks away.

I walk back into the marquis. Nobody has moved. Not a single inch. They sit lazily waiting for something to happen. Like for the models to turn up. Muriel has put on a pair of sunglasses. She is losing it. I can feel it. She knows that we're heading toward a tragedy.

"Is everything fine, Lynn?"

"Everything is fine. We might be five minutes late, but that's it."

I look at my watch and there are forty-five minutes left before the start of the show.

My cell phone rings. I look at the screen and see Nicolas's name.

What does he want?

I have a very bad feeling about him calling now. I walk away because I don't want Muriel to hear me.

"Nicolas, I'm a bit busy right now," I say defensively, but something tells me he's not phoning just to chitchat.

"I want you to know, I had nothing to do with it," he says, and my legs are just giving up. "I'm phoning to warn you. You've been set up."

Breathe.

"What do you mean by *set up?*"

"Lynn, you have to trust me. I phoned you as soon as I discovered it."

"What do you mean by SET UP?" I yell.

"They screwed up your booking. You won't get any models."

"Who's they?"

"Xavier Urbain."

"Oh, that's really surprising," I say and try not to faint. "Where are they?"

"The models? They are working elsewhere."

"Where?"

"Lynn, they are doing more important shows. Everywhere! I'm sorry. If I can do anything…"

I hang up on him.

I look at my watch. Forty-one minutes left.

I phone Louise again, only this time I get through to her.

"I don't understand the problem, Lynn," she says. "We have fifteen girls booked for you, tomorrow at five, not for today. This has been confirmed twice by your office."

"Who confirmed it to you?"

"I…" I hear her shuffling through some documents. "I received a couple of faxes."

Shit!

"Louise! Where are the models?"

"They're working. Some at the Carrousel. Some are doing—"

I cut her off. "What time will they finish?"

"I don't know. I need to call them."

"Louise. I'm going to the Carrousel right now. Tell them to wait for me. I'm going to pick them up and bring them back here. Tell them not to take off their makeup and to keep their hairdos."

"Lynn, it's impossible. You cannot arrange to get those fifteen girls now."

I look at my watch. Thirty-nine minutes.

"Please, Louise, phone them. Tell them that I will be at the Carrousel in five minutes. We will pay double rate to any girl who will do the show."

"I cannot promise you anything."

I hang up and my phone rings immediately. It's Nicolas again.

"You have to cancel, Lynn. Do you want me to phone Muriel and explain what happened?"

"We're not canceling anything," I tell him and hang up again before going back into the marquis.

Carolina, Muriel's girlfriend, has joined our bored little group.

"Ah! Carolina! Good that you're here." I turn toward the makeup artists and hairdressers. "You can start with her and I'm going to pick up the other girls. There was a traffic problem. I'll be back in about ten minutes."

"Muriel doesn't want me to work on her show. She says

that it's not right," Carolina says, but I can see how excited she really is.

I turn to Muriel. "Today Muriel is all right with it, aren't you?" I say and drag Muriel away from the rest of the staff.

"The two dancers? Your girlfriends from New York? Are they coming?"

"They're invited," Muriel says mechanically. She knows that something terribly wrong is happening.

"As soon as they arrive, get them in the marquis and prepare them for the show."

"But…they're not models! The clothes aren't fitted for them."

"Squeeze them in! I'll be back with the rest of the girls."

I walk away thinking I need a magic car, and turn back. "Muriel!" I call. "Whatever happens, don't let anybody cancel the show until I'm back. Okay?"

I walk along the catwalk. A small crowd is starting to gather around it. It's hard to say if they are guests or simply passersby. The press stand is still completely empty.

I try to avoid the security girl, but she sees me trying to sneak out.

"It's a complete mess," she yells at me. "We can't control anything."

I shrug and walk away. All I can see is the major traffic jam on the main road in front of me. Cars are literally frozen. Reaching the Carrousel by cab would take about one hour. I look at my watch. Thirty-two minutes left.

I take my phone. Oh, God, I hate to do this! I dial. He answers. Bless God, he answers. I tell him immediately, "Listen, I hate to do this."

"Lynn?"

I look back. I've walked far enough. Nobody can see me, not even the security girl. "Hubert, I need your help," I say and start to cry.

I run through the Carrousel gallery.

"Where are they? I can't see them," I say into my cell phone. I can hear Louise talking in French on another line while staying connected with me.

"Louise?"

"They are in front of the Virgin store."

I reach the inverted glass pyramid in front of the Virgin Megastore and I see a group of tall girls, dressed casually but with outrageous hairdos and makeup.

"Bless you, Louise. Bless you!"

I wave at the models. They look at me suspiciously. They're not sure they should follow the crazy-looking little woman. I see one of them talking on her cell phone and I know for sure that she's talking with Louise.

"Louise, tell them to follow the crazy little woman waving at them."

I reach their group and say, "Girls, follow me. Quick, quick!"

I hang up on Louise and speed-dial Muriel. She picks up but remains silent.

"It's Lynn."

Silence.

"We're on our way." I look at my watch. The show has officially started ten minutes ago. "Twenty minutes max. Hang in there, Muriel."

Silence.

I hold the door to the street and count my models as they walk out. I have nine of them.

"Be there," I pray out loud and look up at the sky to thank our Lord when I see Dave's Mercedes pull up in front of us. He jumps out and opens the back door for the girls.

"God bless you, Dave."

"No, Miss Blanchett. God has given up on me."

We manage to squeeze eight ultra thin models in the back and the extra one has to sit on my lap in the front seat.

"Get us there quick, Dave."

"Sure thing," he says and passes me the car phone.

"Where are you?" Hubert asks.

"On our way."

"I'm already at the show. People are starting to arrive here. It's great stuff."

"Is there any press?"

"They'll be here. I made a couple phone calls."

Prince Charming!

"Can you put Dave on the phone again?"

I pass the phone to Dave. He nods then hangs up.

"What did he say?"

Dave looks at me and smiles. "If I make it in five, I'm rich."

He makes it in five and we've even managed not to kill anyone.

We're about to reach the stage and Dave asks me if he should park the car nearby but—

No!

I…I phone Muriel. She answers.

Silence.

"Muriel," I say. "Ask the technicians to put the music on!"

"What?"

"Ask them to start the music."

I ask Dave to head straight for the catwalk with the car.

I open my window to tell the security people to let us go through.

It's all right, guys. I have another one of my great inspired ideas.

Something as mind-blowing as Jodie's paper collection.

The lights come on.

The music is blasting.

The Mercedes glides slowly through the crowd. They applaud it. Dave parks right at the end of the catwalk. He jumps out, opens the door and the models pour out and make their way toward the backstage area, just like that, in their casual clothes. The audience goes wild.

It looks cool, so glam.

Nobody pays attention to the Mercedes anymore. I get out. As soon as the models have disappeared backstage, Dave drives away and Carolina appears in the first dress.

The music pumps. The crowd sparkles. It's champagne!

She looks amazing. It looks like a perfectly rehearsed and synchronized performance.

I look at my watch. We are forty minutes late but the show has officially started. And it's hot!

There is a huge crowd gathered around the catwalk.

Most of them are not guests. Just regular Joes and Janes attracted by the light and the hope to see some glitz.

And glitz they get. They cheer Carolina. They've never seen anything so beautiful in reality. They've heard of it. They've read about it. They've seen it on TV. But never has such a goddess appeared for real in front of them. For them!

They're part of something for once.

I turn to the press stand. It's invaded. Not only by journalists, but by regular people. They are passersby who want a better spot to peep at the models. But among them, I can see a few photographers and a couple of television cameras.

And I see him. Hubert stands beside one of the cameramen. He looks professional and concerned. He hasn't seen me yet, so I sneak away to hide backstage. I don't know how to thank him. I'm ashamed. I'm really ashamed! Here is the man I pushed away. He comes back to save my butt and I run away.

I make it backstage and regroup with the models.

They slide into the first set of dresses and off they go on the catwalk.

We can hear the crowd screaming. I mean screaming-screaming!

Muriel sees me. She smiles at me. We made it. We're family. I nod. My nerves are wrecked. I need to sit.

Muriel B is all that. Young, crazy, fun, street-wise and in your face.

I go to the far side of the marquis. I turn my back to the mess.

I cry.

You know, a good cry.

I look at them. The girls are jumping in and out of dresses.

I look around.

I wish he was here.

You ungrateful idiot! You should be crawling on your knees to Hubert and beg for his forgiveness but no, all you can really think about is how great it would be if Nicolas was here to see how you triumphed.

I call him on his cell phone.

"We made it, Nicolas."

"What do you mean?"

"The show, it's going great. Listen…" I walk toward the catwalk. "Do you hear? We made it. They love it."

"Lynn, Lynn, *c'est mon tour,*" Marc calls for my attention. *"Regarde!"* He has just finished fitting the spider wedding dress on Carolina. She looks amazing.

"I have Nicolas on the phone."

"Why isn't he here?"

"Talk to him."

I hand him the phone.

"Bien alors, où t'es mon chéri? Oui, oui, c'est la folie ici. Ils adorent. Ils adorent je te dis!"

He gives me back the phone.

"Come over, Nicolas. Please."

"You know that I can't, Lynn. But…I'm so happy for you two! So fucking happy!"

"Nicolas! We couldn't have done it without you, you know."

There's so much noise I can't hear him anymore, so I just shout, "Come right now," and hang up before he has time to say no again.

I try to get to Muriel but she's too busy making a hit to notice me.

And just before I manage to reach her through the packed models, hairdressers and makeup artists, Carolina grabs her arm and drags her onto the catwalk.

It's their personal dream come true. The groom and the bride. The rest of the models follow. I walk to the edge of the catwalk to see them.

Carolina lifts up her veil and kisses Muriel. I mean, she gives her the real thing. The lovers' kiss. The French kiss. The crowd goes crazy again! They want more, but it's finished. Muriel bows to her audience. She's shining.

I take a good look at the crowd. Even the security girl is cheering up. Obviously, she never had such fun at any event. It's so good, she forgets everything about checking in and checking out, and beside her, I can see Kazo.

He doesn't smile or anything. He claps mechanically. The master approves, emotionless, yet satisfied.

I know! He's going to buy Muriel B.

We're rich!

"J'ai jamais vu ça, chérie, jamais." Marc is so excited, he hugs me. Hugging is good. We're all very proud. Muriel B rocks. The girl's a genius. She's better than butter and I'm so proud of her.

I open the freezer to get another bottle of Veuve Clicquot.

The caterer has done an amazing job in Muriel's apartment. It looks like a surreal nightclub packed with fancy drunks.

"Lynn!" Muriel calls. "Don't you leave me like this, bitch!"

She stands among the crowd, getting the attention she's starving for.

"Don't listen to her, she loves me."

"I love this girl," she yells. "I LOVE HER!"

She throws herself in my arms. She wants more of everything! More champagne! More love! More of me! She laughs. She's excited. Out of control. Champagne and success do that.

"Lynn, you know what you are?" Oops, she stumbles. She looks up and says, "You're by far the best thing that has happened to me."

"And you know what you are?"

"A fucking genius," she yells for everybody to hear.

"You're drunk out of your face."

A lovely waiter with foie gras canapés comes up to us. "Foie gras?"

Muriel grabs a canapé and looks up at him. "You're cute!"

He gives us his ten-thousand-volt smile and walks away again.

"Hey! He can't walk away from me like that. I'm a genius."

Muriel forgets that I'm the best thing that has ever happened to her and follows him into the kitchen to convince him that she's better than butter.

Where is Carolina anyway? I look around for her, but instead of Carolina I see Marc and… Goddamn it! Nicolas!

Marc hugs him. Nicolas looks confused and distant.

Poor thing!

He sees me.

I see him, and immediately all my guilt is gone. Hubert is gone. I just think, *He's the one I want. He's the one I need and nothing else matters.*

I smile at him. I want him to come over. I want to soothe him. I know I can.

"I'm so sorry," is the first thing he says.

"Don't worry, everything turned out great, finally."

"I shouldn't be here."

"Nicolas, you have to let go. Drink some champagne. This is your moment, too."

"If Urbain finds out that I'm here, I'm done."

"Did you hear what I said?" I grab his hand. I drag him into the kitchen. Once we are there, I pass him a flute.

"Drink, that's an order, and listen!"

He takes the flute, but doesn't drink the magic liquid.

"Tonight, we drink to victory."

"Yeah, you win, Lynn."

Oh, boy! Enough!

I launch myself at him and kiss. And I'm not talking about those sweet brother-sister sort of kisses. I go for the big one. The Carolina-Muriel official kind.

I know he feels lost because he's on Muriel B territory.

I know he is defenseless here.

I know I'm sort of taking advantage of him.

And so what?

Nicolas eases back, obviously embarrassed.

"It's all right," I say, and take Nicolas's hand in mine again. We need to get away from the party, find a place for just the two of us.

"I have to go," he says abruptly.

Nicolas releases my hand. What's the matter with him?

"You just arrived," I say. "But fine, let's go together. Let's go to my place. And we're going to…" I try to get his hand back but he won't let me.

"I can't do that," he says and it sounds somehow familiar.

Hey, that's exactly what I said to Hubert, because I… Because I wanted him to know that I didn't love him.

That sobers me up.

"You can't do what?"

"It's just not right."

"Not right? What do you mean by *not right?* Define *not right!*" I hear the anger in my voice and so does he. He goes for the door and leaves me alone. I run for the door, too. I squeeze through the crowd. I push people away. I don't want Nicolas to go. I don't care what every-body thinks. I don't care how it looks. I just want to be with him.

"Stop," I order him. Did he hear me? I manage to grab his sleeve and I shout loud and clear, "I want to be with you!" and oops, he actually stops. Only, it's a bit strange. It looks as if he's frozen to the spot.

Am I some kind of witch?

No, just a damned unlucky fool, because when I turn to see what Nicolas's staring at, I freeze just like him.

We stand side by side, looking at Hubert Barclay in the hallway.

I let go of Nicolas's sleeve.

Barclay looks at us, and well, there is no need to make it any clearer for him. "I'm late," he says. "I wasn't sure you wanted me to come at all."

"I…"

"It's okay. I'll see you around."

He leaves.

He didn't even give me enough time to say how sorry I am. Or thank you for saving my ass today, Hub. God! I can't believe how horrible I can be to such an incredibly nice man.

Nicolas turns to me.

I recognize the look on his face.

It's I've-resigned-and-it's-all-your-fault Nicolas.

It's jealous-to-the-bones Nicolas.

"It's never going to go away," he says sadly and walks off.

You don't need to decide anymore, Lynn.

Hubert or Nicolas?

Mr. Wealthy or Mr. Lovely?

Well, neither, my dear. They're both gone!

★ ★ ★

I push open the door to Muriel's bedroom. It's very quiet in there. Muriel is sleeping. I lie beside her on the bed. She mumbles a few words. She's having a nightmare. I hush her and caress her hair. I close my eyes.

It would be so easy if men didn't exist.

It would be paradise.

Step #20:
Success will bring more success.

Flip-flap. I look at my feet thrashing in the villa's swimming pool.

"Does anybody want anything? I'm going to town."

I look up and take off my shades. Carolina has slid into a thin summer dress and wears a straw hat.

"Get me *Paris-Match,* I think they're talking about us," Muriel says. "And *VSD.*"

"You look sunburned," Carolina says and she's right. I'm about medium rare.

Muriel drops her copy of *Marie Claire* to look at me. She hisses and *tsk, tsks* at me. She never sits under the sun herself. She lies nonchalantly on a chaise longue, under an olive tree, wears a silk kimono and screams "cancer" each time a ray makes it through her parasol.

"Sunshine gives us vitamin D and—"

"And melanoma and chemotherapy and wrinkles,"

Muriel says, shuffling through the pages of her magazine like she was reading those harsh words on each page.

"Listen to this," she reads. "Muriel B has succeeded where most brands have failed, giving us something innovative and meaningful. Full stop."

She drops the magazine. "We might be the flavor of the week."

She can't get enough of it. She picks up French *Vogue* and turns to the article about our show. She wants to read it again.

I duck underwater. Think about it. I'm one of the ingredients that make the flavor of the week. I emerge and say, "Carolina, would you mind buying some of that delicious cassis sorbet?"

"Did you know that so and so was at the show?"

I don't answer. She has asked me the same questions about a hundred times. Yes, we had them all. All the celebrities were there.

"Plus jolies les unes que les autres, les stars sont descendues dans la rue pour assister au défilé haute couture de Muriel B," she reads once more.

I drag myself out of the water and sit on the edge of the pool. I look into the *pinède*.

We're back at the Boutonnière villa, and it is really wonderful. The pungent pine smell and the zealous noise of the crickets....

"Did you know that Paco Rabanne said that I'm the best thing that has happened to fashion *this year*? What does he mean by *this year*? Is *this year* a way to diminish the impact of my collection?"

"I don't like cassis sorbet," Carolina says. Like me, she

stopped listening to Muriel talking about herself days ago. Muriel's like the crickets. She's background noise.

"Come out of the sun, Carolina, you're hurting me." Muriel pats the chaise longue next to her. "Are you in a hurry to look like my grandmother?"

"I'll take the motorcycle," Carolina says. "Give me some money." Muriel reaches for her straw bag and passes Carolina a bill. "I should have been paid for the show."

"It was exposure for you, exposure is everything. Ask our PR expert."

Carolina hisses at me.

My presence at the villa has been hard on her. The two of them were supposed to escape Paris and come to the Rivier all by themselves. But Muriel insisted that I join them.

"Should we go out tonight?" Muriel asks me.

"I'd rather stay at the villa and get drunk," I say.

Muriel and I, we're having the time of our life.

We do nothing but eat tuna salad, get drunk on chilled rosé and lie lazily around the swimming pool all day. We declared the villa a no-man's land. Get the men out of the equation and you get a quiet, calm, perfect retreat.

"We've done nothing but drink rosé and watch TV. We should go to town and enjoy a bit of our fame. Let's go to Cannes. We're invited to the Gucci party."

What Muriel really means is that *she*'s invited. Carolina and I could be her +2.

"I'm not sure…."

"Everybody will be there. Everybody who is somebody! You can get more contacts for us."

I pick up the *Marie Claire*. I flip through it randomly, but Muriel has tamed the magazine and it instinctively opens onto the Muriel B–collection pictures. I look at Kazo posing with supermodel Magdalena Kurkowa.

"I'm not interested in everybody that's somebody."

She slides her shades down to take a good look at me. "It's your job to know everybody. That's what you do."

I hate it when Muriel is right.

It's a hot night and all the doors and windows are wide open.

"I wish we'd take the helicopter again, like last time," Carolina says, looking away from the giant TV screen.

Muriel shrugs. "I don't like flying. Too many people die trying to fly." She sits in the dark brown leather sofa and flicks through the channels the way someone normally uses a machine gun. We're waiting for our chauffeur to turn up.

"It's the Icarus syndrome," I whisper and glide to the huge library, which covers a full wall of the living-room area.

I reach for a book in French. By chance, it's called *Villa Triste* and it's written by a French guy with an impossible name. It means *Sad Villa*. I know that much and tonight that's exactly right. I'm sad because Muriel is forcing me to get out of our retreat. I wish I could read the book and find out how the story ends. I open it. I pretend that I'm reading. *French blah-blah-blah*. Oh, we look so civilized. Three rich girls in their perfect Riviera villa waiting to be picked up for a Gucci party while reading books written by impossible-named writers.

We look very high society. *Vanity Fair*'s favorites.

"Where's the party?" I ask, exaggerating the annoyed-slash-bored tone in my voice.

"At Palm Beach," Muriel answers. When she watches television, she responds to everything with a delay, as if her brain needs to register your sentences, filing them first and then returning an answer.

Carolina shakes her head. Where do I come from? "Everything is always taking place at Palm Beach."

I drop the book nonchalantly on a pile of other books waiting to be read and walk to the terrace.

"You look so…*romantic*." For a second, Muriel thinks that I'm more interesting to look at than the commercials on TV.

People, you wouldn't recognize me. I'm wearing Muriel B. Muriel had one of the dresses made to fit me.

"It's because of the dress. Anybody would look romantic in that dress," Carolina snaps, and poses, waiting for her own compliment.

"There is something very…*littéraire*…about you tonight, Carolina. You look like the lesbian heroine of an old book."

"There are no lesbian heroines in old books," Carolina says.

"You know what I mean, and anyway, get us some champagne, Carolina."

She's back with a bottle, when we hear a male voice calling. *Bonjour! Il y a quelqu'un?* It's our driver. He's come to take us straight to hell.

"We're in love with you," somebody says. They mean with Muriel. She is not just the rich Boutonnière heiress anymore. She is the fashion genius that everybody wants to be seen with.

"Your show was just… There are no words for it."

"Were you there?" Muriel asks while gulping her champagne.

"No, sadly enough! But I heard all about it. Grand, that's what I heard. Grand!"

"I'm not sure *grand* is the right word," I say.

"And you are…?"

"Lynn works with me. She's is like my right hand," Muriel says.

"Oh, really?"

"She's Jodie Blanchett's daughter, you know."

"Mmm?"

"Muriel, *ici,*" a woman calls. She's the same photographer that took our pictures in the Mean Ray in Paris.

Muriel takes my hand and Carolina's. We stick our cheeks together. We send a kiss toward the camera. The picture, if ever published, will be titled Muriel B with Two Friends at Palm Beach.

"Another one, Muriel. Just by yourself," the photographer asks. We move out of the way. She takes a few snaps while Carolina and I stand, slightly embarrassed, on the side.

I don't want to be the bitter friend. Instinctively, I feel I deserve some of the attention, but I know that I won't get any.

I give up and walk away.

Carolina, unlike me, doesn't give up. She tries to stick close to her girlfriend. She is ready to feel neglected and ignored, just to stay in Muriel's radar.

I'm not happy. I want to go to the bar and wait for this party to be over, then go back to the villa and drown myself in the pool.

"Lynn!"

I turn and see Roxanne Green making her way toward me.

"So you made it, darling," she says. "I've read all about you, everywhere. You are my prodigy."

She hugs me.

"You know, until you, I never thought my step book actually worked!"

"I'm not sure it does, Roxanne."

"What do you mean? It did wonders with you."

"Roxanne, I'm not happy. It doesn't add up. I am exactly where I wanted to be when we first met, but it doesn't matter to me anymore."

"Here you go, darling." Brian passes her a glass of red wine. "Hey, I know you," he says when he sees me.

"Yeah, you say that all the time."

"My cocktail days are over," Roxanne says. "Brian is turning me into a wine expert. Darling, go get a drink for Lynn. Bloody Mary. Go go."

He is only too happy to comply. "Isn't he adorable?"

Just the perfect lapdog.

"Lynn, I think that I'm in love with this pathetic creature," she whispers. "How embarrassing!"

"Roxanne, I'm miserable."

She takes a good look at me. "Did you read the last chapter?"

"Yes, actually. I read it just before coming here tonight. Step #20, success will bring more success."

"Success schmuccess! You're right. The guide cannot finish like that. One final step is missing."

"A final step?"

"It's actually the most important one."

Brian is back with my Bloody Mary.

"Listen to this one…."

Roxanne put her arm around his shoulders. She's much taller than him. They look comical together but they don't seem to care.

"Step #21! Bonus Material! Always remember, only love can bring happiness."

She winks at me. Brian turns to take a good look at his goddess. Isn't he the lucky one?

★ ★ ★

"A Bloody Mary," I order at the bar. I end up alone, lost and confused. But I have a plan. Get drunk for the rest of my life. I look at my reflection in the mirror behind the bar. That's funny. I look good. Really good. Just looking at me you wouldn't guess the mess that I am inside.

The barman slides the cocktail in front of me.

"I'll have the same, thanks."

I was so obsessed by my own reflection I didn't see him coming. My heart starts to pound so hard, it's going to explode in my chest. Yes, I knew it from the moment Muriel said that everybody that's somebody will be there.

"Bloody Marys have worked miracles before," Hubert says as he sits on the stool beside me.

I wave at the barman. "Hey, can you change mine to a virgin." The barman gives me a *yeah, whatever* look.

I turn to look at Hubert. "Well…"

"Well, what, Lynn?"

"I never had the chance to thank you for saving me."

"I told you once. I want to be there for you."

"Are you having fun here?"

"What?"

"Tonight? This party?"

"It's just another silly party."

"Let's get away."

We walk on the promenade along the beach. He notices that I'm cold. He lays his jacket over my shoulders. The moon is up and full. It's perfect again. Hubert is very good at being there at the right moment. If he knew we would meet at the Gucci party, I'm sure he would have brought a diamond and asked me to marry him.

"Do you want to have a last glass at the Martinez?"

"No, I don't want a last glass, and I don't want to go back to your place."

"Well…we could just…walk, then."

"I don't want a last glass, I want a last talk." I stop and look at him.

"You're not going to dump me again. You dump me every time we meet."

I smile, turn my back to him and look at the sea. "Hubert, I like you. I think you're a nice man. You're rich. You're gorgeous. You're charming and you can give a woman all she ever dreamed for."

I turn back to him and put my hands on his arms. I want his full attention. I look him straight in the eye. "I don't want a relationship without love. I want the real thing. I want the fireworks. The sparks! You see, the last chapter of the guide was the most important one."

"What guide?"

Hubert is everything I used to want before I came to Paris. He is the symbol of a life I desired so much, but one that doesn't make sense to me anymore. Success doesn't bring happiness. Only love does.

"Hubert, could you spend the rest of your life with a woman who didn't love you?"

"Lynn, we could be very—"

"Answer me."

"I want to be with you."

"Answer the question."

"I like being with you very much."

"Okay, I'm going." I'm too frustrated with this whole night to argue.

"Wait! How can you expect me to answer such a question?"

"Try."

He thinks about it. He opens his mouth. He is about to lie, I know it. He knows it. He wants to say that he could spend his entire life with a woman who doesn't love him but it doesn't come out. Even Hubert Barclay, the media guru, the king of words, cannot lie about love.

I give him back his jacket and kiss him softly on the cheek.

"So that's it?" he says softly.

"Yes, that's it."

I start to walk back to the party.

"Lynn," he calls. I turn to look at him one last time. He's all alone on the sidewalk. "Would you send me a copy of this damned book you keep talking about?"

I nod and turn my back to him.

Forever.

Step #21:
Bonus Material!: Always remember,
only love can bring happiness.

"Are you sure you know what you're doing?" Muriel asks.

We walk quickly toward my gate.

Of course I'm sure, that's why we walk so quickly. So I can make it on the next plane to Paris. I'm on a mission!

"The guy must have developed an allergic reaction to you by now."

Oh, Muriel, you don't know anything about Step #21, the most important of all the steps. You wouldn't understand.

I throw my Adidas bag on the X-ray machine, kiss her briefly on the cheek and say, "Wish me luck."

"Trust me, girl. You'll need more than luck. More like a fish net, chains and a couple of padlocks."

Okay, okay, very funny.

I need something to straighten me up before I get on the

plane, so I walk to a bar and ask for a mini bottle of champagne—oh, no, make it two.

They're so tiny.

I can do this! I was made to do this! It's just that I needed
to know about Step #21. After that, everything became clear.

The champagne works its magic. I take my cell phone and
speed-dial his number.

*"Bonjour, vous êtes sur le répondeur automatique de Nicolas
Bouchez… BIP!"*

Just spit out what you have to say to his voice mail, Lynn.

"Hi, Nicolas… It's Lynn here. I'm in the Nice airport." I
lift my champagne glass. "Drinking champagne."

What are you talking about?

"Sorry, that's not why I'm calling. I'm calling because…"

I love you.

I want you.

I need you.

"I'm flying back to Paris. Because…I want to see you. You
see, I thought about everything that's happened. And…oh,
my flight is boarding now, so…well…what I wanted to say
was that…that…I love you. I can't imagine myself without
you. Oh, if you didn't hear what I just said, I just said that I
love you, right, and… Oh, God!"

I hang up.

Look at me, I'm trembling. I wish I was mute and living
in a box somewhere in the middle of Antarctica.

A short flight later, I'm back in Paris wondering what the
hell I'm doing. Once you know about Step #21, you don't
get much choice but to work your ass off to get the one
thing you really need.

I went to his apartment but it was empty.

So, now I stand in front of the new Xu store in Saint Germain.

Life didn't turn out to be the way I expected it to be. I spent my childhood hiding in Jodie's room, thinking that one day my prince would come and free me. And, well, now I'm the one attacking the dark castle of the Evil Xu to free my prince.

Cell phone in hand, I stare at the windows above the Xu store to see if I'll see him stand and answer my call.

I repeat in my head what I need to say this time.

I won't sound confused and insane.

Loud and clear: Nicolas, we were meant to be. Please drop everything and come down and kiss me!

Second ring.

Here goes nothing!

There's a click and I'm sent to his voice mail again. Did he see my name on his cell-phone screen and block me out?

"Hi, Nicolas… It's me! Again! Ha, ha, ha!"

There's so much noise in the street. I find a sort of retreat in a small passageway.

"I'm in Paris now. I want to see you. No, I actually need to see you. It's about…what I said before. It's about us. It's—"

Shit!

I've been disconnected. I didn't have time to tell him what's really important in the story of us. I dial again and a female voice tells me that his voice mail is full.

I hate modern life! Why can't we communicate with long romantic letters soaked in tears and perfume anymore?

I cross the street and enter the dark castle of the Evil Xu.

I rocket like a torpedo to a long micro-thin shop attendant with far too much bright red lipstick.

"I'm looking for Monsieur Nicolas Bouchez."

"Who?"

"He works here?"

"No, I don't think so. We don't have any male staff in the store."

"I mean, he works in the offices, upstairs."

"Oh, let me check for you." She picks up her phone and exchanges a few words in French. "Did you say Nicolas Mouchet?"

"Bouchez!"

She speaks more French. "Oh, Monsieur Bouchez is away."

Yeah, right! Like they haven't done this to me before.

"So…I need to see Fran Wellish."

Gosh, what you have to do to get a chance to talk face-to-face with the guy you love.

"And you are…?"

"Lynn Blanchett, from Muriel B."

In under a minute I'm ushered upstairs.

"Here you are! What a coincidence! It's the return of the prodigal daughter!"

Xavier Urbain stands on the landing, waiting for me. "I knew it. I told Chloe. You're a miracle worker. Look what you've done for Muriel. Brilliant! You're a genius! A genius!"

I'm not going to say thank-you or anything, not after the models business. So I spit out, "Yeah, sure" briefly. "But I'm here to—"

"I know! I know! Come, she's here and dying to see you."

Who? Fran Wellish?

"I'm going to phone Muriel, you know. I should have phoned her earlier but I was waiting for you two kids to take the first step. Now I'll make the next one."

"So you like Muriel now?"

"What do you mean? I've always liked her. She's a genius! Ha, ha, ha!"

Muriel B isn't the little spoiled brat anymore. If you can't kill it, I guess you have to live with it.

"Here she is." He points at an office door. "She only talks about you. Lynn this Lynn that. She's giving us headaches. She's *so* proud of you."

Proud of me? Fran Wellish? But…we never met.

"I really came for Nicolas Bouchez," I say.

Xavier lifts an eyebrow. "Nicolas? What about him? You're not trying to snatch him back, are you?"

"It's a personal matter."

"Ah! Personal! You youngsters! Like rabbits, really!"

Okay, he's starting to get on my nerves. "I need to see Nicolas. Now!"

"Nicolas took the day off. Now that I think about it, he mentioned something about a personal matter, too."

I'm about to ask when he's due back, but Xavier opens the door and pushes me in.

"Hello, dear."

She puts aside a Xu brochure and lifts herself up from the sofa. Jodie.

"What are you doing here?" I hear myself say.

"I phoned Muriel. She said you might come here."

"I'll leave you two. I'm going to phone Muriel! She's a genius! Ha, ha, ha!" Xavier closes the door on us.

It was a trap! Now Jodie is going to ask me to join the dark side and cut off one of my hands.

"You're here to see me?" I ask her.

"Sure."

Here we go again. Lately, nothing she does fits the person I believe to be my mother. There was the visit to the Riviera, the worried phone call to Dad, and now her presence at Xu, claiming she came to see me.

"No, not *sure*," I snap. "You came to see Fran, didn't you?"

"Fran used to work for me, dear."

"I know." I look around. "And this is her office, and…that's why you're here, you came to see *her!* Not me!"

She takes her shades off. She has such lovely eyes, it's a pity she hides them most of the time.

"I came to congratulate you."

"For what?"

"The show, dear, the show! What else?"

Jodie?

Congratulating me?

For something I did?

"Do you have plans for tonight?" she asks. "I need to talk to you."

Okay, it's official, I've lost my mind and I'm imagining all this.

"About what?"

"I did some thinking. Moscow had a weird effect on me. Something about the weather."

I'm about to say, sorry, no time to discuss Moscow's weather, I'm busy fixing my life, when a stylish woman enters the office.

"Ah, Fran!" Jodie says. "This is Lynn, my daughter."

★ ★ ★

After our introduction, Fran suggested we all have lunch together, and sent Jodie and I to wait across the street in her apartment, where we are now. Jodie opens a cupboard, looking for tea, and I sit at the bar and watch her going through Fran's stuff utterly confused.

She finds a pot. She puts it under the tap. Oh! She jumps when water springs out. She looks so lost, this tiny woman, my mother.

I come behind her, take the pot from her hand. "Let me do that."

"Thank you," she says, relieved.

She walks into the living room.

"Shitty taste, *new money,*" she says, looking around and standing in the middle of the apartment, like she couldn't touch anything or sit anywhere. "I hope your flat looks nothing like this."

My flat? We don't get the kind of money to rent places like this at Muriel B. My flat looks more like a cupboard with a bed and a bidet. "My place is more *real.*"

"*Real,*" she repeats, amused. "I guess that means small and dirty."

She looks through the window. Fran has a direct view of the Xu store.

"A real leech, this Urbain," she says matter-of-factly. "Fran has as little flair as she has taste."

I set two cups of tea on the bar.

"Now, Muriel and you are another story."

"Muriel and me?"

"Her earlier work. It was interesting but unfinished, messy, confused, going in all directions at once, just as if she was rushing toward or away from something. You came, and her collection becomes…together."

Jodie sees things differently than you and me. Where we see style, she sees sense. You talk garments, she means life.

"We've worked a lot. We've…improved," I say, trying to bring us back to earth.

"Yes, improved. That's right."

She breathes uneasily. First, I thought it was the petit bourgeois setting that makes her so uncomfortable, but then she says, "I had a terrible time in Moscow. Terrible!"

"More flight problems?"

"No, because of you!"

"Me?"

"Last time we met, you were so *troubled!*"

"I was stressed, forget about it."

"No, I…I spent lots of time alone in my hotel room. I was thinking… I thought about what you said. You said you were tired of me and—"

"There's no need to do that, Jodie. You're bad at some things and great at others. I've accepted it. Let's move on."

"Right. Right," she says. "Well…"

She closes her eyes. When she opens them she stares straight at me. I need to escape her gaze, so I look down. Her hand is going toward mine clumsily. She's like a virgin coming to bed—awkward and shy. And I know she feels very embarrassed to take her daughter's hand like that in a stranger's apartment. But she must have decided that something needed to be done, sometime late at night while overlooking Moscow from her hotel room thinking, *shit, is this my life? This is what I did to myself? That's how I've wasted all that love, for some fucking garments and a scent!*

And I don't feel warm.

I don't feel good.

There's no happiness honeying down my spine.

I feel rage. We've missed out on so much.

I'm ashamed to be this horrible person scared to death when it comes to holding her mother's hand.

I look at it.

There it is, in her hand, locked. My left arm is paralyzed. I freaking wish she'd say something so my life would stop flashing in front of me, and I'd stop looking for a precedent, a moment in my existence where she was holding my hand just like now. Or walking me to school? Singing a lullaby? Baking a fucking cake? Even just warming up a meal! But all I see is her telling me *not to touch the fabric, not to touch this, not to touch that for Christ sake* and *what a pain I am* and how *she can't wait for William to pick me up so she can resume working*. And now she's holding my hand because the weather was crap in Moscow and she was alone in her hotel room and had an epiphany while watching cable TV.

But that won't do.

Because this is *Jodie Blanchett!*

The woman who would rather wrap you in paper and call it fashion than care for her daughter.

And don't you go thinking that she would have cried over what she realized about us in Moscow!

This woman can't cry because she's dry as hay, has always been dry as hay and if my arm wasn't paralyzed, if I could just move it, or cut it off, I would run away from her. I would run away from this apartment and this city and make a fucking pilgrimage to Mars!

"I remembered something in Moscow."

"Jodie, I'm okay, let's leave it at that."

"You were the most beautiful thing I ever saw," she says and it cuts straight through me. "You were so beautiful, it frightened me. I was waking up at night. Going to your room. I was checking that you were still breathing. My life at that time was…" She puts her lips together, blows, that's how mad and sickening her life was at that time. "But there, listening to you breathing… It was all I always wanted to be."

You'd imagine a couple of violins and a heartbreaking angel choir psalming to this, but no, it's Marion's latest tune on my cell phone.

"I have to…you know…" I finally manage to move my hand away and look at the screen. It says the magic word: "Nicolas."

"I need to take this one," I say.

"Lynn…" is all Nicolas has time to say before my battery dies on me.

I shake the stupid thing. It finds just enough energy to ring again, but as soon as I pick up, it turns off.

Lynn?

What about the rest?

1. Lynn, leave me alone, please.
2. Lynn, Clarice Kleron and I consider your message a real winner! Ha, ha, ha!
3. Lynn—why don't you just not exist?

"It was Nicolas," I say awkwardly.

Jodie looks exhausted. Communicating simple emotions takes a lot out of her.

What am I going to do with her? *My* mother.

"Hell of a time in Moscow, then," I say.

"Hell of a time most of the time, Lynn."

I look at her. Really look at her not as Jodie Blanchett, but as a regular woman. There used to be a place, back then, in my room. A place I knew nothing about. A place where I was sleeping and she was listening to me breathing and everything was *right*.

It's not much. But it's a start.

It's my turn to do her hand trick. "You know, Jodie, we're messed up, but in the end, we'll be fine," I say.

I've walked all the way back to Rue des Martyrs. I wanted to think about my next move.

I will find Nicolas, wherever he's hiding and whatever it takes. I will turn each single stone in this freaking city if I have to. I will start by recharging my cell phone and see what he has to say other than *Lynn!*

I walk upstairs to my apartment.

"Hi…"

So that's where he's hiding then, right in front of my apartment—where I least expect him.

"Hi… How long have you been waiting?"

Nicolas is sitting at the top of the stairs, at the edge of the last step. Step number 21.

"I don't know. Since you started to hang up on me."

"I wasn't… It was my cell phone," I say awkwardly and show him the damn thing as if it would explain all.

"Anyway, I was not really waiting. I was preparing what to say."

"And…"

"I repeated it again and again…."

"And…"

"It doesn't matter anymore, because the second I saw you walking upstairs, I forgot everything."

He shows me his cell phone. We're into a showing-each-other-our-cell-phones mood. "I got your message from the airport. The one where...*you know*..."

"Oh, that silly message! Yes! You should clear your voice mail sometime. I had much more to say."

"You said...anyway, I came to pick you up at the airport. But...I missed you. And then, well...so your battery died, right?"

I nod. I'm afraid if I speak he'll quit talking forever and I'll never know what he wants to say.

"Lynn...I...can't imagine myself without you, either."

Am I still standing? Because I swear I feel myself falling.

"We make a clumsy couple."

Did he say *couple?*

Nicolas runs a hand through his hair and sighs. "We made a big mess out of this."

Nicolas, Nicolas, NICOLAS!

"Do you want to come in?"

"Do you want me to?"

There's only one way to answer that. I hop over a few steps and we kiss.

Kiss.

Kiss.

Kiss.

You shouldn't worry about the future when you kiss the man you truly love.

It's not the right time to think about tomorrow.

Tomorrow?

Who knows?

Paris? New York? Milan?

What's important is right now, and right now, I unlock the door to my apartment and we make it over the last final step.

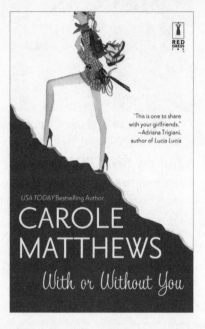